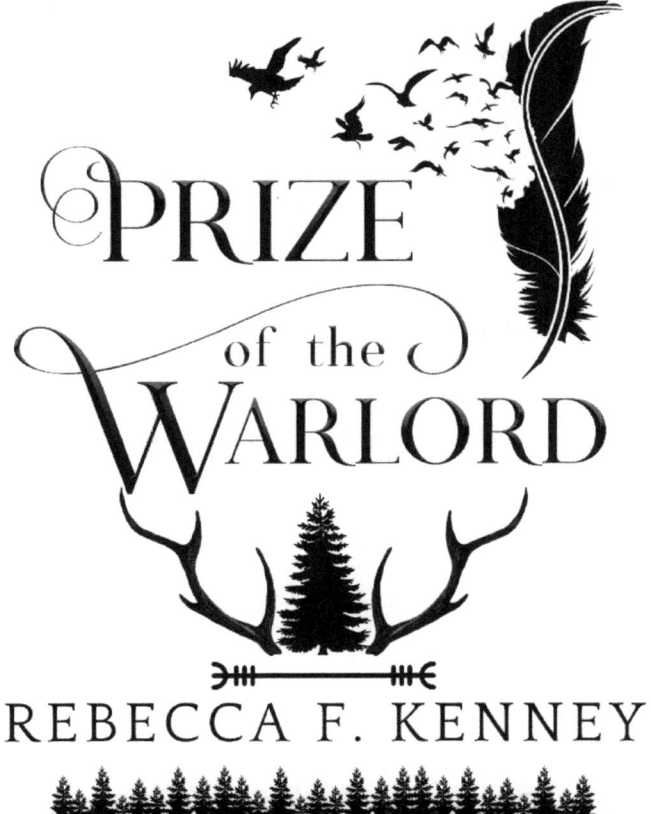

PRIZE of the WARLORD

REBECCA F. KENNEY

This book is a work of fiction. Names, characters, places, and incidents are the product of the author's imagination or are used fictitiously. Any resemblance to actual events, locales, or persons, living or dead, is coincidental.

Copyright © 2022 by Rebecca F. Kenney

All rights reserved. In accordance with the U.S. Copyright Act of 1976, the scanning, uploading, and electronic sharing of any part of this book without the permission of the publisher is unlawful piracy and theft of the author's intellectual property. If you would like to use material from the book (other than for review purposes), prior written permission must be obtained by contacting the publisher at rfkenney@gmail.com. Thank you for your support of the author's rights.

First Edition: March 2022

Kenney, Rebecca F.
Prize of the Warlord / by Rebecca F. Kenney—First edition.

PLAYLIST

"Warpath" —Tim Halperin, Hidden Citizens
"Don't Follow" —Shelby Merry
"Your World Will Fail" —Les Friction
"Viva La Vida" —Katie Herzig cover
"Become the Beast" —Karliene
"Into the Woods" —Fay Wildhagen
"Lilac & Violet" —Miracle of Sound, Karliene
"Freya" —Christian Reindl, Lucie Paradis
"Skywards" —Atrel, Christian Reindl
"Unstoppable" —Christian Reindl
"(It's not about) Running" —Tuvaband
"Wolf" —First Aid Kit
"Border of Lies" —Luke Phillip
"Heimta Thurs" —Wardruna
"O Valhalla" —SKALD
"Grotti" —SKALD
"The Empire of Winds" —Alpine Universe
"Warchild" —Nekokat
"The Still, Cold Wold" —Piotr Musical
"The Wolves" —Cyrus Reynolds, Keeley Bumford
"Let Go of Me" —Karmina
"Mares of the Night" —Glen Gabriel

1

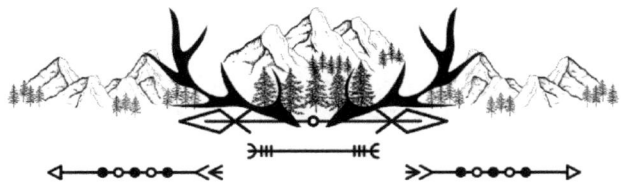

AUTHOR NOTE

This book was originally a serial story on Kindle Vella. I've kept its episodic format in the ebook version, so that's why the chapters are quite short. Hopefully that makes them snackable,
like potato chips.
Thank you to all the readers who propelled this story to the top 20 of Kindle Vella romance!

TRIGGER WARNINGS

Violence, captive/captor romance,
Kissing/touching without asking,
Threat of sexual assault

I'm used to being left behind. It doesn't bother me anymore. Especially not today.

My family left me behind in our stronghold because I'm sick, as I often am during the winter. Too sick to go with them to Cheimhold and make the final arrangements for my wedding to Prince Havil.

If I were feeling healthy and strong, I'd be huddled under furs in the carriage with my mother, my father, my sister, and my brothers. It would be uncomfortable, steamy, and damp. My sister Joss would spend the whole journey sniping at my brothers, while my parents debated border defense tactics in low voices. I'd be miserable, uncomfortable, and bored out of my mind.

Sleet flings itself at the leaded glass of my bedroom window. I hate sleet. Nasty malevolent stuff, too warm to be snow and too cold to be rain. I snuggle further into my nest of puffy pillows. Deep under my covers, my maid placed a hot stone wrapped in towels, and I press my toes against it to keep them warm.

The book in my hands is a lovely fairy tale, full of glimmering candlelight and sparkling gowns and elegant men who know how to dance the perfect waltz. Men like Prince Havil. My heart does a tiny pirouette of pleasure when I think of him. I've known him as an acquaintance for years, and we've spent more and more time together during the past several months as our parents spoke of the potential engagement.

My family isn't royal, exactly. My father rules a small independent territory, one of four districts that form the Confederation of Efhwen. We're allies with Prince Havil's kingdom, and a closer connection there might mean more aid with the defense of our beleaguered northern border.

"The arranged marriage between the Crown Prince of Terelaus and the princess of Brintzia seems to have gone well," my mother told me months ago, back when the idea of my engagement was first being discussed. "Their two countries are at peace. In fact, Terelaus has ceased attacking other nations. And it is said that the newlywed royals are madly in love. So you see, strategic marriages can be a wonderful thing."

"But it was a forced marriage between enemies," my sister Joss cut in. "By that logic you should be marrying her off to one of those vile northern warlords who keep raiding our borders. Those are our real enemies. But you're pairing her with one of our allies, a mild milk-toast slip of a prince, not even the *Crown* Prince, just the third Prince."

"I *like* Havil," I said stoutly, frowning at Joss. "He's gentle and quiet. He likes books and fine tea and beautiful clothes. And since he won't take the throne, he doesn't have to worry about producing an heir, so he doesn't mind that I'm not very strong."

"You could be stronger," muttered Joss. "If you'd quit lilting about the house with your embroidery and your music and your books. You should take up some kind of exercise or training."

"Your sister doesn't care for such things," my mother interrupted. "She has always been more delicate than you and your brothers."

"You coddle her," Joss said under her breath as she swept out of the room.

I can only imagine what Joss would say if she could see me now, snuggled up with my book and my tea, with a warm fire on the hearth. She would probably sneer and charge off to the training ring to practice in the harsh weather. She's the kind of person who considers self-indulgence a weakness, who drives herself hardest when she's feeling low. What she doesn't understand is that sometimes, self-indulgence is necessary to move through weakness, to get past it.

But Joss can't disturb me tonight, and the sleet can't touch me in my cozy room, halfway up the corner tower of our family fortress.

I submerge myself in stories, barely registering the sharp whine and whistle of the gale outside. But when those whistles begin to be followed by loud cracks and crashes, I lift my eyes from the book and notice odd orange flashes somewhere in the dark, far past my window. Some kind of lightning, maybe?

A low thud sounds from below, and a thunderous rumble shakes the whole room. An earthquake and a thunderstorm combined? No, that's not possible.

I set aside the book and push back the covers, but I can't bear to pull my feet out of their warm hole, so I lunge across the bed and tug the cord to summon my maid.

A violent crackling smash, an explosion of fire, and my window blows in with a blast of acrid heat. A black boulder smashes onto my floor, cracking the glossy white tiles. I recoil with a scream, trying to make sense of what I'm seeing—not a boulder, but a grappling hook of coarse black metal, launched through my window and attached to a thick chain. The hook skids backward, raking up more tiles until it lodges secure against the window ledge.

I toss the covers aside and hurry for the door of my room—but something whirs past my ear—a knife, thunking into the wall by the doorjamb. Shrieking again, I cower and cover my head. A quick peek backward reveals hulking figures clambering through my bedroom window.

Raiders, invaders—rovers from the north, the ones who constantly pillage and plunder the disputed border territories. They've never come this far into our district—certainly not to my family's ancestral stronghold. What could they possibly want?

2

I scoot backward on my bottom, away from the advancing figures. They're enormous—like giants. Cold air eddies around them, filling my cozy room with its icy breath.

"Go away," I screech, tears starting in my eyes. A stupid thing to say. I can't stand up—I'm shaking too hard, so I rise on my knees and scrabble for the door handle, planning to throw myself out into the hall, where there are bound to be guards who can protect me—

But as I press the handle, giant fingers engulf my wrist, and another hand clamps around my waist. In half a second I'm spinning, whirling in midair as the big ruffian slings me over his shoulder.

"Go," he grunts to the other two massive shapes. They're all bundled in so much fur and armor plating and leather I can't make out much of their bodies, and their faces are shrouded by hoods, fur hats, and shaggy manes of hair. They look beastly.

Draped over the metal pauldron of the ruffian, I can't breathe very well. I struggle, but feebly. My breath comes short sometimes, even on the best of days, and right now I can scarcely sip enough air to push back the darkness threatening to consume my vision.

My heart is kicking into a frantic tempo I know all too well—one that usually sends me into a faint if I don't sit still and breathe methodically for a while.

"Please," I gasp. "I—I can't—"

But I'm jogged hard against the pauldron as the ruffian halts at the window, preparing to descend by the chain he climbed to get to my room. The other two are already gone, vanished into the dark.

With one burly arm around my torso, the ruffian swings us both out into the hissing sleet. My breath stops at the painful chill that soaks instantly through my soft nightdress, trickling along my spine, slicking my hair to my cheeks and neck. I can't scream, and I can't fight. I have only enough strength to feed slivers of icy air into my lungs so I don't pass out. Shards of cold pierce my lungs, and the pain is enough to keep me partly alert.

Blinking through the freezing drops on my lashes and the matted locks of my wet hair, I can see parts of the stronghold burning. The fires don't look too big—the sleet will quench them soon. Around the fortress is an outer ring of stonework, and more firebombs keep blasting against that wall—but they're a distraction, to keep my parents' soldiers from noticing what's happening.

To keep them from knowing I'm being stolen away.

My captor is running now. With every ponderous stride my body slams against his metal-covered shoulder. Pain shoots through my ribs and stomach.

We pass through a smashed portion of the outer wall, and then we're in the fields beyond the fortress, running across broad plains that slope down to the river.

My captor stops and slings me off his shoulder. I'm flung into the thick grass, where I hunch over, desperately trying to scrape a deep breath into my battered lungs. But every breath is too shallow. I can't fill my lungs all the way to the bottom, and it's making me panic.

"This is the one?" says a deep voice from somewhere above me. "You are sure?"

"It's her. Look." The ruffian grabs a fistful of my hair and jerks my head up. A knife scrapes against leather as it's unsheathed, and then the cold edge of the blade jabs my skin, right in the groove above my collarbone. That's where my mark is—the delicate blue tattoo that identifies every ruling family in our Confederation.

3

For a long moment the man with the deep voice—a monstrous black figure astride an equally monstrous black horse—sits unmoving. Staring at me, maybe, though I can't see his face in the dark.

Sleet stings my face, and I shut my eyes against it. I'm shivering helplessly, conscious that my white nightdress is probably soaked to transparency.

The deep-voiced man grunts. "She looks like a drowned woad-rat."

I don't know what that is, but it doesn't sound very nice.

"Do you want her or not?" asks the ruffian. "Should I put her back?"

"Put her *back*?" snaps Deep-Voice. "After all we did tonight to capture her? Idiot. Bring her here."

The ruffian drags me over to Deep-Voice, who reaches down and grabs me by the shoulder, hoisting me bodily as if I weigh no more than a tankard of ale. Clumsily I manage to get my legs astride his horse—no point fighting unless I want to fall off and break an ankle. My bare feet dangle on either side of the horse's massive body, and my rear is tucked against Deep-Voice's groin. I nearly pass out right then, because I've never been this close to any strange man.

Deep-Voice reaches backward and procures a large animal pelt from somewhere—from a saddlebag, maybe. He drapes it over me.

I'm shaking against him, trembling like the feathers of a songbird in a high wind. He's a boulder at my back, all armor and thick hides, and his two great arms are like walls on either side, holding the reins, hemming me in.

Earlier Deep-Voice spoke in the Common Tongue, but now he shouts something in a language I don't know, and with a rumble of hoofbeats, he and his men charge across the plains, toward the river.

I'm being carried away from the only home I've ever known, the place I've rarely left in all my twenty-three years. When I did leave, it was with my family, and we were always headed south, or west.

The raiders are taking me northeast. That way lies a string of border villages and outposts, scattered through the foothills. Then there's the Altagoni mountain range, like a ridge of broken teeth.

And beyond that sprawls the domain of the northern warlords, the expanse of savage wilderness we call the Bloodsalt.

My captors take the river bridge boldly, galloping past the lumpy forms of slain guards. They killed their way into the heart of my father's territory, and now they're racing back out of it the same way they entered. Which means their primary objective was to kidnap me. Somehow they knew I'd be alone in the fortress, and that most of my father's soldiers would either be accompanying my family to Cheimhold or stationed along the north border.

My father doesn't have enough men at his disposal. They're stretched thin along the north line, barely able to keep out the raiders. That's why my marriage to Havil is so important. Maybe these men know that, and maybe that's why they're trying to prevent the wedding. Or they want to hold me hostage, to bargain with my father for money or land.

If they planned to kill me, they would have done it immediately, in my room.

Cold as I am, it's hard to unclench my jaw and manage enough muscle control to speak through my numbed lips. "What do you want?"

Deep-Voice doesn't answer.

"My feet are going to freeze and fall off," I say.

"Then you will not be able to run from me." His voice rolls through my back, a vibrating force that sends more chills over my skin.

"Tell me what you plan to do with me."

He switches the reins to one hand and wraps the other hand around my throat. His fingers are thicker and more powerful than those of the ruffian who slung me over his shoulder.

"Such a tiny neck," he says.

I whimper, cringing from the throat-hold, but the movement only presses my back harder to his chest.

"A scraggly mewling imp," he growls. "And you're the one who's to marry the prince? My dick is thicker than this little neck of yours."

The image of a male member as thick as my neck rises in my mind, and I squirm, terrified. "Am I your hostage?"

"You're my prize. My new leverage." He barks a laugh. "That is, if you survive long enough. We've got a rough ride ahead."

4

The cold stabs my feet, shooting bright agony along my nerves. I'm crying, and I don't even try to hide it or stay quiet. I sob openly, jolting against Deep-Voice's chest while we ride. He's holding the reins in both hands again, and from the sharp hiss of his breath I guess my crying is beginning to wear on him.

Finally he slaps the reins into one hand and clamps the other over my mouth. "If I put something on your feet will you shut up?" he snarls.

I nod, while my tears leak onto his fingers.

"Hold!" he shouts, and the rest of the riders pull to a halt.

We're at the fringes of the wood that blankets the foothills. Somewhere in this forest, more of my father's men are stationed. I wish I'd paid closer attention to all my parents' talk of border reinforcements. I was never any good with maps, not even when I had a tutor, and my sense of direction isn't worth horse-shit. Even if I ran right now, I wouldn't know which way to go.

Still, I have to try.

Deep-Voice dismounts, pulls me off the horse, and throws me onto the ground, into the wet litter of the forest. With the fur covering gone, I feel more naked and frozen than ever. At least the black canopy of leaves overhead keeps out most of the rain.

I still can't make out much about my captors—too dark. Deep-Voice seems to be rummaging in a saddle-bag.

Now's my chance.

When I try to stand, my frozen feet scream, but I grit my teeth and half-stumble, half-scamper away, into the forest. My hands flail in front of me, brushing against tree trunks and branches in the inky dark.

Behind me, the men are laughing. *Laughing*, because they know I'm trying to escape, and they're mocking the foolish attempt.

Jaw clenched, I try to run faster—but a band of sinew and leather slams around my waist—a burly arm sweeping me off my feet.

Even my scream is thin and weak, and my flailing doesn't seem to affect the man carrying me at all. He plunks me down on the ground again and jams a pair of thickly furred soft shoes onto my feet. Then he tosses me onto the horse and swings up behind me.

Squeezing a fistful of my hair, he jerks my head to the side. His thick warm lips brush my ear, and the rush of hot breath is almost painful against my cold flesh. "Next time make it a challenge," he murmurs.

I lose track of how many hours we've been riding. At one point, Deep-Voice's men dismount and clear a tangle of trees so the horses can enter a narrow gap, a rocky cleft in the heart of the mountain. It's a secret pass, practically a tunnel. The horse can barely fit through, and the rock walls rise high and sheer on either side.

Far, far above us, the night sky has cleared a little—just enough to allow a watery silver moon to shine through the clouds. With that hazy white glow so high above, and the black slabs of rock hemming me in, I feel as if I'm at the bottom of the world, or at the bottom of an infinitely deep well.

After a while the cleft in the mountain widens, creating a sort of rocky room. There are a few spindly trees and a thin rivulet of water. The raiders dismount, drink, and piss against the rock.

My captor doesn't move from his horse, and I shift uncomfortably, conscious of my own bladder and its needs. I have to speak up now, or be forced to ride in agony for who knows how long.

"I need to relieve myself," I murmur.

Without answering, Deep-Voice dismounts and yanks me to the ground with him. He takes a handful of my hair and pulls me toward the rock wall before letting go. "Do it then."

I scan the dozen burly fur-clad figures. The faint trickle of moonlight sharpens their rugged features and glints in their shadowed eyes.

Deep-Voice takes my throat in his hand, pulling me closer. His face is still shrouded in the dark shadows of his fur-lined hood. "I said, do it."

"I can't with everyone watching," I whisper.

"You're not pissing yourself on my horse. Take care of it now." He braces both hands on his hips, which makes his heavy cloak spread wider—almost like a curtain between me and his men. He's still facing me, but their view is mostly blocked.

Turning my back to him, I shimmy off my wet useless underwear and hold my nightdress so that I'm sort of covered while I do my business. Somehow I avoid splashing my soft shoes and my skirts, but the lacy underwear is muddy now, so I leave it behind.

Without being told, I walk around my captor toward the horse. He lingers for a moment, maybe to relieve himself as well—and his men are already beginning to move forward along the passage.

I have another opportunity to escape.

My captor's words echo in my mind... *Next time make it a challenge.*

5

I want to flee, and I have a bare instant in which to make the attempt.

My entire body is practically convulsing with cold. I can't feel my fingers or my nose.

But if I wait until later to run, I'll be even farther from home.

Desperately I lunge for the big black horse, gripping the saddle and trying to pull myself up. But I'm too short, too frail—I can't make it. I don't have the strength to steal my captor's horse and ride to freedom.

With my foot stuck in the stirrup, I hang there, a breathless sob escaping my throat.

"Stealing my horse would not end well for you," says Deep-Voice, pulling my foot free and placing me bodily onto the saddle again. "He is loyal to me. He would toss you and trample you."

With numb fingers I try to pull the fur covering around myself. "I'm so cold," I whisper.

For a second Deep-Voice hesitates. Then he unclasps his hooded cloak and flings it over the horse's rump.

I dare not look too openly at him, so I only catch a glimpse of strong features and a mane of hair the color of ripening wheat. Many of the northern raiders are blond, so his hair color doesn't surprise me. What does surprise me is the bold straight line of his nose, the granite slash of his jaw, and the swell of his cheekbones. His face has a fierce, unexpected beauty.

He unbuckles his breastplate and cinches it to a loop at the back of the saddle. Beneath the breastplate, he's wearing a big, loose, fur-lined tunic, folded over his chest and secured by a belt. He picks the knot of the belt free before putting on his cloak and mounting the horse again.

Divested of his chest armor, his body at my back feels different—still hard, but less metallic.

And then—he opens the flaps of his tunic and pulls me straight against his bare chest.

He wraps the tunic around both our bodies and pulls his cloak over us both as well, followed by the fur covering he gave me.

Now I'm flush against the hard, hot planes of his torso—and I'm too stunned and petrified to protest.

We pick up the pace again, riding on through the secret pass. Against my will, against my desire, the heat from my captor's body begins to seep into me, softening the knots of freezing pain in my chest and gut.

My bare legs are still nearly frozen though, half-draped as they are by my damp nightdress and the edge of the fur. My head bobs with weariness as we ride on, and on, and on…

…

A jolt, and the back of my skull slams against the gigantic collarbone of my captor. My eyes fly open—and I nearly scream.

It's morning, misty and gray, but clear enough for me to see that we're picking our way down a steep mountainside. The trail is a series of switchbacks, bordered on one side by a pebbled slope that looks as if it might avalanche at any moment, and on the other side by steep drops, sheer cliffs of rock plunging down to the plain below.

"Just kill me now," I gasp.

"And waste all the time I spent fetching you?" My captor's voice reverberates through my spine, my ribs, my lungs. His skin is so deliciously hot against my back—I wish I could curl up my cold legs and press them into the heat as well.

"How much farther?" The words leak through my clenched teeth.

He doesn't answer.

As we keep riding slowly down the mountain, I become aware that without the scant protection of my undergarments, the area between my legs has been rubbing against the saddle. Wincing, I squirm, tilting my hips up so I'm sitting more on my ass and less on my sensitive parts.

The man behind me lets out a strangled huff of surprise, and too late I realize that the motion ground me against him more firmly than I intended.

Something stiffens against my rear—a hard column of flesh.

6

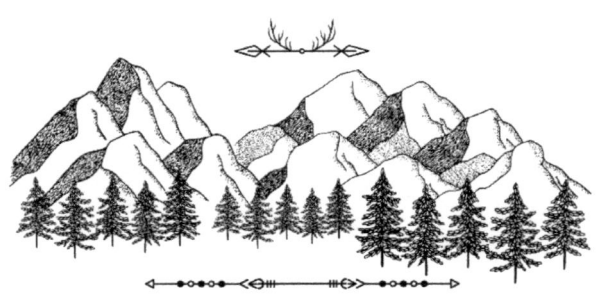

I try to stay still, I really do. But the saddle is hurting my bare privates and I don't want raw patches of bleeding flesh there—so very carefully I adjust my position again.

My captor's body hardens still more, and he snarls, "Stop moving."

"I can't help it. The saddle is hurting me because—because there's nothing between me and it."

"You are the worst kind of prisoner," he grumbles. "Weak, needy, always complaining." Then louder, in a tone rough with frustration, he calls, "Halt!"

The company halts while Deep-Voice spreads another fur across the saddle, leather side down. Once we're seated again, the ride is much more comfortable—perhaps a little too comfortable. The fur is so soft, and it tickles against my sensitized skin in a most illicit way.

It's still cold, but there's barely any wind, and no rain. The sun shines through a thin veil of cloud, looking as pale and wan as I feel. The fever I had before my parents left, the one that kept me home in bed—I think it's returning. It's the only explanation for the rush of heat through my body and the icy chills that follow.

I don't dare speak of it, though.

Beyond the foot of the mountains lies a broad, ridged plain, white with red streaks here and there. The expanse of scarlet and snow stretches nearly as far as I can see, until the very edge of the horizon where I think I can make out the smudgy line of a forest.

"This is the Bloodsalt," I murmur in awe. "The fields of salt and red clay, where nothing grows. No wonder you want our land. This place is terrible."

"Your land?" my captor grunts. "Your father's domain used to be my people's land, generations ago."

"No, it wasn't." I frown. "My people have lived in our district for three hundred years, ever since Ashring the Bold discovered our valley."

My captor snorts. "Ashring the Bold? My people call him Ashring the Bloody." He rattles off several more words in his language, then translates. "It means Bane of Solace, Banisher of Light. He expelled us from our home."

"That can't be true. No one lived in the valley when our people came here. It was our intended home, prophesied by the ancestors—"

Deep-Voice's palm clamps over my mouth. I inhale sharply through my nose, getting a deep whiff of his scent—sweat and leather and dark spice, like the heated peppers Joss likes to sprinkle over her food.

"Close your mouth, little fool." His hot breath gusts across the entrance of my ear. "Or I'll put something in it to keep you quiet."

My skin stipples with panic, because I'm not sure if he means a gag, or—something else.

By the time we pause for a respite, my temporary burst of talkative energy has dissipated, and I'm little more than a limp rag of chilled flesh, fever, and pain. My inner thighs and knees are chafed. My ribs and stomach still hurt from being bounced against the ruffian's pauldron when he took me from my room. The area between my legs is sore and sensitive, and I have to relieve myself again. As if that wasn't enough, my belly is hollow and aching with hunger.

But there's nowhere to rest, or hide, or run. The entire plain is thick with red clay, caked with a layer of salt. My tutor told me this desolate area was the work of a mage who lost control of her powers; but I don't mention it aloud. My captor probably has an alternate version of that story, too.

When Deep-Voice takes me down from the horse, I collapse into the crust of powdery salt. It feels like snow, crumbly yet granular. Dizzily I draw a line in it with my finger, down to the crimson clay beneath.

A huge shadow falls over me. "Get up," says Deep-Voice.

I look up, and for the first time I get a clear view of the man who has taken me.

7

My captor is enormous—I knew that much already—but seeing the girth of his arms and the bulky wall of his torso in the sunlight turns me watery inside. His legs are like leather-clad tree trunks. Through the gap of his unfastened tunic, his chest bulges with mounds of muscle.

There is no escaping this gigantic warrior.

Above a thick, powerful neck, framed by long blond hair, is his face—rugged slanting cheekbones and a jaw sharp as a mountain cliff. I think his eyes are green. They're glaring at me from beneath straight dark brows.

"I was wrong," he clips. "You're not a rat. You're a mouse."

"And that's... worse?"

He scoffs, lip curling.

Then he stalks a few feet away and turns slightly. I can still see him in profile as he unlaces his trousers, pulls out his dick, and begins to urinate on the salt.

I whip my head away, embarrassed. Some of the raiders are relieving themselves openly as well—and I realize not all the warriors are men, after all. A handful of them are women. One squats and pisses skillfully and carelessly, as unafraid to show her parts as the men are.

She pulls her pants back into place and eyes me. From beneath her fur cap, several long blond braids drape her shoulders. As she stalks nearer, I notice bits of something hard and white woven into the braids. Are those—tiny bones?

"I am Zeha," she says.

"Ixiana," I reply. "But you knew that."

She nods. "I will be a wall for you, if you like." She spreads her cloak out like a shield.

I almost thank her, because it's a kindness I'm grateful for—but then I bite my tongue because she aided in the attack on my family's stronghold. She has attacked my people, probably killed some of them. She has stolen things from my father's land. And she's kidnapping me.

I don't owe her any gratitude.

I'm weaker than I was last night, and taking care of my business is a little messier. When I'm done, Zeha walks away without another word. I crawl a little way from the spot and collapse, my mind a fevered blur of agony.

This is a nightmare. How I wish it was a nightmare. Stolen from my home, wearing nothing but a nightdress, when normally I would never venture out of my room without a thick padded dressing gown over my nightclothes—and I'd never go beyond the fortress walls without a fine gown and multiple layers beneath it. I'm used to taking care of bodily needs in a privy stocked with delicious-smelling herbal soap. I've never been pressed against a man I don't know.

And now—I'm nearly naked, my scanty garment hitched up to my thighs, freezing and burning by turns while I lie in the salt a scant few paces from my own piss. My hair is a tangled mess, and I hurt everywhere.

If there's one good thing about the fever and pain, it's that I haven't been able to truly panic about my fate. I just want to feel better. I crave the physical comfort I'm used to with all the power of my being, and I *hate, hate, hate* the man who has taken me away from everything safe and delightful.

Zeha returns and holds out something to me—a dry, grainy, bready sort of thing, studded with wrinkled fruit.

I almost retch at the bare sight of it. "No," I wheeze.

Squinting, she presses a wrist to my forehead. Abruptly she stands and calls, "Cronan!"

Deep-Voice strides over.

"Your prize is sick," Zeha says. "Feverish, and I don't like the sound of her breathing. Is she injured anywhere?"

"She spoke of some—chafing." He practically seethes the words while glowering at me, as if he despises every bit of my weakness. "What in the gods-rutting pit is wrong with this girl? I've never seen such a flimsy scrap of flesh. They're not going to want her back—she's worthless. We should have taken the older one."

"We couldn't get to the older one," Zeha says calmly. "Not without great loss of our people."

"I'm not worthless," I whisper.

Cronan sinks into a crouch beside me. "Tell me your value."

His face blurs before my eyes, and when I try to speak, only a ragged exhale comes out.

"As I thought." He rises and speaks to Zeha. "We'll wait here until the others catch up. I want to know if there were casualties from the diversion attack."

My thoughts swirl, trying to assemble reasons why I'm of value, why I'm worth anything to anyone except my family. Maybe I'm not even worth much to them. Maybe they only love me because they have to.

Maybe they won't want me back.

8

I can feel myself sinking, dropping into the infinite azure, spine curved and limbs relaxed, drifting slowly away from the light into a darker, more desolate place that is a colder, deeper blue.

I think I might be dying.

It doesn't hurt like I thought it would, but it's so lonely. The enormity of the vast nothing around me and beneath me shrinks my soul, and instead of *me*, whole and pleasant and interesting and *human*, I'm a fluttering scrap, a speck, a mote of light in the cosmic emptiness.

And then a male voice, raw and coarse and annoying, scrapes against my consciousness. "Do you have a spine? Any will to fight? Or are you just a weak little mouse after all?"

I don't want to fight. What people don't realize, not even my family, is that I fight every day of my life. I fight harder than everyone else just to seem normal, because my body is always battling me. When I'm not succumbing to one sickness after another, I'm struggling through periods of shortened breath, or suffering with aching bowels because my stomach suddenly decided that every food is now cause for horrendous cramping.

I'm tired of fighting.

I thought I had a future, safe and secure, with Prince Havil. I could live quietly, pleasantly, well-cared for and probably loved, with few significant demands on me besides the occasional court event. That future might be gone. And even if it's not, I'm not sure I want it badly enough to struggle upward through this dark and mystical blue.

But that voice... that persistent, grating, growly voice...

"Pull yourself out of this, little mouse. Show me you have teeth. Bite and scratch."

I could float away, let my consciousness dissipate. But the gravel of that voice disturbs the peace of my death, shattering the lethal calm with ripples. I growl back, and I begin to struggle.

Something twirls down toward me, golden tendrils winding around me and helping me, healing me. Glimmering ropes, drawing me back to the surface.

My eyes flare open.

First I see a slanting roof of leathery skins, stitched tightly together and coated with something waxy along their seams.

Then there's a man's face—skin like black onyx, and dark eyes flecked with gold. As I watch, the gold fades. Maybe I imagined it.

"She's back," says the face. "You owe me for this, Warlord."

"If she lives I'll have plenty to pay you with." It's Deep-Voice—he's the Warlord. Zeha called him Cronan.

Of course he was only urging me back to life because he wants the ransom. He's hoping my father and my betrothed will pay a hearty sum for my safe return.

"I should have let myself die just to spite you," I murmur.

"You did your work well," the Warlord says to the healer. "Until next time."

The man near me moves away, out of my line of sight. There's a brief gust of cold and a flash of light, then a slapping sound as the tent flap closes—because that's where I am, in a tent, buried up to my neck in blankets and furs. It's warm—almost too warm. There must be a fire in the tent, because a thin trail of smoke disappears through a circular hole in the dome-like roof.

Slowly, experimentally, I ease my arms out of the furs. My shoulders are bare—oh gods, I'm entirely naked.

I lock eyes with the Warlord, who stands a few steps away with his barrel-sized arms crossed over his mountainous chest. He's naked from the waist up, and the sheer magnificence of his physique steals my words for a moment. Every valley and ridge of that muscled torso is a wonder of male topography.

My mouth has fallen open, and I close it quickly.

Mentally, unintentionally, I compare the soft slim physique of Prince Havil to the brute standing before me. Havil is attractive. He is civilized and gracious. This hulking warrior terrifies and repels me. I don't admire him at all. Why can't I stop staring at him?

"You're a pain in my ass, little mouse," he says.

"Good." I settle deeper into the furs.

"You almost died. I had to summon a healer."

I shrug, which seems to infuriate him. He closes the distance between us in a single huge stride and grasps a handful of hair at the back of my skull, dragging my face closer to his. "No dying," he growls.

"Because you plan to ransom me?"

"There's more than one kind of ransom," he says. "We will see what price we can get. Money, land, penance for what was stolen from my people."

His breath carries the heavy tang of alcohol mixed with a savory smell—whatever he ate last. My stomach churns with hunger. My head feels swimmy, partly from hunger and partly because the expanse of that massive chest is so close to me, and I can't help remembering how smooth and hot his skin felt when we rode together.

Not that I care about smooth, hot skin. I frown, focusing on the two tiny scars on his chin, and a bigger one along his throat. More faint scars etch his pectorals and arms. Battle marks. The trophies of a warrior.

"My betrothed is only the third prince, and my father has little to offer," I say. "They may not be able to give what you ask."

I gasp as he hauls me closer still.

He jerks a knife from its sheath and sets the tip under the corner of my jaw. "You're saying I should kill you now."

"No," I whisper, trembling. "No. Please don't."

9

The Warlord's teeth are clenched and bared. His beautiful, brutal face nearly touches mine. "You make me so angry," he whispers. "The weakness of you. You're pathetic. Even now, you beg for your life instead of facing death bravely."

"You summoned a healer to save me," I breathe. "It would be stupid to kill me after all that trouble. And weren't you the one who called me back?"

His green eyes widen. "Called you back?"

"I heard you speaking to me. When I was— sinking. Why would you call me back only to kill me?"

His hand at the back of my head relaxes, releasing my hair, and the blade leaves my throat. He recoils, staring at me as if I've grown two heads.

"Rest." He barks the word like a curse, and charges out of the tent.

What a very strange ruffian. Maybe I only imagined his voice in my death-dream. I just met the man. Why would his voice be the one my mind conjured to drag me back? Why not the voice of my kind mother, or my devoted father, or one of my brothers, or even Joss? Come to think of it, Joss and this ruffian would make a perfect pair—warriors, both of them, with the same belligerent attitude and the same disdain for my weakness.

The tent flap opens and closes again, but I don't see anyone walking in. I push myself farther up among the furs, peering around. "Is anyone there?"

Something moves—something enormous and furry, striped black and white—a gigantic tiger, with a head the size of a carriage wheel. Its muzzle hangs slightly open, showing long fangs and a pink tongue. Blue eyes blink at me.

I shriek, scrambling away from the magnificent monster. It hesitates—then with a bunching of shoulder muscles it leaps onto the bed with me and flops down onto the blankets.

When the warlord bursts in, I'm standing on the corner of the bed, stark naked, cringing away from the cat.

He rolls his eyes. "Kaja!" he snaps at the tiger. "Off. Now."

The tiger curls back its lips and snarls at him.

"Kaja." The warlord's voice deepens, and he seems to grow taller, more dominant. "Out."

Still growling, the tiger rises fluidly and leaps off the bed, stalking out of the tent with a baleful glare at its master.

The warlord looks back at me. His gaze drags from my tangled hair down to my bare chest, then to my belly and thighs, all the way to my feet.

"You'll make a poor wife," he says.

"Excuse me?"

"Your hips. Too narrow for babies. And your tits—much too small. All of you—too small." He strides forward, placing his giant hand along my ribs, casually. My skin quivers at the unfamiliar touch. "You had bruises here, but they're gone now. The healer did his work well."

His hand sweeps lower, down to the curve of my waist. His thumb grazes my navel, while his fingers wrap around nearly to my spine.

He's staring at my stomach, head cocked aside. Experimentally he cups my waist in both hands, as if he's curious whether or not he can circle it entirely. Long as his fingers are, he can't quite manage it.

My mind is a tremulous whirl of sensation. I can't tell if I'm scared or embarrassed or—something else.

A whispering tension vibrates through the air between us—me, standing bare and defenseless on the bed, and him, holding my waist, staring at my body like a man entranced.

"My messenger will speak to your father today and make my demands," he says, rubbing his thumbs along my skin. "You'll be gone from here soon."

"Where is here?" I venture.

"A camp."

"Do your people have towns?"

"Settlements further north. Lodges that can be dismantled and moved elsewhere." He's eyeing my too-small breasts now, and he leans in a little closer. Instinctively my body responds, a barely perceptible arch of my spine, a slight sway toward him.

Instantly his grasp tightens, and there's a scintillating, terrifying moment where I think he might put his mouth on my breast—but instead he throws me backward, onto the blankets. "I'll send food for you. And clothes."

I claw one of the blankets over myself. "My betrothed thinks I'm beautiful," I throw at him.

"Ha." And with that single caustic laugh, he stalks out.

10

A bony dark-skinned girl with delicate white glyphs painted across her brow enters the tent soon after, carrying a tray, with some clothes draped over one arm. Her arms and legs are covered in furs, with leather straps banding her wrists, forearms, and elbows. Her leggings are soft dark leather, tooled with symbols like the ones on her forehead. Her curly black hair is banded at intervals and knotted with bone, like Zeha's braids.

"Why do you wear bones in your hair?" I ask.

"To keep the *jäkel* away," she answers. "If they smell death on you, they will not come for you. They prefer fresh things, live things. See, the Warlord gave me some bones for you as well." She plunges a hand into her pocket and brings it out filled with tiny bone fragments.

I wince. "No thank you."

"If you do not wear the bones, the *jäkel* will take you."

"The Warlord doesn't wear the bones." I don't remember seeing any such bits in his long blond hair.

"He does wear them, underneath." She reaches behind her ear, to the nape of her neck. "We all do."

I'm guessing the *jäkel* are some type of evil spirit, and probably not real, but I nod my assent. Wrapped in the blanket, I let the girl comb out my gnarled waist-length locks while I nibble tentatively at the food she brought. "Is there milk in this?" I ask, touching the bowl of creamy soup.

"Musk ox milk," she says.

"I can't eat it. It will make me sick."

She giggles. "The Warlord said you were difficult."

"This isn't me being difficult. My body can only handle milk in little bits, like in baked goods. Isn't there anything else to eat?"

"Not right now," she says. "But when you are dressed and your hair is done, you can ask the Warlord for something else." Another stifled giggle, as if she's anticipating the scene that will cause.

I manage to eat some bread and dried fruit, and I pluck chunks of vegetables and potato out of the soup, but I don't drink the broth.

When the girl is done, my hair has been elaborately looped and braided, with bits of bone knotted here and there. There is no mirror, but I pat the coiffure gingerly. I must look a far cry from my usual self. And the difference between captive Ixiana and free Ixiana only widens once I'm dressed in thick red wool and gray furs and soft brown skins. A corset of stiff leather, glossy as acorns, secures my waist and ribs. Scarlet wool and silky gray fur layer my shoulders, and fur-lined boots encase my feet.

I hate that I look like one of *them*, but I'm finally warm and fed and comfortable, and thanks to the healer, I feel stronger than I have in a long time. I know the effect is temporary—my parents have hired healers for me before, and while they can remedy fevers and repair flesh wounds, they cannot reach deep enough inside me to permanently repair my body.

For now, though, I feel good. Which means I need to steal a horse and escape, before my health wanes again.

When the girl leaves with my dishes, I hold aside the tent flap for her and use that opportunity to scope out my surroundings. I can see a few other tents, two fires, and a makeshift shelter under which three burly horses stamp and snuffle, their breath steaming into the cold.

My heart sinks as I realize we aren't in the Bloodsalt anymore. We're in a forest, populated by a few birch trees and some other trees, black ones threaded by red veins. The leaves overhead are skeletal, translucent and colorless, with webbed veins of scarlet just like the trunks. Overhead, the sky is the darkening gray of late afternoon, lanced with pink streaks from the setting sun.

No one is guarding my tent. They probably think I'm too weak and foolish to escape.

I ease out through the opening and shuffle along the outside of the tent. I look like one of them. All I have to do is pretend I belong, that I'm supposed to be walking around the camp.

The raiders are enjoying their evening meal. They cluster around the fires, talking and belching and slurping soup. There seems to be a handful of additional warriors, probably from the diversion group the Warlord mentioned. They must have caught up to the dozen ruffians I was traveling with.

I don't see the Warlord anywhere.

11

Casually I walk between two tents and then furtively skirt the second one until I'm approaching the horses' shelter from behind. It's a latticework of birch poles and leafy branches, barely high enough for the heads of the great shaggy beasts. They're munching noisily from a temporary trough made of sticks, filled with hay.

These horses are much too big for me to mount alone, especially without a saddle, and I have no time or skill to equip them. I've saddled a horse or two in my life, but it's so much easier to ask our stable-boy to do it for me. Now I wish I'd made the effort more often.

I know these raiders had more than three horses. Where are the others?

I scan the clearing, peering into the trees. Finally I see them, a short distance away in a hastily-constructed pen. The posts of the pen have animal skulls tacked to them. Another superstition to keep away the imaginary *jäkel*, no doubt.

I slink through the trees to the enclosure and pick out a horse that looks small enough for me to handle—not much more than a pony, really, but it will do.

Carefully I slide between the poles of the makeshift fence and approach the pony, hand outstretched. "Come here, girl," I murmur. "Come on."

The pony approaches me, curious, probably expecting a treat. I back away, urging her closer to the barrier. Then I step on one of the fence poles and launch myself onto her back.

The pole falls with a faint thump—not very solidly built, this fence. The pony shudders and blows out a disgruntled huff, but she doesn't buck. Gripping two fistfuls of her mane, I urge her toward the fence, which is lower now. "Go," I hiss. But she backs away, chuffing. It's still too high for her to step over.

Despite the biting cold, I'm sweating under my new clothes. Every second that passes is another moment in which the raiders could discover my escape. I turn the pony, trotting her around until we have a decent space to charge the fence. Then I kick her flanks, and she finally breaks into a run.

She and I are both light and small, and we sail easily over the bar. There's a whinny of interest from behind us as we gallop away, and I can't help a smirk at the thought of the raiders' other horses escaping now that we've shown them the way. It would serve the Warlord right if he had to chase his animals all over this strange scarlet forest.

Shouts break out behind me, and I lean low over the pony's neck, legs bent and knees pressed tight. There's enough sunset left to tell me which way is south, so I head in that direction, with the sun on my right.

Joss would be better at this. Better at riding, better at escaping—she probably wouldn't have let herself be taken in the first place.

I hope I see her again, so she can tell me all the ways I could have handled this better.

My pony must be used to the forest, because she runs lightly, leaping easily over fallen trees and other debris in our path. Up ahead, the trees are thinning, and there's a pale, flat expanse beyond. The Bloodsalt. We must have crossed it while I was unconscious, but we didn't get far into the forest before they made camp and summoned the healer.

How long was I unconscious? Hours? Days? The Warlord said my father had received his ransom demand today—how long has my family known of my capture? And how is the Warlord planning to communicate the terms of my release from so far away?

More shouts from behind me, and the thunder of hooves. When I glance back, I can't see the pursuers yet, but they have bigger horses, and they know the terrain better than I do. They'll catch up to me quickly.

My heart sinks.

Maybe I am the mouse after all. The mouse, chased by cats, unable to outrun them.

But what does a mouse do best?

It hides.

I'm coming to the edge of the forest, and the Bloodsalt sprawls ahead, snow-white tinged with a pink sunset glow.

Sharply I tug on my pony's mane. She screeches a protest, but she skids to a halt.

I fling myself off and smack her rump as hard as I can. Whinnying again, she charges forward, through the final fringe of trees and out onto the flats of the Bloodsalt. I duck sideways and scurry through the undergrowth, dodging trunks and ducking beneath branches.

With any luck, the raiders will follow the pony, and they won't realize she's riderless until they get closer. Meanwhile, I'll find somewhere to hide, and then I'll cross the Bloodsalt at night, when it's harder for them to see me.

It's a flawed plan, but it's the only one I've got.

12

I scramble up a ridge and down again, over a ditch and around a tumble of red-stained rocks. Shadows are deepening, night falling in ever-thickening veils between the black pillars of the forest.

My boot skids on dead leaves, and I almost topple headlong into a narrow ravine. It's deep enough for me to walk along it without my head sticking above its edge, so I slide down into the gully, hoping I'll find a hiding spot. I've been running for what feels like hours now, and my lungs ache from laboring so hard. I can feel the telltale tickle in my throat, the dry itching sensation that often precedes one of my breathing attacks. I need to stop and rest.

The mucky bottom of the ravine plunges lower, and I find a shallow, half-frozen pool among some rocks. I plunge my fingers through the skin of ice on its surface and wet my lips and tongue, but I don't dare drink much of the water in this strange forest.

As I stagger along, I rake the braids and bones out of my hair, mentally cursing the Warlord and his ruffians. Thieves and brigands, the lot of them, rewriting history so they can claim my people's home. Absurd. I throw the last piece of bone as hard as I can, and it pings against a tree before dropping into the leaves.

Barely any light now. I've never spent the night outside, alone, in a forest.

I've been riding and running and scrambling, so I didn't feel the cold until I slowed down. Now it crawls through my leathers and furs, seeping into my skin, eating down to my bones. My fingers sting with it.

I can't hide anywhere. I can't stop moving. If I do, I'll freeze.

I need to go back to the Bloodsalt and try to cross it in the dark.

But the sun is gone, and I don't know which way is south anymore.

Gods, what have I done? I should have stayed in the camp. Healer or no healer, I'm not strong enough to survive a night without shelter or fire in a northern forest. And I can't walk all the way across the Bloodsalt alone. Even if I managed it, I doubt I could locate the mountain pass we used to get here.

What was I thinking?

A shrill, faint shriek echoes distantly through the trees. It's an inhuman sound—a manic, strident cry of rabid craving.

A rush of goosebumps breaks over my skin, and my heart drops into my gut.

Another keening shriek, much closer. And a third.

Something is hunting me—something worse than the Warlord.

Frantically I stumble along the floor of the ravine, nearly blind in the dark. My hands scrabble over some arching roots, thick ones from a great tree. Half-sobbing, I crawl between them, tucking myself behind them so the roots form a cage between me and whatever is coming.

A sharp cry, shrilling up at the end, repeated three times. It's loud, just steps away from me. I tuck myself into a ball and squeeze back against the earthen wall of the ravine.

Crunch, crunch—soft steps in the dead leaves, prowling closer. Lighter than human feet. These are paws, and whenever they land on rock instead of leaves, there's a telltale rasp of claws.

The creature makes a chittering sound, a sort of satisfied predatory purr, and four lavender eyes wink into existence in the dark. They are sharp, narrow eyes, with slitted pupils. I can't see the body they belong to but I can hear the shift of its steps as it prowls, and waits.

Why doesn't it attack? I'd much rather die quickly than sit here in nerve-wracking suspense. At this rate, the frantic pounding of my heart and the tightening of my lungs will kill me before the monster does.

It shrills again, three times, and two more cries reply from different places in the forest. The creature is waiting for its companions, pinning me here until they arrive. And then they will kill me.

13

The clouds scud away from the moon at that moment, releasing a flood of blue light just in time to show me my doom. A sleek black head with a tusked snout—tusks curving down past the creature's jaw and another set jutting up, curving inward until they nearly touch its double set of glowing lavender eyes. Antlers sprout from its skull, but they're not graceful like a buck's—they're crooked and cracked, asymmetrical. Coarse black fur sprouts wild from the creature's neck and shoulders, and its legs bend wrong—they bend in too many places, jointed and quivering, hitching and ratcheting toward me.

I don't pray, not usually. The chapels in my district are poorly attended, and offerings are few, or so my mother says. She's one of the faithful. Her two favorite gods are Hlín, goddess of protection and consolation, and Hœnir, the silent god. I whisper to them while the monster paces on the other side of the scanty net of roots.

The other two beasts scream, and scream again, closer. They're nearly here, nearly insane with the desire for my flesh.

The moment crystallizes. I'm hyper-aware of everything—my breath frosting the air in ghostly puffs, the raw earthy scent of the roots, their grainy texture. The scatter of leaves, twigs, and muck, rough beneath my palms. My knees, tucked close to my chest, pressing the furs and fabric against my skin. The blue-black fur of the creature, the glint of moon on its antlers and tusks. A twig snaps under its clawed foot.

This is my last memory. I'm so close to Death now I could touch it.

I would have preferred to sink quietly into the emptiness. I would still have existed somewhere then, but now, facing this creature, I have the horrible sense that it will rend not only my body but my soul as well. This is something Other, some monster of magic and curses.

With a flurry of scattered leaves and a rippling growl, the two other monsters skid down into the ravine and come abreast of their companion. They champ and huff, foamy lather spitting from their jaws.

They squeal and garble to each other, and prowl nearer, their misshapen legs bending, crouching, ready to spring.

Then a giant figure leaps into the gully, boots thundering solid on the ground, a deep roar rushing from his chest. He wields a massive sword, a big clumsy weapon with a giant blade designed for one thing—slaughter.

Shock blasts through me, bright and paralyzing.

The Warlord.

The creatures whirl, their lean bodies heaving as they howl their displeasure at his appearance. Their heads whip back toward me, nostrils flaring—they like my scent better than his. But they can't ignore him, for he charges them with the giant sword, bellowing again.

With shrieks of thwarted craving, they fling themselves at him. Dodging the swing of the massive blade, they rake his arms and shoulders with their tusks. Their claws scrabble at the bracers on his wrists and the breastplate over the center of his bare chest. One of them seizes the pauldron on his right shoulder and gnaws into it, trying to reach his flesh.

He roars and struggles, gripping one by the leg and flinging it aside. But then he goes down on one knee, while the other two demons swarm over his body and snap at his face.

I don't care if he is my enemy. I will not cower while this man fights three monsters alone.

Frantically I hunt through the forest debris in the hollow where I'm hiding. My fingers close on a thick branch. I shove my way out through the roots, and I deliver a solid blow to the head of a monster.

At least, that's what I try to do. But as I'm swinging the stick, the knot of fighting bodies jerks suddenly aside, and I end up hitting the Warlord in the jaw.

"Oh gods," I gasp. "I'm so sorry."

He snarls at me, and with a guttural roar shoves his sword up through the belly of one of the creatures. It lurches, vomiting purple slime, and he jerks out of the way as the liquid splatters his arm with an acidic hiss. With his skin still steaming, he yanks the sword out of the creature's belly and swings it into the neck of a second monster.

But then the third is on his back, jaws wide, angled for the nape of his neck.

14

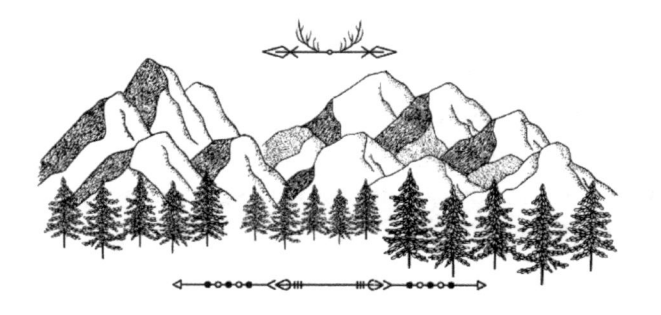

With a thin scream, I charge forward again, and this time I manage to strike the monster before it can bite the Warlord's neck. The creature spins around, wailing, and leaps on me, bearing me down to the ground. Hot claws sear into my flesh. I shove the stick between the monster's snapping jaws and push as hard as I can, while it strains to gnaw through the wood, to get nearer to me. There's a sickening crack, and the beast's lower jaw loosens suddenly, hanging limp and broken.

Howling, it leaps off me and scrambles up the side of the ravine. Its agonized keening fades into the forest.

Shakily I rise on my elbows. The Warlord stands in a shaft of moonlight, dark red blood gleaming on his sword. He's battered and bloodied, and his arm smokes where the acid vomit struck him. His hair shines white, tossed lightly by the night breeze.

I have never seen anything so violently beautiful. A wondering softness expands in my heart as I stare at the silvered warrior who saved my life.

And then he stalks over to me and drags me upright by my hair.

I squeak a protest. "Stop grabbing my hair, you tyrannical fiend!"

"Pardon, Your Highness," he seethes. "Anywhere else you'd like me to grab you instead?"

My pulse quickens, but I manage to gasp, "What were those things?"

"*Jäkel.* Flesh-eaters, spirit-swallowers. You were supposed to be wearing the bones." He runs thick fingers through my hair, and his hand tangles in it. "Gods, why couldn't you behave? Now I'll have to tie you up. And Jili will have to fix your braids again."

He's still yanking on my hair, so I reach back to help him get free. My thin fingers brush his huge ones as I manipulate my tangled locks.

"This is why the women of my people do not wear their hair loose when it is this long. Without braids, it goes all wild and knotted. I'm not used to hair like yours. Soft, like the silk of winflowers." He speaks low, rough and reluctant. "I grab your hair because I like the way it feels."

My fingers pause, halfway through extricating his. A twisty, thrilling sensation races through my stomach.

"Your hair is long too," I murmur. His locks are shoulder-length, and mine reach my waist, but it really doesn't matter what nonsensical words I'm saying. What matters is the heaviness of the air between us, the throbbing pull, the cords tightening between my chest and his.

"Yours is much softer." His voice is still deep, but achingly gentle. The sound of it seems to enrage him the next second, and with a cruel jerk, he yanks his hand free.

Pain shoots along my scalp. "Ow! You rutting bastard."

"Consider that the first part of your punishment."

"What's the second part?"

He towers over me, the mountain against the mouse, and I tremble, but I hold his angry gaze.

"I know how I *want* to punish you." His voice is living stone and the dark of lakes, deep and cold. "Like I would punish any other prisoner of war—strip you naked and beat you until that fair flesh of yours is blue and purple, like the night sky between the stars. But you are no captured warrior, and you are too weak to bear it."

The way he speaks of the beating—it's blunt and harsh, but there is poetry in it, too. "You want to beat me?" I whisper.

"No."

"But you just said—"

"I said you could not bear it. Come with me, fool girl, before any other *jäkel* find us." He clamps a hand around my arm and starts walking, and then he stumbles and releases me, with a cry of real pain.

"*Faen*," he barks. I think it's a swear in his tongue.

"Are you hurt?" I ask.

He glares at me, and I wince. Stupid question—he's bleeding from a dozen different wounds, not to mention the acid burns on his arm. "It's nothing," he growls. But when he takes another step, he says, "*Faen*" again and drags apart the thick leather on his right thigh. It's been split by claws, and dark blood is soaking through. More blood gurgles out as he probes the wound.

"Stop poking it," I say, cringing. "You're making it worse. Where's your horse?"

"Just outside the ravine. I didn't want to risk him down here, with those creatures."

"Kind of you. Tell me exactly where he is, and I'll go get him and bring him down to you."

He presses a palm against the wound, a groan grating between his teeth. But when his eyes find mine, distrust roils in them.

Of course. He's afraid I'll steal the horse and leave him here to bleed out.

What a good idea.

"I'll come back," I tell him, with the most wide-eyed, innocent look I can manage. "The mouse has learned her lesson. I can't survive out here alone, and I can't make it back home by myself. No more escaping—I just want to go back to camp and sleep. After all, you saved my life. I owe you this."

15

After a moment's hesitation, the Warlord nods, apparently deciding to trust me. "Walk that way about twenty paces, climb the left side of the ravine, and walk another ten or twelve paces straight into the forest. You'll find my horse tied to the big leaning tree."

He unbuckles one of the belts from his waist and loops it around his thigh, tightening it just above the wound.

I pretend to hesitate, confused. "So I walk east, and then—"

"No, not east. North. That way."

"Oh." I blink my lashes, inwardly gloating because he just gave me the directions I need. "I'll hurry."

I follow his instructions, walking along the ravine, trudging up the bank, and locating the horse. The enormous stallion tosses his head and eyes me malevolently.

"Shh, hush," I murmur. "Remember me? I rode you before, with the Warlord. Your master's hurt. I'm taking you to him."

I edge closer, talking quietly until the horse calms. Then I step on a nearby branch, and with a gasping, flailing scramble, I manage to get astride the saddle.

And I laugh because I have a horse now, saddled and ready. This horse can take me across the Bloodsalt to the mountains. The Warlord is incapacitated in a ditch, so he can't follow me.

I reach over and untie the knotted reins from the branch. Then I lift them and urge the horse forward. He obeys without throwing me off.

Because I want the Warlord to know that I've bested him, I ride along the edge of the ravine until I can look down and see him there, leaning against the wall of the gully. He glances up, and our eyes meet. I allow a cocky smile to spread across my face—a smile I don't use often, because it feels more like Joss than me. But in this case, it fits.

"Go," I tell the horse, squeezing my legs and leaning forward, lifting the reins. He responds at once, moving on through the trees, away from his master.

The Warlord will bleed out in the frigid dark, between the carcasses of the beasts he killed. He'll die like the animal he is, like a thief and a murderer.

I don't owe him for saving me. If he hadn't stolen me in the first place, I wouldn't have needed saving.

On we ride, through the dark forest, in a southerly direction. Once we're out of the trees, we'll be able to pick up the pace. But the horse has been going hard for days now—all the way to my family's fortress and back again, carrying two people for the return trip. I'll have to take it easy on him so he doesn't keel over. Maybe, when I get home, I can give him to my husband-to-be. Prince Havil would appreciate such a magnificent animal, and there would be a satisfying justice in giving the Warlord's prize stallion to the prince he ridiculed.

Yes, that's what I'll do. I'll give this horse to Havil. But first, I have to make it across the Bloodsalt and find a way over or through the mountains. My father has outposts at every pass—I simply need to locate one, and the guards there will help me.

I've never done anything this clever or bold by myself, and it feels glorious. I take a deep breath of sharp cold freedom, and immediately regret it as my lungs spasm. I bow over, coughing uncontrollably, coughing so hard I can't suck in any air. Black spots dance before my eyes.

Desperately I clutch the reins and focus on tucking my chin down to my chest, opening my throat, and slowly drawing breath through my nostrils. There's a delicate divide with these episodes of mine—they either ease on their own, or they become much worse, until my airway closes and I pass out. I've nearly died a few times. But usually Mother or the maids are there to apply a special herbal rub to my chest and nostrils, and to give me two puffs of magical mist from the bottle the healer gave us on his last circuit through our district.

This time there's no one but me, and nothing but the creepy veined trees and the skeletal leaves and the Warlord's steed.

By luck or the gods' intervention, my fit fades, and I'm able to breathe again. I'm just about to urge the horse to go faster when a clear, distant whistle pierces the night.

The stallion lifts his head immediately, whinnies, and turns around, plunging back through the forest toward the ravine. Toward the master who summoned him.

"*Faen*," I spit.

16

The Warlord waits as the horse picks his way down the side of the ravine, with me hunched grumpily on his back.

"I gave you a chance to honor your word and turn back to my aid," says the Warlord. "You did not."

"So this was a test?"

"To see if I could trust you, yes. I already suspected I could not. Look where you came from—a land of thieves and swindlers." He sneers, teeth flashing in the moonlight. He limps closer to the horse and attaches the great sword to a loop on the back of the saddle. Then, with many a *faen* and a grunt, he hoists himself up, settling behind me. There's an awkward moment as we both adjust ourselves until my rear nestles neatly between his legs. Then the horse begins to move, clopping along the ravine until the Warlord finds a place where we can climb out and continue on through the forest.

"Where are your men?" I ask.

"I told a few of them to fetch the pony, and sent the rest back to camp once I found your trail. I did not need their help to capture a mouse."

"Too bad they weren't around to help with the monsters," I snap at him. "You needed *my* help. That must rankle."

He grunts. "Some help. You struck me in the face."

I twist around until I catch a glimpse of the dark bruise on his scruffy jaw. Then I face forward again, smiling to myself. "Yes. I did hit you in the face." I give a little wriggle of satisfaction.

"Stop moving around."

Just to annoy him, I shift again.

And he stiffens against my rear, a distinct hardness pressing through his pants, just as it did during the trip down the mountainside.

Thanks to Joss and the maids, I know exactly what that hardness is, and this time I'm not so out of my mind with fear and cold that I can ignore it.

He hates me, yet his body is reacting to me against his will. It's a shard of power in my hands, and after the humiliation of nearly escaping and being summoned back, I'm all too happy to use it. The mouse can play with the cat, too.

My heart pounds hot and heavy in my chest, because I've never done anything like this—I've never tempted a man. Prince Havil and I have exchanged lovely kisses—kisses that left us both breathless, warm, and wanting. But this is different. This is the vicious armored warrior who stole me from my home. And I am the soft weak thing who makes him feel irresistible sensations, even when he doesn't want to.

I twist and writhe, rubbing my rear against his groin. Even through my own trousers and his, I feel the increase in hardness and girth, the subtle twitching strain of that part of him.

"Stop," he says hoarsely. "When you move like that, it makes the pain in my thigh worse."

True, I felt the strap on his thigh shift when I moved. But I'm not above causing him pain, too. I hate him, after all. He foiled my escape plans.

Savagely I wriggle against him, and he gasps—I can't tell if it's agony or pleasure. Maybe both.

His enormous hand closes around my neck and squeezes, just enough to threaten my airway. "Stop, or I'll make you ride behind me."

But I'm beyond caution, beyond meek obedience. I've nearly died too many times lately, and the horror of those near-lethal moments bursts out of me in a fount of boiling anger. With my nails I tear at his hand until he curses and lets go. I have an instant of freedom before his entire arm slams across my body, pinning my arms and immobilizing them.

"Bitch," he hisses.

"I hate you," I spit back, my voice full of tears.

"I hate you more."

I wrench my body, grinding it against his.

He leans down and takes my earlobe between his great teeth, biting just hard enough to send a flood of warning pain along my nerves. I freeze, terrified that he's going to bite it through.

His heavy breathing gusts into my ear, pain and desire mingled in a thick panting rhythm. Suddenly I realize I'm mirroring that rhythm, breathing in tandem with him as we ride, locked together, bound by hate.

The Warlord's teeth release my earlobe, but his lips stay there, brushing my ear. After a minute he inhales deeply, as if he's sniffing my hair. Then he straightens in the saddle again.

A delicate wetness is seeping along the crevice between my thighs. With my legs spread astride the back of the horse, I can't press them together, or do anything about it. I'm desperate for pressure, so desperate I nearly scoot forward and press my core to the pommel of the saddle.

My eyes latch onto the large hand of the Warlord, the hand holding the reins. His thick fingers are bloodied and bruised. I imagine that bruised hand settling between my legs, one of those big fingers sliding into—

I pull myself up short, terrified at the fantasy I was about to indulge.

17

When we return to the camp, nearly everyone is already asleep, either in tents or in blankets near the fire. Two men and Zeha remain watchful, awaiting our return.

Zeha hurries to the Warlord's horse. "You're injured. Shall I call back the healer?"

"No," he rumbles. "I can heal on my own."

She makes a harsh sound of frustration, staring at the blood that has soaked his entire pant leg. "I'm sending for the healer."

"Stop worrying."

"If I don't worry, who will?" When he dismounts, she kisses his cheek.

Something clenches inside me—realization, anger, a sense of loss—the same emotion I feel when I watch Joss train, when her healthy, strong body moves so flawlessly through the dance of wielding a sword, spear or ax.

Jealousy.

But it can't be jealousy after all, because I hate the Warlord so deeply, and I would never want to be someone who would kiss him, or receive kisses from him.

"Call the healer then." The Warlord waves her away. "Have him come to my tent."

"Promise you'll rest," says Zeha.

"I have something to deal with first." The Warlord gives me a baleful look. He points sharply at me, then at the ground. "Down, mouse."

Stiffly I swing one leg over the saddle and slide to the ground. My legs nearly buckle from exhaustion, but I manage to stay upright, and I'm rewarded by a brief flare of approval in his eyes.

Or maybe I imagined it, because the next instant he grips me by the back of the neck and marches me to the tent where the healer cared for me. He's limping as we go, but the halting steps don't detract from the storm of feral dominance emanating from him. The strength of his grasp on my neck turns me tremulous and hollow inside. That hand could end me easily. Perhaps I shouldn't have played with him.

Once we're in the tent, the Warlord pushes me toward the center post. "Stand there."

Mutely I obey, while he limps to a corner and drags some chains from a satchel. "Until now I have treated you more like a guest than a prisoner," he says. "That changes tonight."

For a fleeting moment I glance at the tent flap, tempted to run. He couldn't pursue me himself. Maybe I'd be able to avoid the guards—

But at that moment, a huge furry head pokes into the tent. It's the white tiger, nosing in, haughtily requesting permission to enter.

"Not now, Kaja," says the Warlord. "Lie down outside, my girl."

With a low burr in its chest, the tiger retreats outside. She's probably lying in front of the exit now, another barrier to my escape.

The Warlord fastens the chain around the post and then catches my leg, shoving aside the boot and the fur-lined trousers to reveal one thin white ankle. His fingers pass lightly over the delicate bones there, before he shakes himself and snaps the manacle into place.

He rises, infinitely tall and broad, crowding me against the post like a wall of hulking flesh and bone and furs and golden hair. He bends slightly so he can look me in the eye. "Try to scurry away now, little mouse," he murmurs, his breath fluttering across my lips.

For a second our mouths hover so near each other I can't breathe. An unbearable tingling sensitizes my lips—a craving to touch them to his. No, not touch—crush. I want to bruise his mouth with mine. I want him to bite my lip like he bit my ear.

But soft delicate daughters of district leaders don't have such savage hidden yearnings. So I cringe back against the post and turn my face away.

He shuffles toward the bed in the corner, the one where I lay earlier. And then, with a pained groan, he begins removing his armor and gear.

With a noble's entitlement, I thought this tent was mine. But of course it isn't. It's his, and he plans to sleep here.

18

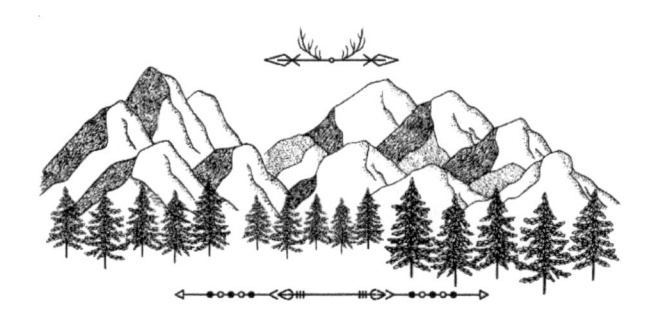

Once all the Warlord's leathers, furs, and armor are off, I get a full view of the knotted muscles of his back, rolling and shifting beneath his skin. He removes his boots—and then he strips off the ruined, bloodied pants.

His backside is perfectly curved, two firm globes of flesh that beg for my hands. I want to touch him everywhere—

He turns, holding the blood-stained pants in front of his groin, and he catches my eye. I avert my gaze quickly, but he chuckles. "You've seen a naked man before, haven't you, mouse?"

I don't reply. I've seen parts of men, yes—but never a whole naked male at once.

Cautiously I glance at him again, this time eyeing the deep gash in his thigh, and the cuts all over his torso and arms. "You're badly hurt. You should call a servant to bandage you."

"I don't have servants."

"But you're a Warlord, a leader."

"And I lead by taking care of myself. But tonight I will make an exception. You will clean and bandage my wounds." He tosses aside the pants and sits on the edge of the bed, pulling a bit of the blanket across his privates. "There is water and soap there, and cloths. Bring them."

Swallowing, I walk to the metal pitcher and basin he indicated. The long chain clinks as I move. I bring the supplies near him and set them on the floor by the bed, along with the small dish of soap and the clean cloths.

"Before you begin," he says, "fetch me the bottle in that satchel." He points to the far corner of the tent.

With a sharp glare in his direction, I go to the satchel and hunt inside it until I find the bottle. Liquid sloshes inside.

As I start to walk toward him, he orders, "Stop."

I hesitate, staring him down.

"Get on your hands and knees, mouse," he says softly. "And crawl to me."

A sharp pulse of indignation rolls through me. "No."

"Do it, or I'll chain both your feet tonight, and your hands as well."

Pinching my lips together, I tuck the bottle into the top of my corset, among the furs. The floor of the tent is covered with woven mats of some kind, so at least I won't be scuffing through dirt.

I sink to my hands and knees, and I begin moving toward the Warlord.

"Slower," he says. "And look at me."

I lift my eyes to his and crawl slowly, forcing every bit of hate I feel for him into my gaze. His own eyes blaze green into mine, and his lips part softly, though his jaw is clenched tight.

"Such a good little mouse," he whispers as I near him. Reaching out, he cups my jaw, and his thumb drags across my lower lip. There's salty blood on his skin, and I can taste it on my mouth when he lets me go.

He reclines on the bed, a giant of a man entirely bared to me except for the scrap of blanket covering his dick. He presses a palm there briefly, and a muscle at his temple flexes. Then he says, "Tend to me, mouse. Start with a little of what's in the bottle—pour it on the cuts. If the healer is delayed, that liquid will prevent infection. Afterward, cleanse the wounds with water and soap."

"Is this my punishment?" I murmur, unstoppering the bottle.

"It will hurt me more than it hurts you."

I choose a cut on his pectoral and tip a few drops of the liquid onto it. He hisses through his teeth, eyes snapping, and his entire beautiful body tenses. My own skin tingles, trickles of delight rippling into my secret places as I torture him with more of the stinging liquid, a little for each wound.

"You're enjoying this," he growls.

"So much," I say softly, spilling a generous amount onto his thigh wound.

He bellows in pain—seizes a pillow and muffles his own cry into it. His abdominal muscles flex tight, hard and bulging. Without thinking, purely on instinct, I lay my hand across them, just to see how they feel.

Hot and smooth, like he felt when he warmed me against his bare chest during the journey. His skin is surprisingly soft, but there's so much power packed beneath it. My fingers trail down to the wisps of golden hair between his hips. He has two slanted ridges of muscle here, angled downward as if his body itself is pointing my way, guiding me.

And I'm entranced, distracted, not thinking, only feeling and wanting.

19

There's a pronounced lump under the bit of blanket the Warlord dragged over himself. He's reacting to me again—he wants my touch, craves it.

He lies perfectly still, gripping the pillow, but he's not looking at me—he's staring at the roof of the tent, his jaw set and his eyes full of anger.

I take my hand from his abdomen and lay it against his inner thigh instead. His hips twitch involuntarily.

My fingers slide a little higher.

"Finish what you began," he says thickly.

I'm not sure what he means for me to finish— but the words break me out of my foolish trance. I take up one of the cloths and begin washing his wounds methodically, sometimes a bit roughly, if I'm honest. Zeha pokes her head into the tent while I'm working, but she only nods and ducks out again, as if satisfied that he's being taken care of.

"She's your lover?" I ask.

"Sister," he replies. "She worries too much."

A knot in my heart eases.

"I have no lover at present," he says. "No time for it."

"Because you're too busy catching mice."

"You are a means to an end. A piece in the game I must play. To redeem you from me, your parents and your husband-to-be must deliver what I ask." He names an exorbitant sum and a strip of land I'm unfamiliar with. "Of course, that land is only the beginning. I won't be satisfied until we reclaim it all."

"And you'll push my people out of the homes they've had for generations?"

"We were here first."

"Let's say I believe you. That was ages ago. Why have you waited so long to push back and reclaim your property?"

"We've been too weak," he says. "We may seem strong, but that's only because we have to be, to survive in this wasteland. The weakest among us perish, and the worthy survive." He turns his face away, his jaw working.

I narrow my eyes at him. "You've lost someone."

"Someone weak," he spits. "Too weak. Pathetic, like you."

"Who was it?"

He stares at the tent wall without answering.

"Tell me." I loop a bandage around his arm and tie it tight—maybe a little too tight. He growls and looks reproachfully from the bandage to me.

"I'll loosen it if you tell me."

"My pain isn't something to be bargained with," he snaps.

"And neither is mine, yet here we are."

He stares at me, and I notice the thickness of his golden lashes, the way they darken at the tips. His green eyes are muddied in the center, a ring of golden-brown. He can't be much older than I am, but tiny lines etch the corners of his eyes, born from squinting into the sky, resisting the bright reflection of sunlight on snow or salt.

"My little brother," he says quietly. "He was born with a body like yours—small and light. Different. His spine, his legs, his lungs—none of it worked right. The healer tried. Nothing we could do. He only lived to his ninth year."

"I'm sorry," I whisper.

"If we had lived somewhere less harsh, less wretched, with better food, more healers and medicinal resources—perhaps he could have survived longer."

"That's why you're doing this. For him."

"Not for him. He's dead. I do it for others like him."

"And when you spoke to me, when I was dying—you took pity on me because of your brother."

He pulls himself into a sitting position, agitation vibrating through every movement. "That wasn't— you didn't hear me speak to you."

"But I did."

"No, you couldn't have!" he exclaims. "It's impossible, because I didn't say any of it aloud. Only in my mind." He stares at me, desperate and panicked, with eyes full of angry denial.

My mouth falls open in shock.

I heard what he said to me *in his mind?*

What does that mean?

Before I can respond, Zeha re-enters the tent. "I've sent a hawk for the healer. You should eat and drink, Cronan. You've lost a lot of blood."

She sets a tray on the bed with her brother and hands me a bowl as well. It's a kind of grain porridge, mixed with berries.

"Made with water, not milk," Zeha says. "Jili told me you cannot stomach milk."

"Yes," I reply. "Thank you."

She gives me a small smile, and I remember that the Warlord's little brother was also hers.

20

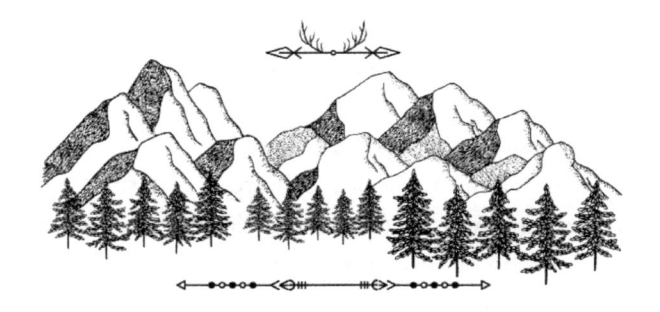

After the Warlord and I finish our food, he throws a blanket at my head before sinking into his furs and falling asleep. The fire burns low, but it's enough to keep warm within the tent. I curl up on the mats with my blanket. It's a lumpy bed, and my bones will ache in the morning, but I'm so exhausted I barely care.

The arrival of the healer wakes me. He tends quietly to the Warlord's thigh and arm while I drowse again, sinking and surfacing through sleep.

When the healer leaves, the Warlord rises from the bed, still entirely naked. I pretend to be asleep, breathing steadily, but I watch him furtively through the veil of my eyelashes. I caught a glimpse of his dick when we were traveling and he pissed on the salt, and I glimpsed it earlier tonight, but now I see it fully. He was exaggerating when he said it was as thick as my neck—but it's still impressive.

He's half-aroused, and as I watch through slitted eyes, he steps closer to me and palms himself briefly, stroking along his length. A soft curse follows, and he fumbles among the saddlebags at the side of the tent, finding clothes and pulling them on. Then he storms out, his heavy steps receding.

Where is he going? Is he going to touch himself, out there in the cold forest? Will he think of me as he does it? Quivering desire traces the seam between my legs, and I slip my fingers inside my trousers, circling the spot that needs tending so badly. I'm hidden under my blanket, but I don't dare splay myself wide and play as freely as I want to. I work quickly, frantically, spurring my body toward the pleasure by imagining the Warlord dragging me to the bed, throwing me face-down, and tearing off my pants. I imagine him planting one huge hand on the back of my head to hold me down while he—

The tent flap opens, and I jerk my hand out. Too quick—the motion catches the Warlord's eye, and his expression shifts. Does he suspect what I was doing?

The white tiger follows him into the tent. "You need to relieve yourself," says the Warlord. "Kaja and I will go with you so you do not run."

He unlocks my chain and with one big hand on the back of my neck, he guides me out into the cold dawn light. I'm still wearing my clothes and shoes from the night before, so the bite of the icy air isn't quite as painful. Still, I can't imagine living here all the time.

"Is it always this cold?" I ask as he steers me through the trees.

"Almost always." He stops. "Here. You can piss and shit here."

I wince at the coarse words. "Turn around."

"Why? I've already seen your body."

"But you haven't seen me do those messy things, and I'd like to keep it that way."

"My people and I do it in each other's presence all the time. It's part of living out here. Part of war."

"So you walked me out here to give me privacy from your people, but *you* want to watch?" I cringe. "You're disgusting."

"I don't *want* to watch," he grumbles. "But I—*faen*, Kaja—*you* watch her." He stalks a few paces away and then stops, keeping his back turned.

The white tiger eyes me blandly while I relieve myself and clean up with snow and leaves. It's not ideal. I would much rather have a privy.

When the Warlord returns me to the tent I wash my hands and then step back to the post, ready to be chained again.

But I don't like the way he's grinning at me, as if he just had a very good idea.

"We'll be waiting here today for word from your father," he says. "And I think, while we wait, I'm going to punish you."

21

The Warlord lets me gulp down some porridge and orders Jili to braid my hair with bones before he takes me outside again. I'm glad to see Jili, though I'm not sure what her role is in camp. She's tough and wiry, but doesn't seem to have the fighting power of the others. And her dark eyes sparkle with a merry, innocent light. With the Warlord's ominous presence in the tent, she doesn't speak to me, but when I thank her for doing the braids again, she smiles.

As usual, the other warriors eye me with a kind of antagonistic interest—not exactly threatening, but not friendly either. Some of them are eating, others are sparring, and others are washing up in the bright, cold air. I wonder if I could persuade the Warlord to have someone heat water for me so I can bathe. He'd probably sneer and tell me to do it myself. Of course he's probably going to chain me again after my "punishment," so heating water myself won't even be an option. Not that I could lift and carry heavy containers of water for as long as it would take to fill a tub, if they even have one around, which seems unlikely—

"Mouse." The Warlord is standing several paces ahead, between the red-veined trees. Impatience tightens his handsome face, but the limpid gold of the morning light bathes his features too, softening them. He braided his hair while I was eating, and the woven locks catch the filtered rays of sun in the most distracting way. When I first saw him he was clean-shaven, but now he has blond scruff along his jaw, partly concealing the bruise I gave him. Why didn't the healer fix that injury when he mended the thigh wound?

"Your face is still bruised," I say.

"I told him to leave it. To remind me not to trust you."

Bars of blue shadow fall across his tall figure—shadows cast by the strange trees of this forest.

"Where are we going?" I ask.

"Not far."

"Are you going to hurt me?"

He walks back toward me, each step deepening the prints he already made in the light powder of snow on the ground. He takes my chin in his hand, pulling at my lower lip with his thumb like he did last night. "Yes," he says quietly. "I am going to hurt you."

I shiver in spite of myself, my flesh and bones cringing, recoiling. "Please don't. I won't try to run again."

"I can't trust you, little mouse. You broke your word, and you tried to steal my horse. If another warrior did those things to me, I would kill them. Now walk, before I make you crawl to our destination."

Trembling, I follow him until we're so far from camp I can't see it, or hear the jangle of bridles and the rough, merry voices.

He must be planning something truly terrible for me, and he doesn't want his people to witness it.

The Warlord prowls the edge of a wide clearing. "Stand in the center, and close your eyes."

Swallowing hard, I obey. With my vision darkened, I focus on the fresh scent of the snow-sprinkled forest, the whispering rasp of the skeleton leaves, the icy breath of the breeze on my cheek.

Then a burly arm slams across my throat, and a massive palm cups my waist. The Warlord has me from behind, in a headlock. I freeze, terrified and thrilled by the power of his grip. My eyes pop open.

The Warlord growls into my ear. "Self-defense is about using your enemy's weak points against them. Sometimes even strength can be a weakness. It can make a man so bold he forgets to be careful. Now show me how you would get out of this hold."

"Wait," I gasp. "Are you trying to teach me—"

His hand leaves my waist, clapping roughly across my mouth. "Show me."

I lurch ineffectually in his grip.

"Your strength won't help you, since you have none. Find my weak points," he says.

I try slamming my head backward, but he's too tall for my skull to strike him in the face. I end up knocking my head against his breastbone, and when I squeal with pain and frustration, he chuckles.

Next I try kicking upward with my heel, toward his groin.

"A good thought," he says. "But now you're off-balance, see?" He lets go of me while I'm still kicking at him. I sway and tumble into the snow. He's on top of me in an instant, his enormous frame braced across mine, caging me. "And now I have you pinned. You should have used your elbow to jab my stomach or side. You should also twist your head into my elbow and then duck your chin and wriggle down. Jab, twist, duck."

"And that will work?"

He stares down at me. "No. Not against someone like me."

"Then why should I try?"

Leaping to his feet, he says, "Again."

22

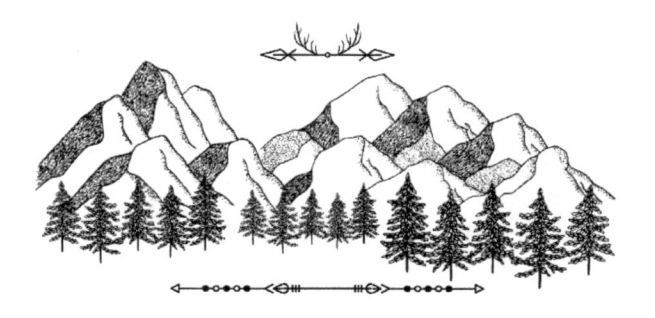

We try the same hold again, several times, and I don't have much better success. Once I manage a glancing blow to his groin, but he only says, "Mm, that tickles," in a mocking tone.

I have no idea why he's doing this. Why would he teach me to defend myself? Whatever his motives, the training is completely ineffectual, because I have no chance against a brute like him. Maybe that's his plan—to discourage and dispirit me so I'll be more compliant.

He retreats, opening distance between us, then paces while examining me from top to toe. He's not wearing a cape or coat, and his loose shirt gapes wide in the front, showing those massive collarbones and boulder-like pectorals.

The Warlord pulls an enormous dagger from the back of his belt. It's as wide as my palm, with gleaming razor edges and a keen tip. The hilt is intricately carved like the head of a hawk.

He flips the weapon casually and holds it by the blade, reaching it toward me. "Attack me with this. Try to kill me."

"What?" I cringe, clasping my hands to my chest. "You're unarmed."

He laughs, a sound as richly golden as his hair, or the sun itself. A quiver of delight pulses through my heart.

"You think you'll be able to touch me with that?" he scoffs. "Take it."

I accept the knife gingerly, horrified by the sheer size of the blade, its power to destroy tissue and organs. That keen edge is honed for spilling copious amounts of human blood. "I don't like knives, or any weapons, really."

He snorts. "Such brazen privilege. What kind of world do you think you live in, Mouse? A safe one? No. Do you think your people cower and whimper when I come for their goods, when I burn their homes? No, damn you, they *fight*. They resist. So fight me."

He takes a fierce step forward, and I swallow, falling back. His eyes snap with a riotous hunger and a lust for conquest. A new fear forms inside me.

"My mother says your men rape our women sometimes," I whisper.

His mouth tightens. "I am not the only warlord of the north, and I do not control all the raiding parties. I don't take women in that way, but it is a war tactic employed for generations by many armies. The act of invading the body as well as the land breaks the enemy's spirit more quickly."

"It's horrible."

"Yes. War is horrible. Loss is horrible. The way my people were uprooted and forced out of their own land was horrible. The way your father's men mutilate my people when they capture them, and hang their dying bodies from the outpost towers—that is horrible."

"But you perpetuate horror," I manage through my trembling lips. "You embrace it and inspire it."

He strides forward until the knife I hold presses to his chest, and he tugs on the braids at the back of my head, forcing my face up. "I took you so I could bargain for my people's rightful inheritance, rather than killing for it."

"So this is you being peaceable." I choke on a laugh.

"Never." He snarls the word in my face. "I will never be at peace with one of your kind. When I look at you, I see blood and pain. I see my people starving through long winters, dying in the cold while thieves enjoy the bounty of our ancestral land. When I look at you," he hisses, his mouth nearly brushing mine, "I see an enemy who deserves to die."

My breath is short and frantic, and his great chest surges with rage as he stares me down. His eyes flick to my lips once—and then he roars, flinging me backward. "I'm going to hurt you, mouse," he bellows as I right myself. "I'm going to take everything from you. Stop me."

23

When the Warlord charges, I flail desperately with the knife. His forearm slams into my wrist, and the weapon flies from my hand.

"Again," he snaps. "Pick it up."

With a whine of panic, I scrabble about in the snow until I grip the dagger's hilt. It's too big for my half-frozen fingers—but I've no time to complain before he's circling me, a tiger ready to pounce. I slash, and he blocks me again, bruising my forearm.

"Your bones are made of stone," I protest.

"Again. Come at me this time." He stands perfectly still, hands at his sides, his breast bared and vulnerable. "I won't attack you, I will only defend."

Maybe I can do this. Cautiously I pace toward him, trying to mimic his style of fighting. Then I charge in wildly, my knife whipping through the air.

A jarring force strikes my elbow, and a palm slams briefly into my chest, sending me flying backward into the snow.

"Don't rush in blindly," he says. "You have to aim for some vital part of me. Pick your target, and attack with purpose."

Gritting my teeth, I rise. I always knew I would hate combat training. I have no idea why Joss seems to enjoy it so much. It's as if she likes punishing her body. My brothers accept their training as a way of life, a necessity, but they don't relish it like our sister does.

I am not my sister. I can't do this.

"What are you waiting for? Choose your target, and come at me," urges the Warlord.

I shake my head. "You're just going to hurt my arm again."

"Mouse. Attack me."

"No. I don't like this. I've never liked training. I'm not a warrior, and you can't turn me into one. I'm not sure why you'd want to."

"Are you defying me?"

Pushing my lower lip into a slight pout, I drop the dagger into the snow and cross my arms.

His face darkens. "You'll attack and accept your punishment, or you'll take my dick in your mouth right now."

Shock blazes through me. "You wouldn't."

"Would you like to test me?"

I picture him moving into my mouth, gripping my head with both his massive hands, groaning with pleasure—it's not an image I ever thought I would like. But the melting heat deep inside my body is proof that I don't know myself as well as I thought.

Still, I'm not ready to fall to my knees for him. "Sick bastard," I hiss. I pick up the knife and run at him. This time I pretend to stab, and then I duck and aim for a different spot.

He catches my wrist easily. "An attempted feint. Good. Try again."

I attack him over and over, trying to get through his guard. I'm the one with the knife, so it should be easy—but he's always ready to block me with his palm, his forearm, even his knee.

Sore, sweaty, and panting, I retreat, stripping off the corset and my top layer of furs. Now I'm only wearing the thick, blousy shirt of red wool and the leather pants and boots. My nose is cold, but my cheeks burn from the physical activity.

The Warlord watches me with a strange light in his eyes and a twitch at the corner of his mouth. "I'm going to attack you again. And this time I won't stop. The threat is real, do you understand? I will do what I like to you, unless you stop me."

A shivery thrill runs through my chest, and my heart skids into a faster rhythm. It's a wonder my lungs haven't given out yet.

24

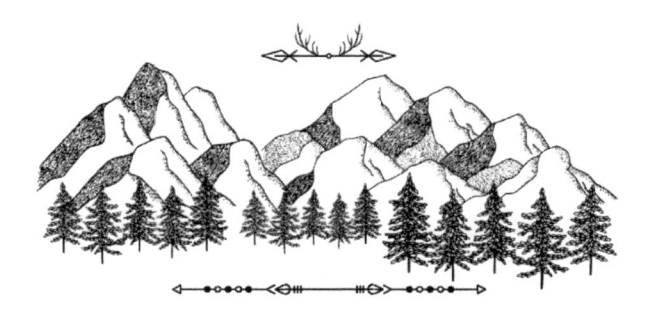

The Warlord stalks me at first, while I bounce on the balls of my feet, dagger at the ready. Then he charges. I try to dodge—I'm not fast enough. There's a crushing impact of bone and bruising weight as I'm flung to the ground. He tries to tweak the dagger out of my hand but I resist, kneeing him in the groin and screaming into his face. My teeth snap just shy of his nose.

"Good, mouse. Very good," he purrs. "See how I've pinned your hands? Twist your wrists, if you can. Make your hands small, and try to slip them out. Do whatever you can to distract me while you get free—spit at me, bite at me, strike my forehead with yours."

"That will hurt me more than you."

He grins, letting more of his weight settle against me. "True."

The cold ground seams to my spine, and his chest presses my front. The telltale lump in his trousers rubs against the hollow between my thighs, a titillating grind. He's hard again, aroused by our proximity, and gods help me, so am I. But I'm furious too, because what he seems to be teaching me is that I'm entirely helpless, no matter how hard I struggle.

"You're not even trying," he says.

"What's the use?"

The Warlord shifts, hovering over me, his knees braced on either side of my hips. He takes my arms and throws them above my head, gripping them both in his left hand, pushing them into the snowy grass. "So you're giving up?" His free hand trails along my waist, thick calloused fingers moving under my shirt and caressing my heated skin. "Not going to stop me?"

I inhale sharply as he thumbs the curve of my breast. I twist my wrists in his grasp. My right hand still clutches the knife, but I release the weapon so I can squirm my fingers downward, wriggling free of his hold. Just as I manage to get one hand out, his right palm leaves my chest and lands between my legs, cupping firmly. I go perfectly still, helpless to the heat rolling through my body.

"This is mine if I want it," he whispers. His fingers flex over me, through the fabric.

A soft whimper escapes me. It's more desire than fear, but he seems to register it as terror, because he sighs and moves off me, rising again.

"You failed," he says. "You got one hand free, but you didn't reclaim the knife. You're right. It's pointless trying to teach you anything. You've got no will, no strength of heart. You'll let yourself die or be claimed by anyone stronger than you."

He turns away and walks back to where he left his cloak. He's not sweating, and that infuriates me. I gave him no trouble at all. He scarcely had to exert himself, while I'm damp with sweat, panting so hard that when I clamber to my feet, I have to bend over and pause to catch my breath.

The breathlessness prompts a very wicked thought in my mind.

I start inhaling erratically, imitating the halting gasps I usually make during a breathing attack. I stagger back from the Warlord, my eyes blown wide with panic. This is a dangerous game, because imitating the symptoms of an attack could trigger them—but I can't resist trying to best him. If he sees me in distress, he'll try to help me. I'm his hostage, his prize. He needs me alive.

"What is this?" the Warlord says, eyeing me with a frown.

Dropping the knife, I clutch my throat, still pretending to struggle for breath. Then I collapse in the snowy grass, with the knife pinned beneath my thigh where I can access it easily. I claw at my throat and chest. Then I extend one trembling, pleading hand toward the Warlord.

He looks stunned and alarmed. After a heartbeat, he rushes to me, bracing one burly arm across my back. "What happened? You can't breathe?" he asks.

"Calm down, mouse. Try to relax." His other hand settles on my belly, a gentle pressure.

I snatch the knife from beneath my thigh and plunge it toward his neck.

25

I almost plunge the knife into his throat. I could, because he doesn't stop me—his hands are occupied with holding me gently.

The point of the dagger cuts a tiny line on his neck, right where his pulse beats.

The Warlord freezes.

I know what he's feeling—the excruciating clarity, the crystallized imminence of Death.

His palm leaves my belly, and his huge warm fingers close around my thin chilled ones. Slowly he moves the dagger down, away from his throat.

And I let him do it.

"You wicked little liar," he breathes.

I didn't kill him. Why didn't I kill him?

My heart is beating even faster than it was when he pinned me and clasped that huge hand between my legs. There's a new look in his eyes—wonder and respect, edged with the sting of betrayal.

"Do you have any honor at all?" he asks.

"It wasn't entirely a lie," I tell him impulsively. "I do have breathing troubles. Sometimes they get so bad I pass out. Our healer back home made a special tonic for me—distilled herbs and mineral water infused with magic. Two puffs in my mouth will loosen my throat and lungs when they're closing up." I allow myself a small smile. "But for healthy lungs, it causes spasms and retching. One of my brothers tried it once, and he was sick everywhere."

The Warlord gives me a stern look, not amused by my attempt to distract him. "You tricked me, mouse."

"I'm not sorry."

"Honor is for warriors," he says. "But there is a law that trumps any code of honor, and that is survival. You did what you had to do. But you also spoiled your last chance of besting me, because I won't fall for that ruse again. You should have killed me when you had the chance."

The image of his great body slumped in bloodstained snow rises in my mind. I imagine his handsome face, perpetually still, and his green eyes empty.

"You're weak," he continues, sliding his arm away from my back and collecting the dagger from my limp hand. "A little mewling soft thing who can lie, but not kill. Your trick gets you nowhere unless you're willing to follow through."

"I prefer you alive," I mutter.

He's standing now, while I'm still sitting on the grass. The height of him dwarfs me, engulfs me in blue shadow.

"Why?" he asks quietly. "You know what I've done to your people, what I plan to do."

"When you were just 'warlords and raiders,' it was easier to hate you," I say quietly. "Easier to condemn and despise. But you have faces now, and families. You have pain and a past. I see you, and I see myself through your eyes. So no—I cannot wish you dead. And I certainly can't kill you myself."

He doesn't move or speak. After a long moment I look up at him—but before I can read the emotion surging in his eyes, a rumbling growl and a flash of striped fur catches my attention. Kaja pads into the clearing, accompanied by Zeha. On a leather bracer wrapping her left wrist, Zeha carries a beautiful hawk, snow-white flecked with red and black feathers.

"There you are," Zeha says. "We've received a reply from the girl's father. They took our messenger prisoner, as we expected, but they allowed him to send back my snow-hawk with this." She holds out a small tube with tiny leather straps attached to it.

A message from my father. Which means he's making arrangements to pay my ransom, and soon I'll be home again, back in my comfortable room with my things and my own privy where there's a lovely big washtub. My body trembles with mingled eagerness and weariness.

26

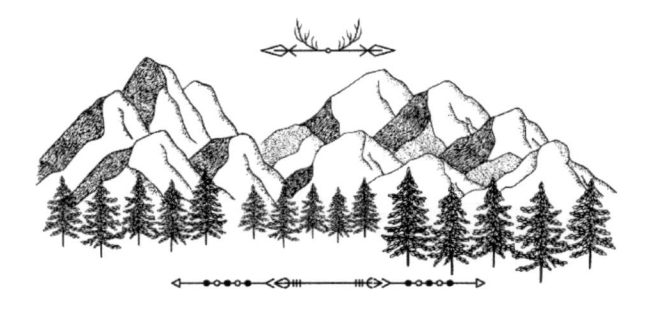

The Warlord takes the tube and tries to extract the message, but it's jammed inside and it won't fall out, even when he shakes it violently.

I stand, brushing snow from my rear. "Let me."

With a grunt, he turns over the tube to me. I wriggle two fingertips inside and tug out the tiny scrap of paper. "I assume you can read?" I say primly. "Or shall I read it for you?"

"Of course I can read," he snarls, snatching the paper. He steps beside Zeha and holds it so she can see the message too. He might be the leader in name, but it's clear he considers her a close partner.

"Well?" I say, when they don't speak. "When can I go home?"

The Warlord's green eyes meet mine over the edge of the paper. "You can't."

My legs quiver. "What?"

"Your parents and Prince Havil have rejected my price, and they make no counter-offer. Which means they are leaving you in my hands." He crumples the message and turns to Zeha. "They may send search parties over the mountains to look for her. We should pack up camp and return home. Once we've withdrawn far enough, we can count on the wilderness and the *jäkel* to take care of our enemies for us."

"And what will we do with her?" his sister asks.

"We'll wait," he says. "When they realize they can't find her and I'm not giving her back, they may be willing to bargain. And if not, I will do what we discussed."

"Cronan." Zeha lays a hand on his arm. Even with the furs and leather she wears, I can tell that her muscles are far bigger than mine; yet even a strong frame like hers looks small beside the Warlord. "I can't let you do that."

Is he talking about killing me? Does Zeha want to spare my life?

"You only get one life-bond," she continues, low. "I won't let you sacrifice that joy by tying yourself to the daughter of our enemy."

"Life-bond?" I quaver. "What are you talking about?"

The Warlord glances at me, his expression unreadable. "If your father and the prince refuse to bargain with me for your life, I will take you as my wife. Among our people, the life-bond is sacred, and can only be broken in the rarest of circumstances. Once the bond is knit by a Shaman of the Bloodsalt, it will link our very souls. And when you are my wife, your father will be forced to acknowledge me."

"Such a bond is usually reserved for the deepest kind of love," says Zeha. "Our people may pair with whomever they wish, share a bed, have children—but they do not Life-bond until they can hear each other's thought-voices through the ether."

"The ether?" I ask, but the Warlord says sharply, "Enough. I will give the order to pack up camp. Zeha, the girl rides with you."

He strides away, and I want to run after him and claw at his massive shoulders and *make* him look at me, *force* him to let me go. I want to hurt him—I think I could kill him now if I had a weapon in hand.

But I only stand trembling, with tears flooding my eyes because my parents refused his demands. They refused. They aren't going to pay for my freedom.

Maybe the Warlord asked for too much. But they didn't even send a counter-offer.

If it had been Joss or one of my brothers in the Warlord's grip, would they have paid then? My three siblings are their *useful* children, the healthy ones. Perhaps I'm an acceptable loss.

I know that can't be what they're thinking. I know they love me—I can imagine my father's anxious pain and my mother's furious agony over my capture. But in this moment, I'm so far from them that the idea of them leaving me, abandoning me, feels deeply true. They've been leaving me behind all my life, even when they didn't realize it, when they didn't mean to.

I can't help crying. I'm so exhausted—the lack of sleep, the failed escape attempts, the Warlord's version of punishment, and now *this*. This rejection, this broken hope. I can't bear it, and I sob quietly into my hands while Zeha waits, stroking her hawk's feathers. She doesn't tell me to stop crying, or hurry me along. She simply waits until I have cried enough.

While I'm sobbing, Kaja bumps her weight against my shins and then settles into the snow across my feet. Which makes me sob even harder. I sink down, heedless of the fact that she's a giant killer beast, and I bury my face in her thick fur.

27

When I'm calm again, Zeha lets me collect the borrowed clothing I took off during the fight, and allows me to relieve myself in the bushes before we return to camp. After tying my wrists together in front of me, she drapes an extra cloak over my shoulders and knots the laces at my neck. "Where we're going, it will be colder than here," she says.

"You're kind," I tell her.

She smiles, and in the sunlight I see tiny white scars on her skin—scars I hadn't noticed before. It's as if a million tiny shards of something exploded in her face, long ago. "I'm kind until I need to be cruel."

I'm amazed at how swiftly the sprawling camp is packed away into bundles, lashed over the backs of saddles and onto the warriors' backs. Within an hour we're ready to leave, and the line of horses files into the trees, led by the Warlord himself.

Riding with Zeha is more comfortable—her saddle has extra padding. But it's less exciting than riding with the Warlord, and I miss the hectic uncertainty of being in his presence.

After a while, I venture to ask Zeha the question that's been burning in my mind. "What did you mean, earlier, when you said that some couples can hear each other's voices through the ether?"

"You may have heard the stories of the Bloodsalt and the northern lands beyond," she says. "How this entire land was damaged from the aftereffects of one woman's uncontrollable magic. I'm not sure if the legends are true. Few of our people are born as mages, and when one of us is gifted, the gift usually relates to healing. But we are magically sensitive in other ways. We are born with a link to this land, so we can sense when a breaking of the Bloodsalt is about to occur, in time to get clear of the explosion. We can discern places in the forest where evil is likely to haunt, so we know to plant our tents elsewhere. And the people of my clan can each hear the thought-voice of their soul-partner, their life-mate, when they are unconscious or asleep. For most people it is faint and distant, and it happens at unpredictable times. For others, the conversation is as clear as the one I'm having with you now."

My heart thumps harder.

"When two people discover that they can hear each other through the ether, it is a sign that their souls have already bonded. They are meant to be a pair until death parts them, and so they request the forging of a life-bond by a Shaman of the Bloodsalt."

"Are there ever times when other souls communicate through the ether?" I ask. "Surely it doesn't always mean a life-mate bond or whatever you said. There must be exceptions."

"None that I've ever heard of."

I remember the voice I heard when I was dying, clear and gruff and annoying. *Do you have a spine? Any will to fight? Or are you just a weak little mouse after all? Pull yourself out of this. Show me you have teeth. Bite and scratch.*

That's why the Warlord reacted with such shock when I told him I could hear his voice in that liminal place. My consciousness was in the ether when he spoke to me. And I heard him.

But I'm not one of his clan. I wasn't born here.

"Could such a conversation happen between two people who aren't from one of your clans?" I venture. "Like if there was one person from the Bloodsalt or beyond, and one from—somewhere else—could they still speak through the ether? And what would that mean?"

Zeha has been riding with her palm lightly against my waist, and her grip tightens as I speak. "Why are you asking me this?"

I consider lying, but I'm desperate to know the truth.

"When I was dying, I heard him," I murmur. "The Warlord. He talked to me, and—and I came back from the dark."

"That's not possible. Ether-speak only occurs between life-mates, among the people of our clans." She lets out an exasperated huff. "Have you told him of this?"

"Yes. He seemed very disturbed by it."

"Of course he did, because it's abhorrent, and impossible." She's speaking through gritted teeth. "Has he bedded you? Touched you?"

"No, and—a little."

"*Faen*," she swears. "I did not expect this. He isn't meant for this. He's not for you, do you understand? He will marry one of the proud daughters of our people, and not the craven, simpering child of our mortal enemies."

"Good," I spit. "I don't want to marry the hulking grotesque bastard of some wretched barbarian clan."

"Then it's settled. You and I will prevent him from carrying out this mad idea of his, this plan of marrying you if a bargain isn't struck." Zeha lowers her voice. "I'll send your Prince Havil another message, with an amended offer. We will see if he bites. Don't tell my brother of it, do you understand?"

"I won't tell him," I promise. "Trust me, I want to go home."

28

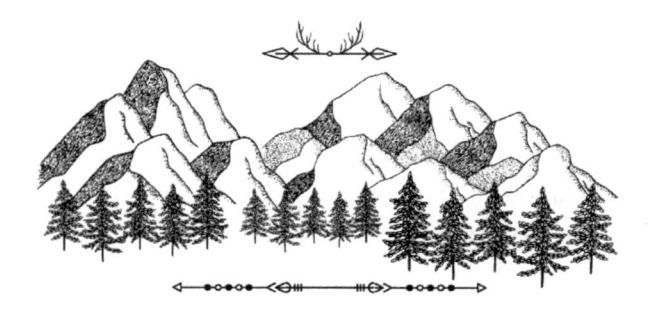

As we ride further into the forest, the trees begin to change. They no longer have the scarlet veins twining their trunks; instead, frosty crystals cluster along the bark and the branches. Most of them glitter white, but some have a bloody, pinkish tinge.

The undergrowth is white, too, but not with frost—the very leaves, petals, and pods of the strange plants are pallid, as if ice infuses their cells. Not an insect or animal is in sight, except for the great form of Kaja pacing beside the Warlord's horse.

After a time one of the warriors in the company begins to hum, low in his throat—a sustained groaning sound that reverberates through the silent, frozen forest. Another warrior joins in with a staccato thrum, like a vocal drumbeat. More of the riders add their voices, each one in a different rhythm and register, until the woods are filled with a perfectly synchronized chorus of rich, wild voices. Behind me on the horse, Zeha lends a soft wail to the song. Even Jili participates, her youthful voice a high counterpoint to the droning note of the female warrior with whom she's riding. The two of them share a similar skin tone and features. Related, maybe, which would partly explain the presence of someone so young in this company.

My skin chills and tightens with a dread delight at the wild song of the raiders. Some cautiously feral part of me, deep inside, wants to crawl out and join the music, contribute my own throaty chant to the rhythm. But I repress it, sitting primly quiet on the horse.

The singing continues for an hour or so, and then gradually drifts into silence. We clop across a frozen sheet of lake or field—I can't tell which—and enter another forest, a thicker one with tall, thin, close-set trees, like pale pillars, naked except for a crown of lacy white branches at their very tops, high overhead.

"'Ware, and keep watch," calls the Warlord. He turns in his saddle, and for the first time since we started our journey, he looks at me. Or maybe he's looking at his sister. He lifts a hand and beckons, so Zeha urges her mount ahead, bringing it abreast of his. We can't ride directly beside him because no space between the trees is wide enough for more than one horse to pass, but we stay near.

"This wood is infested with ice-wyrms," says the Warlord in a low voice. He doesn't look my way again, but he must be speaking to me, since Zeha already knows the territory. "The swarms usually stay in the treetops near the eastern edge of the forest during the day, so we should be safe."

"What are ice-wyrms?" I ask.

"Pray to the gods you never find out."

"That's not much of an answer," I grumble. "Why even mention them if you won't tell me—"

But a shimmering, tinkling sound interrupts me, and the Warlord holds up a broad hand, his face tightening with apprehension.

He's afraid. And that, more than his warning, drains the blood from my face and sends ice into the pit of my soul.

Another chiming ripple of sound, and the Warlord bellows, "Weapons! Spread out in pairs, and run for the open!"

The company of warriors obeys him instantly, breaking into groups of two and racing ahead through the maze of trees. Zeha urges our mount into a gallop, and I clutch mane and saddle to steady myself as the mare pitches this way and that, dodging the pillar-like trunks.

Up ahead, several silvery-white lines zig-zag through the forest, zooming in parallel to the horses' heads. They whip against one of the riders, and he falls with a cry. Zeha releases an anguished shout as we plunge past the fallen man, but she does not stop. His blood is already jetting onto the white foliage. We cannot help him or his horse, who crashes onto her side, spewing blood from a torn throat.

As we pass them, I catch a glimpse of slim, shimmering creatures like eels, beautiful things with pearly, iridescent scales and tiny fins along their bodies. They lace and coil around the fallen corpses, moving impossibly fast, slitting and biting.

29

The Warlord has his great sword out, wielding it one-handed while he grips the reins in his other fist. His blond braids lash as his head turns, watching all sides, glancing behind. "Faster!" he roars.

But the horses cannot run full out among these close-set trees. When I glance to my right, I see the glimmering shapes of more ice-wyrms. They're approaching at my eye level, writhing up the slender trunks and flinging themselves from tree to tree. When they leap through midair, their fins flare and they glide for a moment. The thin lancing rays of the sun flash on their pearly scales.

"How do they move so fast?" I gasp.

"We shouldn't have taken this route," Zeha mutters. "Grab the reins. Just hold them—the mare will guide herself."

I obey. Zeha's body shifts, and then there's the gleam of a long blade on my right. I'm not thrilled with the idea of her brandishing that sharp weapon so close to me, but I have to trust her skill.

The ice-wyrms snake toward us, tree-to-tree, and then one flings itself directly at our galloping mare. Zeha slices through the wyrm neatly, then smacks another one aside before it can strike. A third escapes her guard and sails straight at me—a line of pure lethal beauty, with a mouth like a rose except instead of petals, there are overlapping layers of razor teeth.

Screaming, I punch at the oncoming creature, knocking it away. A few of its teeth lacerate my knuckles—better that than my face or throat.

They're all around us now, a glittering flurry of eel-like bodies falling from trunks, whipping through midair, snapping at our flesh before falling to the ground and wriggling back up the trees to try again.

They're so impossibly quick. Zeha cries out and nearly drops her weapon, but she rallies and keeps slashing.

One of the ice-wyrms dives straight for my chest, latching onto the furs and gnawing straight through them, burrowing as if it wants to screw a path to my heart.

With a shriek I grip the ice-wyrm around the body and yank it free just as its teeth burn into my skin. I fling it wildly away, and it hits two of its companions and knocks them out of midair too.

My eyes focus on the shape riding nearby—the Warlord. He saw what I did, and for the tiniest of suspended moments, I relish the approval in his eyes.

But there's no time to speak. A swarm of the toothy, pearly eels flutters between us, shimmering, snapping, clouding my view of him. I catch one glimpse of Kaja leaping into the air, snarling and twisting, batting the serpents aside with her paws.

Zeha yells to her mare, begging for more speed. With a panicked whinny the horse complies, charging even faster between the trunks while Zeha whips her sword to my right, then to my left. One of the wyrms skims past the horse's neck, opening a long cut. I switch the reins to one hand and clamp my palm over the wound, trying to stem the flow of blood. It pulses warm between my fingers.

Tiny teeth rake across my shoulder, and a sharp tail scratches my cheekbone.

And then we're out of the trees, thundering across open land. As I look back, several of the ice-wyrms fling themselves frantically at us, but most of them fall short, writhing on the pale ground, scuffing up the layer of white salt to reveal scarlet clay.

"The Bloodsalt?" I wonder aloud. "I thought we left it behind."

"The largest section of the Bloodsalt is near the mountains," Zeha says, tugging the last ice-wyrm from the horse's flank and throwing it away. "But there are smaller strips of it throughout these lands. The magical corruption extends far into the North."

Most of the warriors in our company have gathered up ahead, and a few burst out of the forest behind us, joining the cluster of survivors.

30

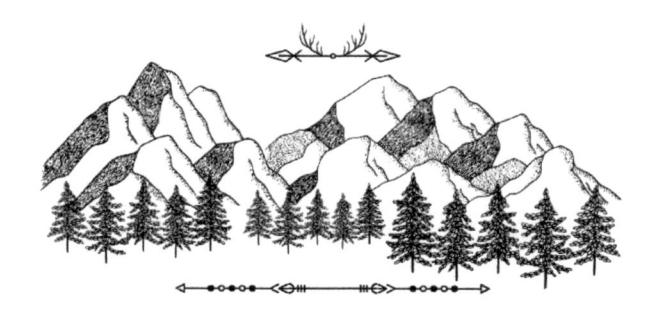

With Kaja at his side, the Warlord rides around the group, his eyes flicking from one face to another. I exhale with relief when I see Jili still on horseback with the female warrior.

"One man lost," the Warlord says.

The others voice a guttural moan in response, a low, blended vocalization of sorrow. My heartbeat is already quick, and the strange, doleful sound nearly sends me into a panic.

The Warlord rides up to Zeha and me, his eyes latching onto the place where my bloody palm still presses the mare's neck.

"We should have gone around," Zeha says.

"It would have taken an extra day and a half."

"And that saved time was worth Belwyn's life?" she says harshly.

"Yes, because it takes us beyond the reach of her kind." The Warlord jerks his head at me. "She is secure now. They cannot get to her. We have our leverage."

"Leverage you have not yet been able to wield."

"When they cannot find her and rescue her, they will be ready to bargain," he says.

Zeha shakes her head. "You cannot decide the fate of every clan. When we reach home, you must summon the other warlords to a council. They should have a say in this bargain, too."

"Why?" he snaps. "All they care about is living as thieves and brigands, wreaking terror and violence. They revel in it. They don't want change. They'd as soon kill her as hold her for ransom."

"Some of them think as you do," Zeha replies. "And if you are going to bargain for a land-price, for a piece of soil south of the mountains, you'll need allies among the clans, or you won't be able to hold onto the land you get. Not that her family will yield any property to you—but in case they do, you'll need a few other warlords on your side."

I'm stuck between the siblings, unable to escape the conversation, so I try to make myself small. My face, chest, and shoulder burn from the ice-wyrms' teeth, but I'm more concerned about the horse. Her head hangs low, and her flanks shudder with every breath. She's practically steaming from the exertion. With every passing second, more of her blood pumps out, despite the fact that I'm pressing so hard on the wound that my arm is shaking.

The Warlord dismounts and approaches, tugging a long scarf from his shoulders and unbuckling one of the belts at his waist. He begins wrapping the scarf and belt around the horse's neck.

"Your questions about my methods can wait," he says quietly to Zeha. "We need to get home. If you can call any of your hawks, and you want to summon the other warlords to our village, I will not stop you."

"You'll meet with them?" Zeha says.

"Yes. You can move your hand now, mouse."

I lift my fingers, and he quickly pads the horse's wound with the scarf and cinches the belt tight.

"She's too weak to carry both of you," he says. "You'll ride with me, mouse."

I slide off the horse, and my legs immediately crumple. Terror has left me weak. My bloodied hand sinks into the crusted salt.

The Warlord drops to one knee, cupping my face and running his thumb along my scratched cheekbone. Then his fingers drift to my chest, where there's a gnawed hole through the furs and leather.

He pulls all of the clothing aside, inspecting the small teeth marks over my breastbone. "Not too deep," he says. "It's barely bleeding."

But he doesn't remove his hand from my chest.

Zeha has dismounted and moved aside to tend to her mare and call her hawks. The others in our party seem distracted with their own wounds. For a moment, the Warlord and I are alone, unobserved.

His fingertips skim along the inner curve of my breast. I inhale raggedly, watching him, quivering at the intensity of the pleasure that rolls through me at that one tentative touch.

His fingers nudge deeper, under the edge of the furs, grazing my nipple. It's hard and tight with need. Color rises in his face, above the blond scruff.

"She's right," he whispers. "I was a fool to take us through that part of the forest. You could have died."

I swallow and suck in a breath, my chest surging against his fingers.

"Sometimes the passage is easy," he continues. "Not a swarm in sight. But this time—" He sighs and arranges my clothes again before unfolding his great frame and standing to his full height. He towers above me, and I tremble with the hunger for him to lift me, to crush me against himself.

My body craves him, and I don't know why. He's my enemy, a killer of my people. His kind have destroyed lives and villages all along the borders of my district.

I shouldn't want him. And I certainly shouldn't be tremulously thrilled at the idea of riding with him again.

31

The Warlord makes me ride behind him this time. I suppose he doesn't want to deal with his body's response to me when he should be mourning his fallen warrior. But I'm not sure that having me leaning against his back with my arms around his waist is any less tantalizing for either of us.

The sun sets and the sky darkens to a deep bluish-purple, like a bruise. Crisp white stars glitter in the arched expanse. Yet still the Warlord does not call for a halt. He seems intent on crossing this stretch of the Bloodsalt before we stop for the night.

The white tiger Kaja has run off, and he doesn't call her back. Perhaps she's not so much his pet as his occasional partner, half-wild, permitted to roam as she pleases.

My body aches, my wounds sting, and I'm so weary I think I might tumble off the horse any second. And it's cold—a deep, dark, bone-cracking cold.

"How much longer?" I whimper against his cloaked back.

"This part of the Bloodsalt is volatile," he says. "We can't stop here."

"Volatile how?"

"Sometimes it bursts open."

"Like an earthquake?"

"Like an explosion of liquid clay. Like a geyser of blood. And then, as it settles, everything is sucked down with it, and the hole seals over. See there?" He points to a branching scar, half-concealed by salt. "That's from a recent explosion."

"I thought the Bloodsalt was safe, or stable, at least. Why do you ride across it if it's so dangerous?"

"Because we have no other choice. Because this is the world we were given—a land laced with ruin, soured by corrupt magic."

"It's my people's fault you were driven out here," I murmur. My limbs are weakening, slackening, no matter how desperately I want to be strong for him, to endure, to show him that I can be tough—

My arms drop from his waist, and I nearly slide off, but he reaches back and steadies me.

"I'm so cold and tired and thirsty," I moan.

"*Faen*," he bites out. And then he calls out to the others up ahead. "Ride on. We will follow."

They don't question him, though Zeha glances back through the frigid gloom, her eyes sharp with suspicion.

The Warlord pulls to a halt and dismounts. He takes a flat bottle from one of his saddlebags and hands it up to me. "Drink."

I gulp eagerly—and then I release a faint shriek, because the liquid inside isn't water. It roars through my mouth and throat, scorching my insides. "Oh gods," I whimper. "What was that?"

"Something to keep you warm." Maybe it's my imagination or the play of clouds across the moon, but it looks as if the Warlord is smirking. "Move forward in the saddle."

I try, but I nearly tumble off. He grunts in frustration, propping me up while he mounts again, this time behind me. "You weak little scrap of flesh."

"But I helped," I murmur. "Back there, with the ice-wyrms. I was useful."

He settles in at my back, and I let myself relax against him with a sigh of relief.

His body stiffens, and then he says, low, "I am not your safety. I am your captor."

"But you like me."

"I hate you."

"Of course you do. And you like me as well. Both."

"You're talking nonsense. Maybe you lost more blood than I thought."

"Maybe it's the drink you gave me. I do feel warmer now." I snuggle deeper against him. "Why didn't you give me some of that on the night you captured me?"

"I didn't want to waste it on you."

"And now?"

"Why can't you ever be quiet?"

I pinch my lips shut for what feels like forever, and then I say, "You touched my breasts earlier. But the other night you said you didn't like them, that they were too small."

He groans, adjusting himself behind me. "Stop."

"I'm only existing, and riding. I can't stop either of those things."

"Stop *talking*."

"I was just wondering if you'd changed your mind about my breasts. That's all." The hazy warmth of the drink is swimming through my veins, humming in my head. "If you like them, you can touch them."

"I'll touch any part of you whenever I want," he says, ragged. "You're my captive, my prize. I don't need your permission."

I tilt my head back on his shoulder, looking up at him. "Do it then. I'm too weak to resist you anyway," I say softly.

"You think I haven't considered it?" His words drag through his teeth, rough and dark. "Most Warlords would set their mark on you, send you back bruised and used. You would look so lovely with the prints of my teeth and fingers on your pale skin, with my seed filling you up. I'd deliver you to your husband-to-be just like that—marked by me, bred by me. He would know that you're mine. Mine."

He tears one hand from the reins and wraps it over my throat—not a constricting hold, but a possessive one. Through the haze of the drink, my body flares with a panicked craving—half terror, half lust. The way he was talking—those primal, brutish words sent a flood of liquid desire between my legs. If he touched me now, he'd find me slick and trembling, eager for him.

32

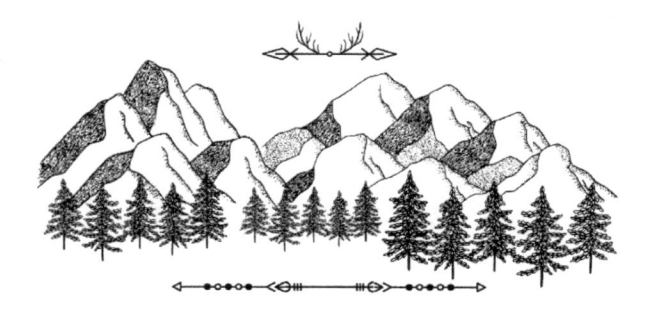

My body has been simmering with reluctant desire for the Warlord, and now, with the aid of that fiery drink, my flesh ignites. My breath puffs short and hot, white wisps in the frozen dark. My very skin feels alive, awake, crawling with fevered lust, screaming to be touched.

My head still lolls on his shoulder, and his massive hand cups my neck. I turn my face toward him, warming my nose and lips against the hot skin of his throat. He swallows hard.

Slowly his hand drifts down my throat, over my collarbones and lower, moving across my breast. Despite the layers I wear, I feel the pressure like a brand on my naked skin. I release a quiet moan into the still air of the night.

A rumble passes through his chest. He's hard against my rear, the length of him clearly tangible despite our clothing. He changes tactics, plunging his hand into the neckline of my shirt. As he massages my bare breast, a wild heat flares at my core, and I arch into the touch.

"I hate that you make me feel like this," I whisper.

He makes a sound—a huff of angry frustration, and he pinches my nipple. I gasp and twist against him, stunned by the spike of pleasure between my legs. Prince Havil and I never got past a bit of kissing and fondling. He certainly never touched me like this.

"What are you thinking right now?" I say hoarsely.

"I'm not thinking."

"Everyone thinks, all the time."

"Not me. Sometimes I only feel. And then I do stupid things, like this." Under my shirt, he spreads his warm, large hand across my chest.

But the next second he yanks his hand out of my clothes and grips the reins, straightening so abruptly that I'm jostled upright. "What is it?" I exclaim.

"People born here, people like me—we can sense the unrest of the land," he says. "The Bloodsalt is about to break. Hang on. We must ride faster."

He bends forward, his great body and massive arms encircling me as the horse picks up the pace. But his horse is weary—I can feel it. The long journey and our combined weight is too much.

The others are so far ahead I cannot see them. They are safe, but the Warlord and I—we are not.

A loud snap behind us startles me, and I jerk in the Warlord's arms. He only leans farther forward and speaks to the horse in his native tongue, a crooning tone edged with panic. The stallion thunders desperately faster across the Bloodsalt.

Tears whip from my eyes as the night breeze scrapes over my face like an icy blade.

Another cracking noise from behind, and then gurgling, roaring explosion. Clumps of wet scarlet rain down on the white salt around us, and crimson cracks begin to snake across the land, splitting crooked like lightning, widening.

"You have to leave me," I whisper. "I'm dead weight. Leave me and ride."

People are always setting me aside while they move on. I'm used to being left behind.

"Your weight isn't enough to make a difference," he snarls. "Mine is. Tell my sister she's responsible for the bargain now. She'll take care of you, and arrange the ransom with your people. You're our hope for a better future."

He's throwing himself off the horse before I can stop him. The stallion slows, whinnying desperately, but the Warlord smacks him and shouts, and the beast catapults ahead, free of his master's weight. The horse and I race the ever-growing, ever-spreading cracks in the ground, a blood-red net of death.

I clutch the reins, screaming. A look over my shoulder shows the Warlord's massive figure, dwarfed by a cataclysmic tower of bubbling red—a fountain of blood soaring high, high into the night, uplit by some molten pit below. The salt and the clay are caving inward, crumbling into some unknowably deep chasm in the crust of the world. In a moment the Warlord will disappear into its widening maw.

"No!" I shriek, and I haul backward on the reins with all my strength. The horse shrills in pain and skids to a halt—just long enough for me to scramble off, and then the stallion bolts, fleeing alone across the Bloodsalt.

33

My boots skid in the powdery clumps of salt, and my knees wobble from the drink the Warlord gave me, but an emotion stronger than fear propels me and I run back, toward the glowing geyser. The Warlord is running too, pounding toward me, bellowing something I can't hear—then the ground splits beneath him and he drops—almost disappears, but he grips the broken crust of the earth. He's struggling on the edge, while more lines snake outward from the spot. He'll go down any minute—disappear forever.

I could leave him, be rid of him.

The thought skates through my mind and I reject it instantly. I skid to a stop at the edge of the broken place where he's hanging, choking on my own fear as I face the monstrosity of the explosion. The rush of the spewing molten clay fills my ears, and the grinding of the earth nearly deafens me.

The Warlord's cloak rips free from his shoulders and flies into the depths, a dark doomed bird fluttering against the red glare. I grip the belt that runs across the Warlord's chest and I pull with all my might, shrieking and sobbing.

Whatever strength I have is just enough to help him clamber back up.

"You idiot!" he yells above the conflagration. "Run!" He grips my collar and practically throws me ahead of him.

"You're welcome!" I yell. I force the fog of the drink aside and I focus on running, running faster than I ever have in my life.

But I've never trained or exercised. My body can't magically become the instrument of escape that I need. I can feel it failing—my lungs spasming from the cold and exertion, my throat tightening, refusing to draw in air.

The ground breaks with a cracking shudder, and I'm thrown forward onto my stomach. There's a roar behind me—a sucking force of wind and something else, something magical and compelling, drawing everything into the molten maw of the Bloodsalt.

I'm skimming backward, toward the magnetic force of it—but the Warlord drives his great sword into the crust of the ground like an anchor, grips it one-handed, and clutches my wrist with his other hand.

For one shearing, agonized moment, I fear my arm will be ripped off as the implosion tries to pull me down with it.

And then the horrible tearing force is gone. A rumble passes through the clay, the snap of cracks sealing, gaps closing.

Silence drops over us like a sheet of black ice. We lie panting on the surface of the Bloodsalt, and when I glance over my shoulder there's no geyser, and no chasm. Everything is whole again. Healed as if it was never there—except for the dull brick-red scars across the surface and the splattered lumps of cooling red clay.

The Warlord releases my wrist and lets his forehead fall against the cold white salt. His shoulders slump with relief.

But I can't breathe. My lungs won't accept the air—it sticks in my throat, refusing to go where it's needed. I cough, sharp and desperate, but I can't inhale more than the tiniest sips of freezing air, and the cold only makes everything worse. I roll onto my back, eyes wide, fingers clawing the salt. Tiny wheezes are the only sound I can make to signal my distress.

"Mouse?" The Warlord crawls to me, hauls me into his lap. He knows I'm not faking it this time. He cradles me against his chest, pressing one big warm hand above my breasts. The heat eases my lungs a little.

"Breathe with me," he murmurs. "Breathe with me, treasure. Please."

"Air—too—cold," I manage. He nods, understanding, and turns me toward him, into the warmth of his body and breath. "Breathe with your belly," he says. "That helped my brother sometimes. From here." He touches the center of my stomach, just beneath my breastbone, where my ribs arch outward.

With my cheek pressed to his bare chest I breathe with him, drinking slow inhales of the warmer air that lies against his skin. I breathe through my nose, carefully, while my hands grip his with the spastic strength of someone clawing her way out of a yawning grave.

At last, at last, I'm able to haul in a deep, satisfying breath, all the way to the bottom of my lungs. I still have to breathe carefully, but the deadly fog is clearing from my brain. And as it clears, I remember what the Warlord called me.

Not rat, or mouse, or weakling.

Treasure.

34

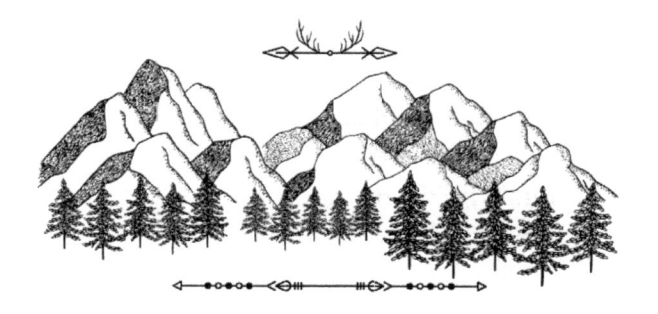

The Warlord carries me the rest of the way across the Bloodsalt plain, to the forested hills beyond. These trees are familiar—evergreens with brushy branches and prickly cones. In the shadow of their boughs the company of warriors waits anxiously. Zeha is holding the Warlord's horse by the bridle.

"We were going to come after you," she says, white-faced. "But I thought you would want me to take our people to safety."

"Yes." He nods to her. "You did right. And we survived."

He doesn't explain how he jumped off the horse, or that I saved him, or that he saved me by helping me through my breathing struggle. He simply puts me back on his horse and mounts again.

Kaja prowls out of the undergrowth, a striped shadow of snow and ebony, her eyes luminous. If she sensed her master's peril, she shows no sign of it—merely takes her usual place by the side of his mount.

"A little further into the trees," the Warlord says. "And then we camp."

The wind picks up as we travel, and by the time we halt and the warriors set up the tents, snow is scouring between the trees, sifting down through the scant canopy of evergreen boughs. The Warlord helps with camp, leaving me alone on his stallion's back. I can't do anything but huddle in my cloak and try to keep my chest and throat as warm as possible while breathing through my nose. The wind seems to slice right through my leathers and furs, straight to my skin and deeper, right down to my bones and into the marrow. I can't feel my toes or my nose, but my fingers blaze with the pain of the cold.

Through the rising storm, Zeha calls, "She isn't used to this—you need to get her warm! Take her in the first tent and make a fire!"

A moment later the Warlord's figure appears through the swirling snow. He scoops me off the horse and bundles me into the first tent they erected. I curl up on the ground, shivering, half-unconscious. Vaguely I'm aware of him starting a small fire, piling skins and blankets nearby as a bed. This tent is far smaller than the first one I shared with him—it's a hastily constructed shelter, barely big enough for us both.

When the Warlord comes to me, I'm shaking so hard I can't speak. He tugs my boots off, cupping my toes and wincing at how icy they are.

"You have no endurance for the cold, mouse," he mutters. "You need warmth, and quickly."

He pulls off my snow-laden outer layers—and then he drags my shirt over my head and throws it aside. I try to protest, but I'm too dizzy, too sleepy. My pants are pulled off next, leaving me entirely naked—and then he's tucking me into the bed he made.

I'm shaking so hard I can't speak. I can barely concentrate on my breathing anymore. It would be easier to stop breathing, to slip into the seamless dark and drift forever…

The blankets lift, and a blast of cold air washes over me for a second before it's replaced by the great heated bulk of the Warlord's body. His *naked* body. He's wearing some sort of loincloth but otherwise he's bare, the warm planes of his chest and stomach pressed fully against me. With a sigh that's nearly a sob, I cuddle closer to that expanse of heated muscle. His chest is lightly garnished with curly blond hair, and it brushes my cheek as I nestle into him. My frozen toes press against his legs.

Slowly his heat saturates me, body and soul.

35

When I wake, my head is tucked under the Warlord's chin, and I'm bunched against him. His arm lies heavy across my body, a soothing weight. From what I can see in the bit of low firelight, he seems to be asleep.

I must have rested a long time, because I don't feel nearly so exhausted anymore. Beyond the taut skins of our tent, the blizzard howls, pressing as if it wants to break through and bury us in snow. But the tents of the Warlord's people are sturdy. This burly son of the North drove the stakes deep despite the frozen earth, and I can rest with him, knowing I have a reliable shelter.

In the dim glow of the flickering fire I can make out his features, half bathed in amber, half shadowed in deep gray. He's beautiful, from the sweep of his brow, lightly seamed with lines of worry and war, to his thick lips, rough from the blast of snow and salt. His nose is perfectly straight, not crooked from battle like those of some in his company. It's a flawless nose, a kingly nose. And his cheekbones are bold and beautiful, jutting against skin flushed rosy with our shared heat.

His jaw is coated in a light blond beard now, but I can still make out the lines of it, the crisp corners and strong chin. His hair has mostly fallen out of the braids, and it sweeps in loose golden waves across the furs.

Godlike he is, yet almost boyish too, with those long, darkly-golden lashes. He has tiny fine wrinkles at the corners of his eyes, from squinting against the winter sun, and maybe from smiling, too.

My gaze travels to the brutal thickness of his throat and collarbones, the bulging curve of his shoulder. The rest of him is under the blanket, with me. My hands are tucked between my chest and his. Carefully I flatten them against his giant pectorals, feeling the soft scattering of hair over his skin. My hand slides lower, moving in tiny increments so I don't wake him. Once again, I want to touch the swells and ridges of the abdominal muscles I admired when I saw him naked, and when I bathed his wounds.

My fingers ripple over the bulging muscles, and I inhale softly. They still feel as amazing as they look.

Lower, and lower, until my fingers encounter more hair, a thickening swirl of it, disappearing under the wrap he wears around his privates. Kind of him not to jump into bed with all his goods hanging free. Although at this moment, I'm not sure I would mind.

My consciousness reverts to my own body, to the warm liquid heat pooling low in my belly, seeping between my thighs. I withdraw my fingers from the Warlord's body and tuck them into that crevice of my legs, trying to quiet the craving—but I only succeed in stoking it higher.

I can't do this now. I can't achieve the angle and pressure I need for release, not in this position. Sighing quietly, I curl my hands against my chest again.

The Warlord shifts, and I freeze—but he's still asleep, his brow dented with troubling dreams.

If we're really bonded, could he hear my thought-voice in his sleep?

Swallowing, I focus my thoughts on him. *I wish I could ease your sleep like you eased my breath. And I wish that the craving I have for you would vanish. I know you feel it too, and you hate it as much as I do. It's only the lust of two bodies put in close proximity. Nothing more, nothing meaningful. Unless you can hear me through the ether, and then maybe it's more. Wouldn't that be a cruel trick of the gods?* Faen, *I am burning up with all this desire. I want you to touch me so badly I can hardly bear it.*

The last thought is more to myself than him, because I don't truly believe in soul-bonds or thought-voices. Do I?

The Warlord's earlier movement dislodged the blanket, and my back is growing chilled, exposed to the cold air by the wall of the tent. Gingerly, by degrees, I twist beneath his arm, rolling over until my bare back is pressed to his front. I tug the blankets to my chest and sigh as the heat of him spreads through my chilled spine.

He stirs, his arm moving down at an angle. The motion brings his hand much too close to the space between my legs that desperately wants tending.

I lie perfectly still, breathing rhythmically like a woman who is deeply asleep. But I burn, inside and out.

And then the Warlord's hand moves again—with purpose this time.

36

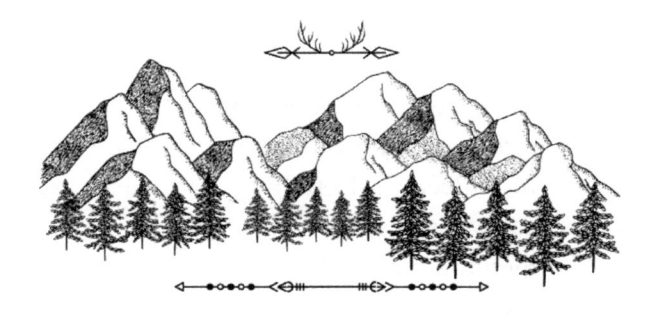

His palm shifts into a gliding caress up my thigh, over my hip, along the dip of my waist. He stops at my ribs, where my arms are tucked against my chest. Then down again, smoothing my warm skin in a long stroke, framing my curves with his hand. His fingers slide across my lower belly, down to the triangle between my thighs. And he nudges there with his fingertips, as if requesting entrance.

Did he hear me when I spoke to him in his sleep?

He cups my left thigh, urging it upright so my legs are no longer pressed together. Now the left leg is arched, and my secret places lie open to him.

He knows I'm awake—my breath is quick and shallow, a telltale sign of my eagerness. But I don't speak, and neither does he. Perhaps if we do not speak, if we stay in the dreamlike cocoon of this tent, whatever we do together won't be real—won't affect our future or complicate our plans.

I know he's thinking it, just as I am. And the certainty of his thoughts frightens and thrills me almost as much as the broad, thick fingers creeping along my thigh toward my trembling center.

He touches me, a delicate caress upward through my folds, and he hums low in his chest, a rumble of satisfaction because I'm so very wet for him. I try to summon Prince Havil from the recesses of my thoughts, but I can't. It's as if the Prince doesn't exist, as if his lips and hands never touched mine. This is the hand that was always meant to caress me. These are the fingers designed to trace the seam of me, to manipulate the delicate nerves and quivering petals of my body.

I reach up and grip the bicep of the arm the Warlord is using to tease me. I wrap my fingers around that giant swelling muscle, and the feel of it, the strength of him—it propels me closer to the glimmering edge of the pleasure I crave.

He's a little clumsy, my Warlord—a questing glide of fingertips, with none of the rhythm I want. Has he been with other women? Perhaps with others he simply plunged his length inside, instead of playing with them first.

My fingers travel down, along the ropy sinews of his forearm, to that fumbling male hand, and I guide him. Tiny massaging circles near the top. A quick venture lower, a shallow dip into deeper parts of me.

More circles, a rhythm both soothing and stimulating. He learns quickly, and I let go, cupping my hand over my mouth while he tries new things, flicking and rubbing and palpating. Every soft whimper of mine is echoed by a rumble from him and a twitch of the rigid member pressed to my backside. Eliciting moans from me makes him harder, and that knowledge sends a thrill into my stomach.

He begins rubbing me lightly, faster, and I let out a series of hitching whines, nearly sobs, because I'm nearly there, nearly there—I squirm, clutching his arm, and I buck against his hand. His fingers circle, slick and quick, and I nearly shriek as a bolt of ecstasy rips through my belly, shearing along my spine. My legs jerk and quiver, and he gathers me to him, growling his triumph, cupping my sex possessively with his great hand. His teeth bite lightly into my earlobe, and I shudder against him.

When I can breathe normally again, I turn to face him. He'll expect reciprocation—a fair exchange, my pleasure for his. Will he be satisfied with my hands, or demand entrance where I've never permitted a man to invade? Can I let the Warlord have all of me, when I'm promised to Prince Havil?

But before I can touch him, or offer myself, he leaves the warmth of the bed, wraps his cloak around himself, and goes out into the swirling blizzard.

37

Did I do something wrong?

Why didn't he let me tend to his desire as he tended to mine? I gnaw my lips, left behind to huddle alone in the fading warmth of the blankets.

When the Warlord comes back and slides into the bed again, he isn't erect anymore. He took care of himself, out there in the blistering cold.

Maybe he didn't mind indulging the desires of his enemy prisoner, but he thinks himself too superior to allow my touch.

I can't bring myself to ask. So I lie with my back to him, quietly seething until I fall asleep again. Until his deep voice, faint and frustrated, invades my dreams.

There is some magic in you that I cannot resist.

I can't respond to his thoughts, because I'm buried deep in a cloud of purple dreams, and they mute my voice. I can only listen.

You hear me, don't you, mouse? As I heard you when I was sleeping. But you don't understand what it means, this ability of ours to commune through the ether.

I do understand, I want to scream. *Your sister told me.*

I wonder if we could talk to each other through the ether if we were *both* asleep or unconscious?

There is a woman in my settlement, he continues. *Someone I thought I would take as my wife one day.*

An ache throbs in my heart, and I struggle against that deep, doleful voice. But he keeps talking.

She is right for me, and you are not, no matter what twisted chance connected our minds. Now that I have sated your craven lust, I will not touch you again. It was a foolish mercy on my part.

With a mighty effort, I break myself out of the dream and wake, sweating and panting, nearly sobbing. The Warlord lies propped on his elbow at my side, watching my face. A hint of alarm flares in his eyes at my sudden waking.

"Next time have the courage to say it to my face when I'm conscious," I gasp, my eyes pooling with tears. "Tell me now, great Warlord. Tell me you think I'm disgusting, weak and pathetic, treacherous and worthless. Say it!"

He scowls at me for a long moment. Then he says, "The wind is dying, and the storm is slowing. Soon we will break camp and travel the remaining distance to our settlement."

"Coward," I hiss at him, and turn my face away.

He stays still for several minutes, then rises. I keep my back to him, listening to the swish and shuffle as he gets dressed and stamps out the fire.

After he leaves the tent, I dress quickly and go outside. I relieve myself behind a bush, and no one fusses about standing guard while I do it. We're so far from my home that even if I did manage to escape, I'd die on the way back. The route is far too treacherous to survive alone.

It's time to face the truth, that my prickly, tantalizing interludes with the Warlord were the only thing keeping my spirits up. The deliciously forbidden possibility of him tempted me, in spite of my better judgment. But he is committed elsewhere, as I am. Not that I ever truly considered a relationship with him—we are mortal enemies, and the very idea is absurd.

Now that he's vowed not to touch me again—now that he has told me about the other woman—I have nothing to hope for, no forbidden future to imagine.

The woman he wants is probably strong, sturdy, and beautiful. She knows the land, and she'll bear him healthy children, not sickly ones. She doesn't have to be cradled and coaxed to breathe, and she can eat the coarse northern food without feeling sick.

I am simply a piece in a game my parents and Prince Havil are playing with the Warlord. I'll be kept in this awful wasteland until a bargain can be made—and if one can't be reached, then—

With a horrible shock, I recall what the Warlord said to his sister. How he plans to marry me if my father won't agree to the ransom. How a soul-bond between us will force my father to pay attention to his demands.

He clearly doesn't *want* to marry me. He wants this other woman, the one he planned to join with. What if he takes me to wife, as a political move, and then sleeps with her, and never touches me again? I might live for years in this deadly place, without ever knowing the loving embrace of a man.

No, it's unlikely that I'll live for years. I'll probably survive for a handful of miserable months before succumbing to the harsh climate, the fibrous food, and the monstrous dangers. I'll die a virgin, touched only by my own hand except for last night.

It's a desolate prospect, almost as distasteful as the cold, lumpy porridge I force myself to swallow. Getting out of this mess is looking less and less likely, and my heart feels heavy and sodden in my chest.

38

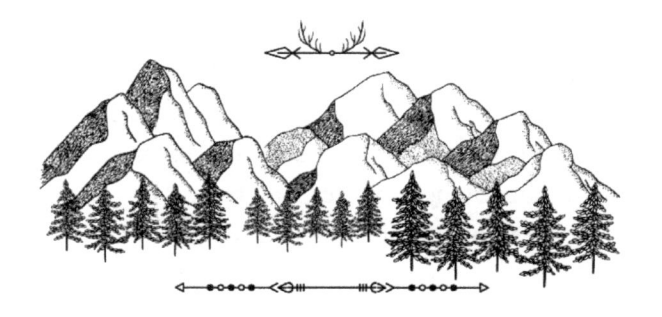

As we prepare to break camp, I notice that the horses look far worse for wear despite the hours of reprieve. They are shaggy, hardy beasts, born in this wilderness, but even they cannot endure a blizzard without suffering. Even though the snow has lessened to a sifting of large flakes, the horses remain bunched together under a scant shelter of skins that someone must have rigged for them when we stopped here.

The humans, too, are looking scruffier and more miserable than they did when I first saw them. They're certainly smellier, and some of them have minor wounds. The one who took me from my room in the stronghold, the one who is nearly as big as the Warlord, has puffy swollen bags under his eyes. Lacerations from the ice-wyrms mar his face and hands.

I can still feel my own shallow cuts from the ice-wyrms. They're stiff and a little sticky, but they barely hurt at all. When I dressed, I didn't see any oozing or swelling.

Only Kaja seems invigorated by our stop. She wasn't in the tent with the Warlord and me—perhaps she took refuge in another tent or preferred to remain outside. She bounds through the drifted snow like an oversized kitten. When she rolls up against a tree, and clumps of snow tumble from its boughs toward her face, she bats at them with enormous paws before leaping upright, chuffing and shaking her head.

Jili and the woman who looks like her mother mount their horse first, then Zeha follows, leading her wounded horse. A handful of others trail after them while the rest of the warriors finish packing up camp. I stand by the Warlord's horse and wait, fighting the urge to help with tying blankets into rolls or attaching them to saddles. I refuse to aid my kidnappers. Especially after their leader indulged my "craven lust" and then rejected me.

He's the last to leave the campsite, waving everyone ahead and then boosting me ungraciously into the saddle with a firm shove to my rear. I hold myself as close to the pommel as I can, trying to create space between us, but he's enormous, and it's impossible to stay clear of him completely. Finally I give up and settle in, though I keep my back rigid, touching him as little as possible.

Kaja paces just ahead of us, occasionally padding away into the trees to investigate some fascinating sight, sound, or smell.

"You're angry with me," the Warlord says.

I vent a scoffing laugh. "I've been angry with you since you kidnapped me."

He shifts behind me. "This is different."

"You don't care that I'm angry," I tell him. "You're my captor, not my protector. You hate me, remember? I'm a filthy worthless weakling with 'craven lust.' You're eventually going to send me home or kill me. Or you'll marry me, which is the same thing as killing me, because I can't survive up here."

"The land isn't all like this," he says. "Our home valley has some fertile soil, good hunting and fishing, and few monsters."

"Fertile land?" I snort. "How do you farm with all the snow and ice?"

"The upper slopes of the mountains receive plenty of sun. We time our plantings carefully, and we have crops that can survive."

"I don't care," I say recklessly. "I don't want to hear any more about it. I won't be staying long, at least not alive. So it doesn't matter."

"It could take weeks for your father and the prince to realize they can't find you. And even then, they may not contact me again."

"And in that case you'd—" I swallow hard.

"I'd take you as my wife, in the hopes that our bond would force your father's hand."

"I'd rather you killed me," I whisper.

A long silence. Then he says, low, "Am I such an unwelcome prospect as a husband?"

39

I almost laugh. An unwelcome prospect as a husband? He's an enemy raider, one who has ravaged my people's lands and taken our goods. Why should he care what sort of husband I think he'd make?

"You told me you're in love with another woman, and that you'll never touch me again," I say. "I'd rather not be soul-bound to a man who detests me, who is disgusted by my body's natural needs. Small and weak I may be, pitiful and pathetic in your eyes, but I'm a woman with the same capacity for love and pleasure as anyone else. And I have the same capacity for honor, bravery, loyalty, and jealousy, too. I'd rather not live to become a laughingstock among your people—the pathetic mouse with the disloyal husband who beds someone else."

"A soul-bond is sacred." He sounds shocked and offended. "If I bound myself to you, I would never stray. Not even if it meant I would never feel the warmth of a woman's body again." His voice sinks deeper. "And I never said I loved the woman in my village. Only that she and I would make a good match."

"But you *could* love her. You could have a strong family with her."

"I could. She is a strong, fertile, desirable woman."

"Yet you would marry *me*. You would ruin your life and mine, all for the sake of winning influence over my father?" My voice shrills, shaking with emotion I can't suppress.

"If it meant my people could gain a foothold in the southern lands—yes."

"That's—that's so godsdamn *noble*," I seethe. "Why are you such a beautiful, self-sacrificing bastard?"

"Beautiful?" He scoffs lightly.

"Yes. You're beautiful. A big glorious god-man in furs and armor. You don't smell great right now—sweat and blood and all—I don't smell like a patch of flowers either—but you're still the most beautiful man I've ever seen, and that's what I hate the most about you. That, and your big, noble, zealous heart. I hate you—" I'm half-sobbing now, clutching the pommel of the saddle and quaking with feelings so powerful I fear they might shake me apart. "I hate you so much, I hate you. Why couldn't you have left me at home? I was comfortable there—I was—I was fine."

I crumble, hunched over and weeping. My tears fall into the mane of the weary horse, onto his bowed neck.

The Warlord doesn't reply. He holds his stallion at a walk, lingering far behind the rearmost horse in the company. I'm not sure if the warriors ahead can hear me crying—until one of them breaks off from the group and rides back to us. It's the big man who slung me over his shoulder the night of my capture.

He stares at me, his thick beard curved in a disgusted frown. "Want me to gag her for you?" he asks.

"No," answers the Warlord.

The warrior pulls his horse alongside ours. "I can take her into the woods—give her a lesson like I gave to that wench in the butcher's shop—you know, the one from the village on the ridge, with the waterfall?"

"No," says the Warlord, in a deeper tone.

"Suit yourself." The raider shrugs. "Let me know if you need me to take the sniveling bitch awhile. I'll keep her nice and quiet so we can ride in peace. Best way to shut a southern whore's mouth is to show her something worth crying about." He sidles his horse closer, reaches past my bedraggled braids, and jerks my chin up. "She's got a pretty face. I'd like to paint it. Got the paint right here." He releases my face and chuckles, cupping between his legs.

The Warlord's huge sword is out and pointed at the raider's throat faster than I can blink. "Ride on," he says, a deathly growl.

The other warrior stares, dumfounded, at the massive blade angled for his neck. Gathering the reins, he urges his horse ahead, returning to the rest of the group.

Only after the Warlord sheathes the weapon do I realize that I've stopped crying.

40

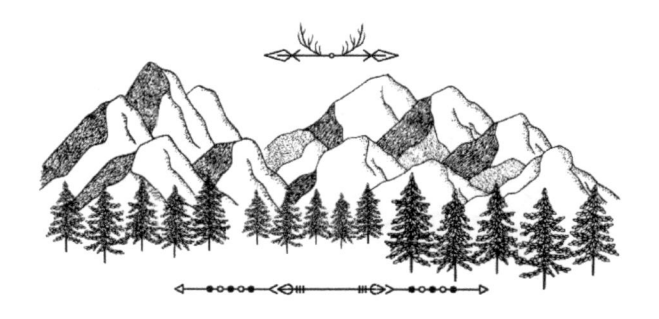

The Warlord's settlement is nestled in a cozy valley between two great mountains. On either side of the cluster of wooden cabins, the mountain slopes sweep upward, one shadowed and the other bathed in sunshine, gleaming so brightly I can't look at it long. The mountains flanking the village seem infinitely tall and sharp, and behind the settlement more mountains rise—beautiful icy spikes in the blue sky.

Smoke trails from the cabins, its savory scent wafting toward us on the breeze.

"Are all the warlords' settlements this pretty?" I ask.

The Warlord makes a pleased hum in his throat. "No."

As we ride into the village, I notice people occupied with cleaning and tanning hides, crafting arrows, salting fish. A sweat-slicked woman hammers weapons at a forge, her heavy coat lying aside over a chair. Several older children, bundled in furs, operate butter churns or small grain grinders, while younger ones run about playing.

The snow is frozen so hard it creaks beneath the horses' hooves as we tread the packed road through the village. Yet, cold as it is, it seems the whole village is out enjoying the sun and light while it lasts.

Up ahead, the rest of the company is already dismounting, and a few people approach to greet them—not a mad rush of giddy delight, but a stoic, pleased acknowledgement that they have returned whole. These forays and raids are commonplace here, and loss must also be commonplace.

A woman rises from whatever task she was doing—something with leather and needles—and approaches the Warlord's horse. She has striking bone structure, cheeks flushed with health, and a mass of chestnut braids crowning her head. She's buxom, wide-hipped, and lovely.

Kaja growls at her approach, and the Warlord orders, "Hush," in his alpha tone. The white tiger retreats, still snarling.

"Someday your cat will learn to like me," says the woman, smiling.

The Warlord dismounts without answering, and she steps forward and kisses his cheek.

My lips pinch together. This, then, is the woman he had planned to marry.

I slide off the horse without help—and promptly stumble because my legs are stiff from traveling. Kaja sidles up to me, and I use her shoulder for support.

"Thank you," I tell her, scrunching my fingers into her ruff. She rumbles, pressing nearer.

When I lift my eyes, I see the Warlord and the woman watching us. Pride threads through my heart. Holding my head high, I walk forward, my hand still resting on Kaja's neck.

"This is your prize?" the woman says. "Daughter of the district leader? Betrothed to the third prince of Cheimhold?" She adds something in her own dialect, but I don't need to understand the words to mark the scathing tone.

The Warlord's mouth is a hard line, his eyes glittering with purpose, anger, or pride—I can't discern which. Maybe all three.

"Two of the warlords are here already, and the third is arriving within the hour," the woman says, reverting back to the Common Tongue. "I put them in the meeting hall and gave them food and drink. You sent for them?"

"Zeha sent hawks for them, yes," he replies. "Have her birds returned?"

"All but one are back in the aerie."

"One is still out?" The Warlord frowns. "Do you think the storm took it down?"

"The hawks know when and how to take shelter," answers the woman. "It should return soon. Or perhaps she had another errand for it."

He scowls deeper, but then he seems to shake off his concern. "I will greet the other warlords. Take the prisoner to my lodge."

"Gladly."

I didn't see Zeha send out those messenger hawks, but I'm guessing when she sent messages to the warlords, she also sent one to my parents and Prince Havil. What ransom did Zeha ask for? Is it a price to which the Warlord would agree?

As he strides away toward a long, low building, the rosy-cheeked woman beckons me. "Come, child."

I want to snap that I'm not a child, no matter how thin and small I may look. But I restrain myself and walk to her. Kaja prowls beside me, her head low. Her posture is almost defensive.

I glance back, concerned for the Warlord's horse, but one of the village boys is already leading it along behind us. I'm glad. The poor creature deserves a warm shelter, some food, and a long rest. Three things I hope to have as well, when I reach the Warlord's lodge.

41

We walk through the village, past tidy homes built of logs and plaster and thatch. A few have walls of red-clay bricks. Most of them are patched in places, sealed with mud and mortar to keep out the wind. It is a solid, attractive settlement, as solid and attractive as the Warlord himself. But the weather-beaten faces of its people and the hate in their eyes when they look at me testify of hardship and suffering. This is a place devoted to the basics of survival, with few items of art, beauty, or comfort beyond what is necessary to keep out the cold. Herbs and medicines must be difficult to come by here, not to mention grain and fresh produce.

"There was a healer," I say suddenly to the woman guiding me. "He came twice, once for me and once for the Warlord. Does he live here?"

"We have one healer here—Mer Azatha," says the woman. "But there is a healer who lives on the border of the Lower Bloodsalt, near the mountains. He has a cabin there, built among the limbs of great trees. He serves the raiding parties returning from the southern lands. Makes good money for his work, too. He does not come this far north."

"Oh."

"And why did the Warlord need a healer?"

"He was injured fighting the *jäkel*," I mutter.

"The *jäkel*? But he wears the bones, always. Why was he fighting with them?"

"Because I ran away and pulled the bones out of my hair." I wince, touching the bits of bone still dangling in my loose braids.

Shaking her head, the woman mutters something that I'm sure isn't complimentary.

At the end of the village, on a low rise, stands a lodge larger and sturdier than all the others. Unlike the other cabins, its posts and lintel are decorated with painted designs.

The boy with the Warlord's horse has been following us, but now he turns aside, leading the stallion to a large stable nearby. Kaja pads away from me too, prowling the outside of the lodge, headed around back. Without her warm fur, the chill air bites my fingers, and I tuck them under my arms.

The woman ahead of me pushes open one of the lodge's double doors. "Inside."

I venture past her, into a huge room of golden firelight and rich wooden beams, sturdy chairs and thick cushions, draped blankets and woven floor coverings. More stenciled art covers the posts and ceiling, and the walls hold wooden brackets with weapons and tools of every kind. There are painted cabinets and heavy tables, stools and benches.

"Sometimes village gatherings are held here, when the meeting hall is too cold," says my guide. "Come." She grips my arm just above the elbow and tows me through the front room. "The Warlord's room is there." She points to a nearby door. "His father sleeps over there." The second door she indicates is all the way across the space.

"His father?" For some reason I hadn't imagined the Warlord having parents. He seems so self-sufficient. "His father lives, and yet he's the village leader?"

"His father was never a leader," the woman says grimly. "And there's no need for you to concern yourself with the Warlord's personal affairs. You're a captive, not a guest. You'd do well to remember it. Now come." She jerks my arm harder, throwing open a door in a back corner and shoving me inside.

The room I stumble into is dark and chilly, barely touched by the heat from the big front room. It's crammed with wooden crates and cloth sacks. Swords, spades, and pitchforks lean against the walls. There's a central post, and from it dangle a pair of manacles. Another pair of cuffs lie on the floor.

"The former warlord kept prisoners here. It's mostly storage now." The woman shoves me back against the post and jerks my hands up, above my head. I'm too startled to fight her—not that I could—

her strength flows through every movement. She's taller and more powerful than I am.

With a jangling click, the manacles snap shut around my wrists. I'm chained to the post, my hands stretched high above my head.

"I don't think this is what the Warlord meant when he said to take me to his lodge," I falter.

"Didn't he tie you up during your journey?" Her eyes pierce mine.

"He did, but—" But he also curled up naked with me, and touched me...

"I wonder if I should chain your ankles too." She cocks her head aside, surveying me. Then she smirks, apparently deciding I'm not worth the extra effort.

Without another word, she leaves me there. No food, no fire, no rest, no chance to wash or change my clothes. At least I relieved myself shortly before we arrived in the village.

Standing against a post with my hands above my head is a new kind of torture. The cuffs are too tight to slip out of, and the chain is so short that my entire torso is pulled taut.

I'm not sure how long I stand there in the dark. My only source of light is the glow from the front room's fireplace, and the slivers of sun leaking through the cracks of the window shutters. But after a while the fire burns low, and the sunlight fades.

I'm tempted to cry out, but who in this village would come to my aid? I'm a prisoner, as the woman said—the daughter of a nation these people hate. At least there's a roof over my head, and a little warmth flowing through the open door from the front room.

But my arms are tired, and my whole body aches to lie down instead of being stretched upright.

At long last, the door of the lodge scrapes and thunks, and a pair of boots clomps across the wooden floor. There's a pause, and a heavy sigh. Then more steps, and a deep voice calls softly, "Mouse? Where are you hiding?"

42

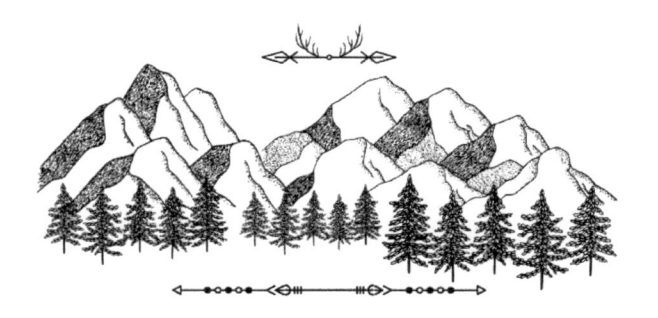

When the Warlord calls me, a shiver runs over my body. "In here," I answer. My voice is raspy, my throat parched.

His heavy steps approach the doorway, and he appears, a massive outline against the dim fire-glow. "Mouse? Why are you in here?"

"Your friend decided this was the appropriate spot for a prisoner of war," I retort.

He doesn't rush to my aid and unchain me immediately. Instead he trudges back into the front room, stirs up the fire, and uses tongs to bring one of the burning logs from the big fireplace to the small one in the storage room where I'm standing. Unhurried, he tends to the second fire, feeding it with kindling until it blazes, lighting me up in all my dejected misery.

Then he steps in front of me, stroking his blond scruff with his fingers. "She's right. This is the place for a captive."

"But I'm exhausted," I whimper. "Please, just let me lie down. You can chain my ankle like you did before."

"I prefer this." There's a spark in his eye, something that I might call mischief in anyone else. But the Warlord doesn't do mischief. "I like seeing my prize displayed for me." His eyes drift purposely lower, to my breasts, which are pushed out further than usual thanks to my position.

"You disgusting barbarian," I hiss.

"Barbarian?" He lifts an eyebrow. "A harsh word, mouse."

"Fitting, in your case."

He steps nearer, reaching out and unfastening my cloak. He removes it, along with the scarf and furs I've been wearing. The torn neckline of my shirt sags, exposing the tops of my breasts and the wound from the ice-wyrm.

The Warlord traces the perimeter of the bite mark with a fingertip, then notches his forefinger into the top edge of my leather corset, right between my breasts. "I met with some of the other warlords. Two of them believe I should kill you, and send your head back as a message to your people, and to your future husband."

I draw a ragged inhale, conscious of the swell of my breasts against the corset edge. The Warlord watches my chest move, and his tongue traces his lips.

Then his teeth clench, and he removes his finger from the corset. He grips one of his knives and whips it out, turning it back and forth so the blade catches the firelight. It's a beautiful weapon, imprinted with the runes of his people's language.

"Are you going to kill me?" I whisper.

"After the trouble I've had bringing you all this way alive?" He sets the tip of the knife under my right ear and draws a slow, grazing line just under my jaw, without ever breaking my skin. "You know how I feel about wasting my time, mouse."

I'm trembling, but there's a slow warmth suffusing my body, too. I press my thighs together, drawing in a deeper breath to make my chest swell again. When the Warlord glances down, I smile. For some reason, limited though my curves may be, he can't resist looking at them.

"It wouldn't take much to cut through this tiny neck of yours." The knife traces down the slant of my throat. When the Warlord meets my eyes, I blink slowly at him and moisten my lips with my tongue.

"Your life would be easier with me gone," I whisper.

"With you—gone," he breathes, and his eyebrows pull together, a thunderous, pained frown. "*Faen.*"

"*Faen,*" I echo quietly.

He shoves the knife back into its sheath and spreads his hand across my throat, his callouses grazing the softness of my skin. His body sways nearer, a monstrous wall of flesh and bone, towering over me. He hunches down slightly, pressing his hips to mine, and I respond with a faint whine, arching into him.

His hand runs from my neck along my body, all the way down to my rear, where he cups a handful of flesh and squeezes, keeping his green eyes locked with mine.

"You said you wouldn't touch me again," I whisper.

With a groan he settles himself against me, his chin on top of my head, one fist resting against the post near my manacled hands. The other hand still cups my ass, pushing me tighter to him.

"I have to make this stop," he says hoarsely. "How do I make it stop? Would killing you end it? Would burying myself inside you set me free?"

I can hardly breathe through the terror and exhilaration spiraling in my heart. "Just wait," I murmur. "If you wait, then maybe the ransom will work out, and I can go home."

He clutches my bound wrists with a snarl, grinding his hips harder against mine. "No."

"No?"

"If I send you home, that Prince gets to marry you and bed you. He gets to put his tiny dick inside you, and I won't suffer it—I can't endure it. You," he releases my ass and grips my chin, "You belong to me."

43

A pulse of utter euphoria flares through my soul. My lips feel swollen and hot, and he hasn't even touched them. His claim resonates in my mind: *You belong to me.*

"But—what about your people, and your plan?" I say. "The ransom—"

His mouth descends on mine, a brutal possession. His lips are rough, hot, and all-consuming, they scorch and sear me, summon and seduce me. The kiss is a demand and a plea all at once. I jerk against the chains, desperate to touch him, but he only voices a broken hum of pleasure and deepens the kiss. Eyes shut, blind to the world, I kiss him back with everything I have.

My tongue quests at his lips, and when he parts his mouth I slide delicately inside him, flicking across his tongue, dancing with him.

The kiss breaks so we can snatch breath, and then he's back, holding my head between his great hands, slanting his lips to mine, giving me full access to the hot sweetness of his mouth. We sink into a blur of incandescent desire, a hazy glow of hectic delight.

But I'm truly exhausted, hungry, and thirsty, and the haze begins to darken as I grow fainter. My body slumps against the post, weak and wanting.

"Mouse?" The Warlord examines my face anxiously. His mouth is flushed from my kisses.

"May I have some water?" I smile weakly at him.

"Gods, I'm an asshole," he exclaims. The next second he's unfastening the manacles, releasing me, scooping me up as I slide to the floor.

He carries me into the great room and lays me on a bench with a curved back. It's cushioned with thin pillows and furs.

Moments later he returns with a wooden cup of water and a piece of flat, coarse bread smeared with preserves. While I eat and drink, he stalks the room, a storm of passion and indecision.

"I told the other warlords I would wait," he says. "One week of waiting, and then, if we receive no message from your people, I will kill you or marry you. So if you'd rather die than marry me, I can arrange that."

"What would you expect from me, as your wife?" I ask.

He swears and begins unraveling his braids with annoyed jerks of his fingers. When he finishes and sweeps the wavy mass aside, I notice that he left one braid intact, a small one at the base of his skull, under the rest of his hair. The bones woven into that braid look different from the tiny animal bones in my own braids.

"I'd expect nothing from you," he says. "Producing my heir would likely kill you. I'm not even sure I could fit inside you."

My face heats, and I murmur, "You won't know until you try."

His pacing halts abruptly, and he plants both hands against the wall. He's in a sleeveless tunic now, divested of his heavy outer layers, so I have an unobstructed chance to admire the bulging curves of his muscled arms.

"You need a bath," he says, low. "You're filthy."

"You need a bath, too," I retort. "You stink."

The Warlord turns, a manic gleam in his eye. "Yes. A bath. I'll prepare it."

He storms off to the back room from which he brought the food. I remove my boots and relax on the bench, watching the play of the firelight, sipping the rest of my water.

A door creaks open—the door that leads to the room of the Warlord's father—and a tall, thin shape sidles out, clutching a blanket around his shoulders. Lank hair straggles from his scalp and chin. There's a haunted look about him, a wild hunger in his faded green eyes.

"Who are you?" he rasps.

"The Warlord's prisoner," I respond.

The man eyes me, drawing his blanket closer around himself. "You look too fragile for this world.

Too fragile, like all the best and most beautiful things." He coughs raggedly. "Is he gentle with you?"

"He is gentle enough."

The man nods. "Our people do not understand gentleness. They call it weakness. Watch him, and you will see when he decides to reject his gentler impulses and return to violence. It takes violence to survive here. Violence, and madness." A chuckle threads from his lips, and he limps toward the back room.

Through the doorway I overhear a muffled conversation between the gaunt man and the Warlord, spoken low in their dialect. The Warlord's voice is harsh, frustrated. His father's tone is bland, apathetic.

After a few moments, his father shuffles back through the front room, carrying a wooden bowl and a bottle. "My sustenance and my poison," he says, grinning at me with rotted yellow teeth. "I'll not disturb you two again."

I'm not sure what to think of the Warlord's father. There's a story behind his condition, and I have a feeling it's closely tied to the Warlord's demands on himself, the goals he pursues with such single-minded passion. He's reacting to the weakness of his family, to the death of his brother and possibly his mother—and to the current sad state of his father. The Warlord is determined to be strong, powerful—a leader and a change-maker for his clan.

His attraction to me stands in the way of what he's planning. It counteracts everything he believes in, everything he intends to do. Which means I can't trust him not to kill me. He seems to hate the idea of letting me go, but he won't let himself want me without feeling guilt and rage.

What if he decides that killing me is better than letting someone else have me?

44

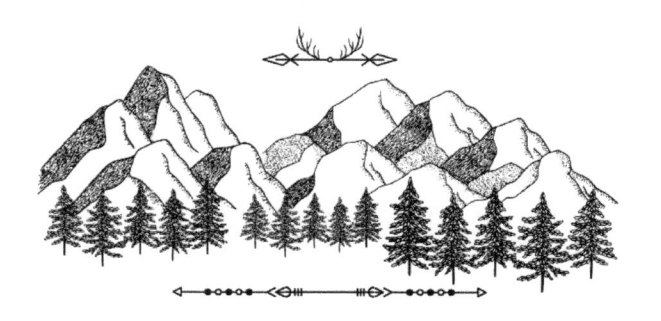

I'm sitting on the bench, chewing the edge of a fingernail and thinking anxiously about how I might defend myself, when the Warlord re-enters the front room. He strides over and picks me up without a word, sweeping me into the back room.

It's a neatly appointed kitchen, with panels of gleaming wood and a smooth hearth made of one massive stone slab. In the center of the room, on stone tiles, stands an enormous wooden tub. The water inside breathes a blessed hot steam.

"Hot water?" I gasp as the Warlord sets me down. "But you couldn't have heated it that quickly."

"There's a hot spring nearby," he says. "At the foot of one of the mountains. Years ago a previous warlord took Southern captives as slaves to serve him, and he made them run copper pipes from the spring to this lodge. We abolished the use of slaves, but the water system remains. See, here." He points to a thin pipe arching over the side of the tub. When he presses a lever, the thin stream of hot water issuing from it diminishes to a drip, then ceases altogether.

"Oh," I breathe. Suddenly every particle of my skin and every bit of my flesh aches to be in that steaming water.

"Undress," says the Warlord.

Startled, I lift my eyes, meeting his burning stare. I expected privacy, though I'm not sure why—by now I should realize that I'm no longer the cherished younger daughter of the district leader. I'm a scared slip of a girl, helpless in the Warlord's palm.

"Are you going to leave?" I ask in a small voice.

"No, mouse." He prowls around the circumference of the tub, to the opposite side, and shucks off his weapons belt and tunic, exposing the glory of his muscled torso. He's grimy and bloodied, smudged and scratched everywhere. Yet he's still beautiful in a way that makes my teeth clench and my limbs loosen.

He crosses his arms, scowling. "I'm going to bathe with you. Now take your clothes off, or I'll do it for you."

I mirror the stance, folding my arms across my own chest and giving him a tiny smile. "Come and strip me, then."

Grimacing, he circles the tub and lunges for me, seizing my corset in both his great hands and tearing it open, laces popping and snapping apart. I gasp, but I'm not afraid, not really.

He grips the hem of my shirt and I let him pull it off, over my head. Then he drags my pants down to my ankles, his calloused thumbs skimming along my legs. In the process he has to bow before me, and I plant one hand on his golden head for support as I step out of the pants.

He lurches upright, chest heaving, and surveys my body. I'm not in much better shape than he is—dirty, scratched, and bruised. I probably smell terrible. But he looks at me as if I'm the most exquisite thing he has ever seen.

"Get in the tub, mouse," he says hoarsely.

I hesitate, wondering how far I should push him. Why is he doing this to himself, adding more temptation to the desire he already feels for me?

In that second of hesitation, he loses his patience, picks me up, and lifts me, naked and kicking, into the air. A moment of breathless suspension, and then he flings me into the hot water.

I tumble into the tub with a gasp, submerging immediately.

Glorious heat. Impossible bliss. I relax at once, letting my limbs float. The tub is just long enough for me, and I don't want to make room for anyone else.

But I don't have a choice, because the Warlord's great body splashes in next to mine. I lurch upright, tilting my head back so the loose strands of wet hair don't cover my eyes. I tug at the twine knotted around my braids, loosening each one—but I leave a few of the bones tied in place, just in case there are more demon-monsters around these parts.

The Warlord grabs a bucket nearby and dunks it into the tub before pouring the liquid over himself. He exhales with pleasure at the rush of hot water, eyes blinking slow, water beading on the dark gold of his lashes.

The firelight gilds both of us as we bathe silently. The Warlord passes a bar of dark brown soap to me and I lather myself with it, from scalp to toes, before handing it back to him. The suds sting my scratches a little, but being clean is such bliss that I don't mind.

In the glimmering amber light we rinse our bodies until they shine. And then we sit opposite each other, elbows hooked over the edges of the wooden tub, reveling in liquid comfort.

The tips of my small breasts peek over the rippling surface of the water, and most of the Warlord's broad chest is exposed, wet curls of hair glistening over his pectorals. He watches me, while a red glow heightens along his cheekbones.

Tentatively I shift one foot under the water, probing toward him. My toes nudge the hard, thick length that arches up from between his legs.

He sucks in a harsh breath, but he doesn't move. He lets me rub my foot along his length, pushing it toward his belly.

Only for a second, and then he leaps out of the tub with a muttered *faen* and snatches one of two thick blankets lying over a chair nearby. He strides to the back door—he has it half open to the cold dark blue of the night when I say, "Wait."

45

The Warlord stops, fingers arched rigid around the edge of the door. "What?"

"You always do this. You go outside to pleasure yourself—out in the cold. Why?"

"I won't take your body," he mutters.

"But you could let me touch you, as you touched me."

"No."

"Because you find me frail and disgusting, not worth your admiration or pleasure." My voice falters.

"No, by the gods! *Faen*, you—you make me hard simply by speaking to me. By moving, by *existing*—"

I almost whimper with the thrill of those words. "Then let me touch you."

"No." He pulls the door wider, heading outside.

"You'll freeze," I protest. "If you won't let me touch you, at least release yourself here, in the warmth… where I can watch." My heart shudders with the wicked boldness of those words, and the Warlord's shoulders tense.

Very slowly, he closes the door.

He turns toward me, half-draped in the blanket. "Stand up in the tub," he says quietly.

I rise, liquid trailing off my body in glittering rivulets. The bathwater comes partway up my legs when I'm standing, while the rest of me is bared to him. Most of my wet hair falls behind me, grazing my butt, but one yellow lock is plastered to my breast and stomach, its slick curled end trailing against my hipbone.

"Spread your legs a little," he orders.

When I obey, he drops the blanket and walks forward, erect and magnificent. He stops opposite me, at the edge of the tub, and curls his thick fingers around himself. His cock looks so long and hot and silky that it's all I can do not to approach him and touch it. My fingers creep toward my sensitive center, aching to tend myself, but the Warlord stops me with a brusque, "No."

Inhaling, I clench my hands and stand, trembling and inflamed, while he strokes himself to the sight of me. Slow movements at first, then faster while he groans and his stomach hardens, every muscle of his glorious body contracting, his great shoulders bending.

"Gods, Ixiana," he moans, and then his release jets across the water, falling in pearly drops onto the surface. A few drops strike my belly, beading there. Dazed, I collect them with a finger and touch it to my tongue, tasting the salty male essence of him. He gasps, eyes locked on me with startled awe.

We stand there, breathing the steam, inhaling our mutual desire. And then, at the same time, we move.

I step from the tub, and he hands me a blanket to dry myself with, and a plain tunic to wear. He tugs the cork from a pipe in the bottom of the tub, and the water drains away, along with the evidence of his lust for me.

When I'm dressed in a soft tunic of spun cloth, I wring out my hair and begin to plait it into one long braid, tightening the knots that secure the bones. The Warlord steps up behind me and takes over the task, expertly weaving the braid with quick fingers.

"Sit," I tell him when he's done. "Fair is fair. You braided mine—let me braid yours."

He scowls, and I waver, remembering what his father said about the Warlord's gentleness always turning back to violence. But then he sinks crosslegged onto the hearth, allowing me to work with his hair.

"I'm not as good as you or Jili," I tell him.

He shrugs.

"Why was Jili with us on the journey?" I ask. "It was a rough trip for anyone, and she's still a child."

"Jili's father was killed on a southern raid. If her mother leaves her too far behind, Jili becomes frantic, nearly demented, terrified that her mother won't return. She's much better when they ride together. She stays in our camp during raids, which is still hard for her—but it means she doesn't need to wait for days for word of her mother's survival. She gets the news, good or bad, within hours."

As I cross the sections of his hair, my fingertip catches on the tiny braid at his nape. "Do you always keep this one in?"

"Don't touch it," he growls.

"The bones in that braid are different."

"They are the finger bones of my mother and my brother. So they can protect me."

Horrified, I swallow hard. "How—nice. You, um—you didn't tell me your mother had passed."

"She cut her own throat after my brother's death."

"Oh gods," I whisper. "I'm so sorry."

"Now you know my shame. The weakness of my line—brother, mother, and father." He releases a harsh laugh. "Zeha and I are the only strong ones. This is why I must never yield, or soften. This is why I must breed with someone hearty and reliable, someone with the health and grit to survive here and produce sturdy children. And this is why I must secure southern lands for those among my clan who need a warmer climate, different food, and better care."

He knocks my hands away from his hair and rises. "Marrying you, bonding with you—it would ruin my chances for the family I want. But it might secure a chance of survival for others."

Meekly I nod. What he says of my frailty is a harsh truth, one I can't deny. My moment of boldness in the bath is gone—spent like his pleasure, and I am my pathetic helpless self again.

"Are you going to chain me tonight?" I ask quietly.

"No."

"Then where should I sleep? On the bench?"

"You'll sleep in my bed. But if you touch me I'll cut off your fingers."

I cringe from the savagery in his tone. Immediately his features soften with regret.

"I won't do that," he admits. "But—don't touch me."

46

A soft yellow gleam slants across my face, waking me.

I'm exquisitely warm, buried under blankets, nestled in the Warlord's arms…

Wait—the Warlord's arms?

He told me not to touch him. But apparently he didn't have the same rule in place for himself, because he's draped over me.

The floor creaks faintly, and I shove his big heavy arm away so I can sit up. Kaja has prowled into the room, her white fur shining in the crack of light between the shutters.

The Warlord's room looks rather like the front hall of the lodge, only much smaller. It's furnished with a solid wooden bed frame, its posts stenciled with runes and simple patterns. On the ceiling above is a crude painting of a woman, legs spread while a man thrusts between them. Around the pair is a wreath of mountains that resemble breasts and trees that look rather phallic.

"It's intended to promote fertility," rumbles the Warlord, and I jump, startled. "Gods!" I gasp. "Warn a person before you wake up."

He laughs then, a rich masculine ripple of humor.

I grin at him. "I love your laugh."

Side by side in the bed, we smile at each other, the air between us rosy with quiet longing. His gaze settles on my mouth, and as his lips drift nearer, I lean in to meet him in that magical place where the sunlight beams into the room, where dust floats like diamond flecks and everything is golden and possible…

And then someone clears their throat from the doorway of the bedroom.

Zeha. And she doesn't look pleased. Neither does the chestnut-haired woman, who stands behind her.

"Tell me you didn't rut with her," says Zeha sharply. "If you did, we're ruined."

"He didn't," I say, and he snarls, "I didn't," at the same moment.

"Good. I've had another message from her people." Zeha holds up a scrap of paper. "This time it's good news."

"Another message?" The Warlord throws back the covers and I whimper as heat escapes and cold rushes in, bathing my legs.

He's bare-chested, clad only in trousers, and he tugs on a loose shirt, to my great regret. I love his body more than I can express—I don't think I will ever get tired of looking at it. I only wish he'd let me touch it freely.

But the message—the message means I might be going home—maybe even today. It means another harrowing journey through perilous lands, back across the Bloodsalt, and through the mountains. It means returning to my parents' fortress where I'll stay under guard until my wedding to Prince Havil, after which I'll live at his family's castle in Cheimhold for the rest of my life, secure and protected, coddled and cared for to my heart's content.

Except my heart won't be content—can't be, now that I know how big the world is, and how many people are suffering in it.

The Warlord steps over to Zeha, taking the note from her, but the woman with the chestnut hair advances, catching his arm. "Why is she in here? I chained her in the storage room, yet I find her in your bed? What does this mean, Cronan? You and I had an arrangement."

"An arrangement, not a vow, Olsa," he says.

"What has she done to you?" Olsa lays a palm along his cheek, inspecting his face. "Do you *care* for this scrawny little whore?"

He jerks away from her and unrolls the missive.

As he's reading, Kaja coils her massive body and leaps onto the bed with me, settling in at my side with her rump on the Warlord's pillow, facing her master and the two women. The tiger's weight presses warm against my leg. I can't deny the feeling of savage victory that rises in me, because I have two magnificent predators under my spell—the white tiger and the Warlord himself. I stroke Kaja's head and risk a tiny triumphant glance at the chestnut-haired woman, Olsa. She's glaring at me. If eyes were spears, I'd be dead.

47

The more of the message the Warlord reads, the deeper his frown grows.

"Don't be angry, Cronan," Zeha says. "I contacted the Prince myself during our trip back, to save you from having to make an unsuitable marriage. The terms of the bargain are different from what you wanted, but still good for our people."

"This is all wrong," says the Warlord, in a tone of utter exasperation. "We need land below the mountains, not in them. I wanted good flat land for farming, with a town nearby for trade."

"They won't yield that to us unless we take it by force," Zeha protests. "Or unless we do what the other warlords suggested—kill this girl as a warning, and take more valuable hostages. We either invade, or we broaden our campaign of terror, kidnapping more of their noble children and killing them if the ransoms aren't paid. Or you can accept this bargain as the best we are going to get."

The Warlord crumples the thin paper and shoves it back at her. "I don't like this deal."

"Money and land. It's what you wanted."

"Not enough money, and the wrong land."

"Take it, Cronan," Olsa interjects. "This bargain will help our clan. We'll be able to pay what we owe to Vinzha's clan and to the healer, and we'll have money left over for medicinal tonics, weapons, and other supplies. And it will rid us of *her,* so you can be yourself again."

He glowers at her. "I am more myself now than I've ever been."

A tiny thrill races through my heart, but I keep calmly caressing the tiger as if I heard nothing, as if my fate weren't being decided at this very moment.

Tension thrums in the air of the room—the shock of the two women at his confession, the angry energy of the Warlord, who probably regrets what he just said. He grabs his weapons belt from a nearby chair, takes a knife out, and jams it into the wall for no apparent reason.

"I'll consult with the other warlords again," he begins, but Zeha cuts him off. "No need. Your meeting with them was a courtesy, and you've heard their opinions. Two of them left for their settlements already and won't appreciate being summoned back again so soon. This is your decision to make. For the good of our clan." She sinks into their dialect, her voice gentle yet intense, unspooling long phrases like delicate ropes winding around him, binding him.

"The girl wants to go home, Cronan," Olsa says at last, interrupting the siblings. "She's too weak to survive long up here, and you know it. The kindest thing you can do is take her back to her people."

The Warlord doesn't look at me, but his shoulders sag at her words. I want to dispute Olsa, to claim that she's wrong—but she's uncomfortably right. In this harsh land, without the magical spray for my lungs and the careful diet I'm used to, I will probably die much sooner than I would at home.

"I will accept the ransom." The Warlord's deep voice fills the bedroom. "Choose some of our warriors to go along with me and take possession of the mountain village they're giving us. And we'll need fresh horses. Once we've secured our new southern village, we can bring some of the weaker clan members there to live."

"The other clans will want a share of the foothold we've gained," says Zeha.

"I will call another council in a week to discuss it," the Warlord replies. "I did this for all the clans, not ours alone. As you said, the other warlords can help us hold onto the village. I don't trust the Southerners not to double-cross us and try to reclaim the place after we've taken possession."

"You know some of the warlords won't respect the tentative peace you've arranged," Olsa says. "They will see this as a chance to drive their raiding parties further into the southern districts."

"Then I'll rely on you both to help me convince them." The Warlord slaps his weapons belt around his hips.

The two women exchange sly grins. I have a feeling that "convincing" the other warlords might involve more force than diplomacy.

48

When Olsa and Zeha leave to accomplish their respective tasks, the Warlord throws on several more layers of clothing, including his big fur-lined cloak. Then he looks at me, where I sit on the bed with my arm around his tiger's neck.

His eyes widen, shot through with pained pleasure. "Kaja likes you."

"She does." I smile, rubbing the top of the huge cat's head.

"You look as if you belong there, mouse," he says quietly. "In my bed, with a tiger under your palm."

My fingers tighten on the tiger's ruff. "Maybe I do."

"No." He shuts his mouth tight, strides over, and smacks Kaja lightly on the rump. "Go! Get your ass off my pillow." The tiger snarls and leaps off the bed, shaking herself before padding regally out of the room. The Warlord kicks the door shut behind her, then returns to the bedside. With his giant hands he lifts me out of the bed onto the cold wooden floor. I yelp at the icy feel of the planks and leap right back into the covers.

"Ixiana," he says, exasperated. "Up. Now. You need to get dressed. You're going home today."

"Can't we rest a little first?" I let a plaintive note enter my voice. "It was such a long and terrible journey to get here."

"More whining?" He scowls. "You know how much I hate whining. Obey me, prisoner, or I'll have to strip you down and dress you myself."

He realizes his mistake the moment I smile at him. "No," he says warningly. "You impossible little lust-creature—no, I won't strip you—you're going to dress yourself, like a good girl, or you'll be punished."

I tilt my head aside. "What kind of punishment? More useless training where I bruise myself against your massive bones?"

"Something worse." The Warlord reaches for me again, and I scoot away from him, grabbing onto the headboard of the bed and giving his hand a petulant kick.

A wolfish smile spreads across his face, and he climbs onto the bed, dragging me away from the headboard while I kick and writhe. My tunic has worked itself dangerously high, nearly exposing tender parts of me to the Warlord. He pins me down like he did during our training session—both my wrists in one of his hands. His other hand rakes the tunic higher, while his green eyes gleam into mine, full of a carnal savagery that makes me pin my legs together.

Deftly he works his free hand between my thighs, and I can't help myself—I open wide for him, spreading my legs.

The Warlord glances down, and his throat jerks as he swallows. His tongue travels his lips. "*Faen*," he breathes. "Why did the gods make this part of you so damn beautiful?"

He's hanging over me, a huge impending destruction of male beauty and power. The thick braids I wove have come partly unraveled, and tendrils of his blond hair fall past his jawline, tickling my cheek. I lift my head from the mattress, my mouth yearning upward. He bites his lip, the tug of one sharp canine—but he doesn't kiss me. He looks down at my parted legs again, at my center spread wide for him. I can feel my own wetness—I know I'm glistening, ready, a dewy field meant to be plowed.

The Warlord's powerful arms tremble as he holds himself over me. He's actually shaking from the force of his desire. A keen rush of pleasure traces along my nerves.

"Unmolested," he gasps. "Those were the terms. I must return you untouched, still a virgin. Prince Havil said you would be examined to ensure it, and that if you weren't intact, the engagement would end and our bargain would be forfeit."

Disappointment and revulsion course through me. "He said that?"

"He wrote down those exact words."

I suppose I'm fortunate the Warlord's fingers didn't dive too deep when he pleasured me before. That incident might have ruined my chances of getting home—a fact that angers me deeply. I hate that Prince Havil would lay such a condition on my surrender. What do my parents think of that? They probably don't like that part of the message, but they depend on the Prince's family for protection and allyship. They're in no place to protest the inclusion of their daughter's unbroken hymen in the contract.

"What if you'd already had me by force?" I say. "Would Havil reject me over something that wasn't my choice?"

"Yes," says the Warlord simply.

"That's not fair, and it's not love. He's not trying to protect me, he's thinking only of himself, getting the first chance at this." I wriggle my hips, and the Warlord huffs out a rough breath.

"He values being the one to claim you," he says. "I understand the urge. It's a primal need, to stake first claim. Though I'd have you even if you'd been with a hundred other men."

Heat rushes into my cheeks. "You want me that badly?"

He lowers his head, his short beard brushing along the softness of my cheek. One word grates into my ear, hot with need. "Yes."

"Take me then," I whisper. "Not like an honorable man. Take me like a beast, like a raider. Like a Warlord."

49

At my wicked plea, the Warlord's jaw tenses and he rumbles low in his chest. His breeches are tight and prominent with his need for me. But somehow, he exerts a tremendous amount of control and shoves himself away.

"I won't enter you," he says. "But I have my limits. And I cannot let you go without first tasting this."

His mouth is on me before I can respond, before I can prepare, before I can think. He grips my thighs, holding them in place while he licks me, through and through—laps and suckles and kisses every crease, every fold, every bit of sensitive flesh. I bite my wrist and whine, scrunching a blanket with my other hand.

He's simply—enjoying me. Savoring all the tender parts of me, coaxing the tiny nub that makes me release sharper sounds of pleasure. When I let a faint scream escape, he lifts his head and scowls, his lips damp.

"Quiet," he orders.

I nod, frantic, and he lowers his mouth again. He laps and lingers until I'm writhing, panting, quivering uncontrollably, whispering, "Please, please—"

And then he stops.

He rises, wipes his mouth, and drags my limp, trembling body from the bed. "Get dressed," he says. "And maybe then I will finish it."

"You evil monster," I gasp. "I'll do it myself."

He clutches my hair in his hand and drags me closer. "If you do, I will know. And then I will chain you to the post again until we leave. Be a good prisoner, and you'll be allowed to move freely. Fresh clothes are there." He points to a chair where there's a small pile of items—among them soft leather breeches, a thick tunic, a sort of corset-and-vest, and a heavy cloak. My boots stand nearby.

As he stalks out of the room, I can't even curse him. I can only mewl with thwarted desire, squeezing my legs together. He hears me, because a low chuckle drifts back to my ears.

Shakily I dress myself. Clearly he doesn't plan on fulfilling his part of the deal and finishing what he began, because how could he touch me with all these layers in the way? No, he was torturing me with desire, the way I tortured and tempted him.

I never realized how deliciously agonizing it can be to need someone like this. When I used to kiss Prince Havil, I wanted him, yes—but in a decorous, genteel, slightly illicit sort of way.

With the Warlord, I crave him deeply, all of him, as if he's the last life-saving breath for my shuddering lungs. I ache to rub my skin against his whole body, to take him inside me, to lose myself in the storm of him. He might break me, shatter me—I don't care. I would die to be plundered by him, to have the passionate force of him centered only on me until I exploded in scarlet and snow, like a geyser of the Bloodsalt. A violent image, to be sure, but in my mind, nothing less will do.

Fully dressed, I sit on the bench in the front hall, still pouting. The Warlord brings me a different kind of porridge—lighter and creamier, with a spoonful of preserves swirled through it. "Does it have milk?" I ask.

"I made it with a milk-like liquid distilled from the *iru* nut," he says. "Very rare and expensive to make. Don't waste it."

I cup the bowl in my hands. "Thank you." My eyes wander to his father's bedroom door. "Will he come out for breakfast?"

"He'll be sleeping off his liquor." The Warlord sits on a chair near me with his own bowl.

Several spoonfuls into my food, with my hunger and my arousal lessening, I feel more prone to conversation. "You've had a difficult life. I understand now, why you are the way you are."

"And what way is that?"

"Harsh. Cruel. A brutal warrior." I savor another spoonful. This is the first food of his people I've thoroughly enjoyed. "You've lost much, and you've had to live and act a certain way to survive. I understand."

"After a handful of days, you understand my entire life?" His green eyes narrow. "So prideful, just like all your people. Assuming you can grasp the depth of someone else's pain."

"I'm human," I say. "Aren't all human experiences somewhat related? We experience them in different degrees, but I can *imagine* how you feel. I've been sad before—I can imagine that sadness multiplied a thousand times in the loss of a brother and mother. I've been angry before—I can imagine that anger so much more powerful, running so deep through generations that it sometimes blinds you to the real cruelty of your actions—keeps you from seeing how you are mirroring the very thing that was done to your people generations ago."

"But we didn't begin this," he says. "Your people started it, by going to war with us and pushing us out."

"That was long ago." My voice takes on a pleading note. "No one who did those things is alive in my district today."

"You are their descendants."

"And so we should pay for their sins?"

"Yes!" He slams his bowl onto a table and rises, burly and thunderous. "Someone should pay. The wrong of your ancestors will be visited on their children. On *you*, little mouse." He advances, seizing me by my braids again and pulling me up. My empty wooden bowl clatters to the floor.

His grip is tighter this time, more painful, and his face is strained with a violent clash of emotions. Something inside me stretches taut and brittle, humming with fear and anticipation, because I sense, in the deepest part of my soul, that this point is pivotal for him. Whatever he decides right now will impact my life and his forever.

50

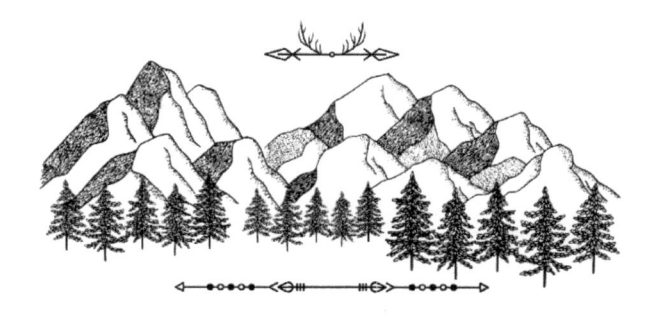

The Warlord holds me up by a fistful of my long yellow braids. I have to rise on tiptoe to ease the sharp pull on my scalp. Wincing, I look up into his eyes, into the agonized swirl of anger and indecision. In this moment, he is determining where we stand, he and I, and his choice will ripple outward, affecting both his clan and my people.

"When we take possession of that village in the Southern mountains," he hisses, "it will be our first foothold. But we will not stop there. I have a plan, one that will spread our influence throughout your districts and shake the grip of your leaders. Your father and the other district nobles are already weak. We will infiltrate, erode them further from within, and then strike. We will take back our birthright, the land of our ancestors."

"And my people?" I say softly. "Where will they go?"

"Those who resist will die. The others will be sent North. Let them live in the wasteland we were given."

"You're no better than my ancestors, then," I whisper.

"No!" He shakes me, and I grimace from the twinge of pain along my scalp. "No, I'm not like them. I'm only reversing what they did. Setting it right."

"How is this right?" Tears form in my eyes, and my voice rises. "How does more violence ensure a bright future?"

"Your people will not hear soft words!" he bellows. "All they understand is violence, and pain, and the theft of the comforts they worship!"

I reach up, laying my thin fingers across his wrist. "Some of them might listen. After all, I heard your words." My lips tremble as I hold his gaze. "And yes, I had to have all my comforts torn away first. But I listened. I hear you."

A muscle along his jaw pulses. "That's because you're different from the rest of them."

"No. It's only because you and I had time together. We were forced to see through the words we use to describe each other. I had to learn to look past 'raider,' 'ruffian,' and 'warlord,' until I could see you clearly as Cronan, heartbroken son of the North, compassionate man, fearless guide to his people."

His grip on my hair slackens just a little.

"And you see me," I whisper. "Don't you? You see past the weakling, the mouse, the spoiled Southern child of entitled nobility. Who do you see now?"

He shakes his head, his eyes bright and wet, his teeth gritted.

I choke on a half-sob. "Cronan. Tell me who you see."

He lets out a long, shuddering breath, and his hand on my hair eases. "I see a girl who annoys me with her whining, her constant challenge of my goals, and her ignorance of my culture."

I swallow, more tears pooling in my eyes.

"And I see a woman, stronger than anyone knows," he continues in a hoarse whisper. "A survivor. A warrior who battles every day and wins. I see a sly trickster, an enchantress who could turn my heart into a lush garden, or into a wasteland as barren as the Bloodsalt."

His fingers slip from my braids and slide along the back of my neck, flexing, urging my face to tilt up as he bends. With a soft cry I throw my arms around his neck and meet his mouth.

Harshly he kisses me, hungrily, his lips and mine sensitized with the pain of all that we carry, with the harsh truth of what this moment means for both of us. I still can't see a future in this, only agony.

I pause to breathe, and then I kiss him again, softly.

"I can't ask you to stay with me," he murmurs, brushing back strands of my hair. "You'll die up here, in this wild land."

"And I can't ask you to come live with me," I whisper. "My people would kill you."

His hands cup my shoulders, tightening. "Why is my life like this? One loss after another. Some days I don't think I can bear it."

The stark hollowness of his tone frightens me. "You have to bear it, because I can't live in a world where you don't exist."

He pulls me in, against the leather and fur of his chest. "I can't let you go to that prince and marry him."

"But if you don't, you'll lose the ransom you were promised. The little village in the Southern mountains, and the money for your people's welfare."

Groaning, he wraps me tighter. "I don't see a way out of this, mouse."

A shout outside startles us both—but it's answered with a merry call. There are people near the lodge, probably getting ready for our journey.

"You have to take me back home," I mutter into the savory warmth of him. "Maybe on the way we'll think of something."

51

The band that leaves the settlement is somewhat different this time. First of all, there's a fresh batch of shaggy northern horses to replace the weary ones. Twice as many warriors accompany us, and their faces are all new—with the only familiar ones being the Warlord and Zeha. The white tiger doesn't seem inclined to come on the journey this time—she pads along near us for only a handful of minutes before bounding back to the village.

The woman with chestnut hair, Olsa, rides with us too, and I'm unhappy about it. In fact, I'm unhappy about the entire situation. Strange as this wilderness is, I have the feeling I could have stayed in that spacious lodge with the Warlord and been happy for a long time—until one of my illnesses caught up with me, of course.

I do miss my family. I miss my brothers' cheerful, open faces and my mother's sweet cleverness. I miss my father's weary brow and kind smile. I even miss Joss's wry expressions and her disdainful comments about my physique. Sometimes she can be kind. And even when she isn't, I think her harsh, prodding remarks are her way of trying to help—to push me to be stronger, as if by will and words, she can make it happen.

On the first day of our journey, we cross the narrower northern band of the Bloodsalt, but the Warlord guides us around the pale forest infested with ice-wyrms. Instead, he moves our company into an area of low hills and twisted bushes. He claims he's taking this route because he doesn't want to lose anyone else, and I'm sure that's true—but I also suspect he wants more time with me.

When we make camp that evening, among scraggly bushes glazed with ice, Zeha sends out one of her snow-hawks again, to let my people know that the terms are acceptable, and we're on our way. I watch her murmur to the bird before she lets it go, crooning to it with tiny chirps and the rippling words of her language. When it takes flight in a flurry of white and scarlet feathers, I can't help a tiny gasp of awe.

"How does it know where to go?" I ask her. As usual, I'm standing near the Warlord's horse, holding the reins and waiting while the others set up camp.

"It is another gift of my people," she says. "Some of us are born with the ability to commune with the creatures of our land. I am a hawk-speaker, and so is the man your people are holding prisoner. We can tell snow-hawks where to go, and they can sense our whereabouts. They have a unique love and loyalty for us." Shading her eyes against the setting sun, she smiles fondly at the receding shape of the bird.

"Your messenger," I say tentatively. "Is he part of the ransom deal? Did you negotiate his freedom?"

"No," she says. "He volunteered for this, knowing how important it is to our people's future. He is loyal to the Warlord, ready to lay down his life, his freedom—whatever is required of him. And truth be told, he is also a master of locks and stealth. Once the bargain is complete, I doubt any cell will hold him for long. He will find his way back to us."

"I hope so," I murmur. "I would hate to think of anyone dying on my account."

Zeha looks at me sharply, and then she steps closer, lowering her voice. "Tell me in truth—did my brother bed you? Because if he did, and your prince discovers it, we will all pay a heavy price."

"He did not," I say through clenched teeth.

"Good." She nods, relieved.

Just to unsettle her, I add, "But he came very close to it."

"Gods, why?" she exclaims under her breath. "I cannot understand the attraction. You are pretty, yes, but he has always insisted he would marry a warrior, someone strong and bold, one of our proudest daughters. Why this fascination with you? Have you spoken through the ether again?"

"Yes."

"Well—stop it." Her voice is petulant, exasperated. She looks so comically flustered that I can't help breaking into a small, blushing smile.

And wonder of wonders, her lips twitch. She fights the smile, shaking her head and turning away, fingers pressing her mouth. "It's not funny."

"I know." My smile trembles. "It's tragic." I drop my voice to a bare whisper. "I think I love him."

She turns back to me, eyes wide with a half-delighted alarm. "No. Oh gods no. Tell me you're joking."

I shake my head.

"And he—" She lifts her eyebrows.

I know the unspoken question. Does he love me?

Biting my lips, I look toward the Warlord, and Zeha follows my gaze. Her brother is driving a metal tent stake into the frigid ground, and when he's done he glances our way. There's a flash of pleased joy in his face when he looks at me. It's subtle and quick, but his sister sees it as clearly as I do.

She exhales, long and weary. "May the gods have mercy on both of you." She strokes the long nose of the Warlord's horse, sighing again.

"What about you?" I ask. "Do you have someone?"

"A man? No. I prefer women," she replies. "Less smelly. Less prone to talk of *seed* and *claiming* and *breeding*." She fakes a deep, gruff male voice as she speaks the last several words, and I laugh. Her eyes crinkle at the corners when she smirks.

"You remind me of my sister Joss," I say. "She's a warrior, and she prefers women too, for those and other reasons. You'd like her, I think."

"Me, *like* a Southern warrior?" Zeha scoffs. "I doubt that."

"Stranger things have happened," I say softly, my eyes fixed on the golden bearded face of the Warlord as he strides toward us.

"Mouse," he says, low.

Zeha rolls her eyes at the velvet in his voice. "You impossible fool." And she smacks him hard on the cheek.

"What?" For a second, he's not a Warlord, but a boy, stung and offended. "What did I do?"

"You know what you did." Zeha stalks away, unwinding the leather hawker's cuff from her forearm.

52

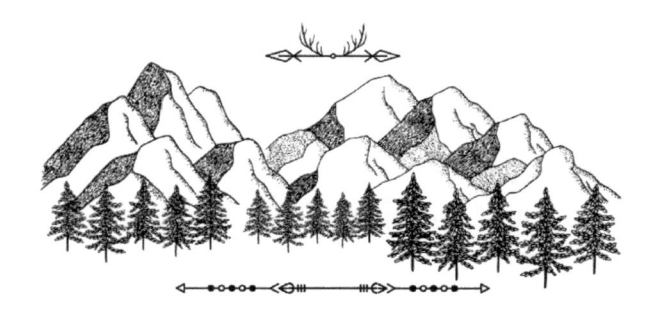

That night, I sit on a log near the others of our company and partake of the evening meal by the heat of the fire. The sky arches impossibly huge overhead, its size compounded by the low stature of the scraggly shrubs dotting the land around us. We're camped in a shallow dip between hills, our small cluster of tents exposed to the black night.

These tents are too small to have fires inside them. Will I be snuggling with the Warlord tonight, for warmth? The thought heats my face and my blood just as surely as the glow from the dancing flames.

The stew we're eating is good, made from some meat with a flavor I don't recognize. But a few minutes after I finish eating, I realize with dread certainty that it isn't settling well.

I can't approach the Warlord about it—he's seated on the opposite side of the fire, between two of his men. They're beginning a song—one of the bone-deep, humming chants they like to sing during our rides. The Warlord tips his head down, opening his throat and voicing a note lower than I'd ever thought humanly possible. He holds it long, while the others thrum and vocalize with him.

I'd like to sit and listen. But I have to go. Now. Before I soil my borrowed clothes.

Thankfully Zeha is beside me, so I whisper my predicament to her and she escorts me far from the fire, into the darkness.

What follows is the worst and most humiliating experience of my life. Back home, when my bowels revolted like this, I had a privy to use. Out here in the frozen wilderness, I have the shallow hole that Zeha hastily scraped for me.

It's a long, messy process. By the end, my thighs and calves are sore and trembling from crouching for so many minutes. I kept my clothes clean, and I was able to wash myself thoroughly with plenty of fresh snow; but my rear is numb with cold, and my face burns with shame. Quickly I toss lumps of snow over the hole and return to Zeha.

She rises from the spot where she's been sitting with her back to me. "All done?"

"I'm sorry," I tell her. "For how long it took, and for the—the sounds, and the smell."

"I've smelled the guts of a dead man," she says bluntly. "I've heard the squelch of flesh being ripped from bodies by the *jäkel*. And I've had a bout or two of sickness myself. It happens."

"It happens far too often for me." I lay a hand over my stomach. "If I'm not very careful what I eat. There's a short list of foods that don't bother me."

"That's why you're so thin and weak."

The blunt truth bruises my soul, but I know she doesn't mean to hurt me. "Yes."

"My brother was like that," she says. "The work of the healer never lasted long on him. Always he returned to the same weak state, until—" She stops speaking. For several long seconds, the only sound is the faint scuff of wind on snow, and the soft crunch of our footsteps.

"I'm sorry about your brother," I say. "And your mother."

"It is the way of things. Those weak in body or spirit die. The strong survive." There's a bleak hardness to her tone. She's not angry about it like her brother is. He is molten clay, where she is cold iron. He burns and roars for change, while she drives toward it, steady and unstoppable, like a spear through flesh.

A dark, broad-shouldered form moves toward us from the camp, while the droning of the fireside song continues. "What happened?" The Warlord's deep voice rolls through the dark. "You were gone a long time."

"The stew didn't settle well." I hate admitting my weakness to him, showing him how ill-equipped I am for a life here—or anywhere, honestly.

"Are you all right now?"

"Yes."

He rumbles assent and scoops me off my feet before I can protest. "You need rest. We'll go to my tent."

"Not so fast," Zeha interjects. "She'll be staying in my tent tonight."

The Warlord's arms contract around my body. "Why?"

"Because I can't trust you not to violate her."

"I would never take a woman unwilling. You know that."

"That's the problem," Zeha answers. "I did not mind you two sharing space when I thought you hated each other. But now—"

"I still hate her," he growls.

"Of course you do. That's why you're holding her so tightly, as if someone is going to steal her away."

"She might escape."

"Cronan, stop." I lay my hand against his cheek. "She knows. About the ether and the thought-voices, and how we both feel."

"The ether-speak means nothing," he mumbles.

"That's not true, and you know it as well as I do," Zeha says. "If it had only happened one time, I could have discounted it as a random oddity. But multiple times? It's the sign of a soul-bond, brother. Admit it."

"Admitting it does no good." He sets me down, and his hands curl into fists. "After everything that's happened—this? When will the gods decide I've suffered enough?"

His sister approaches, and at first I think she's going to hug him—but instead, she sets a fist to his chest. "Stop whining. You sound like *her*." She jerks her head toward me.

He knocks her hand aside. "I do not."

"You do. So quite mewling like an infant, and start thinking about how you're going to secure the mountain village and keep it safe against repossession. I'll take Ixiana to my tent."

She grips my arm and marches me to a small tent cluttered with two bedrolls and an assortment of saddlebags, arrows, and hawker's gear. "Sleep," she orders.

I've pushed her good graces far enough for one day. She needs time to process this, just like Cronan and I do. So I obey her, and I slither into the blankets, grateful for the rest.

But the rest doesn't last nearly long enough. I wake in the night, paralyzed by the certainty that I just heard someone scream.

53

The scream—if it was a scream and not my imagination—did not wake Zeha. She's snoring quietly in her bedroll.

I'm still fully clothed, boots and all, but I'm cold and scared. The glow of the firelight through the tent beckons me, so I slip out of the blankets, drawing one around my shoulders, over my cloak.

The icy night air bites my cheeks and nose as I emerge from the tent and walk toward the fire. All is still, except for the hiss and crackle of the logs as they cave to the gnawing flames.

The Warlord sits on a fallen tree, holding a chunk of firewood in his massive hand. He's staring deep into the writhing fire, his handsome face gilded with its light. Cautiously I pad to his side and sit with my arm brushing his.

"Can't you sleep?" I whisper.

"No."

"I heard a scream."

"*Jäkel.*"

"But why? We're all wearing our bones."

"They can't smell your spirit when you wear the relics of the dead," he says. "But sometimes their lust for flesh is so strong that even the relics are of little use. There is only one, though, I think. And it won't venture too close to a camp with so many humans. You can sleep, mouse. I will watch."

I press my shoulder more firmly against his arm. "I would rather stay up with you."

"You need rest. We'll be riding all day tomorrow."

I reach up, stroking his golden beard. "I'd rather be kissed than rested."

For a moment he keeps staring into the fire. Then, with a swift lunge, he drops the hunk of firewood and drags me onto his knee. He's wearing leather gloves, but I tug them off him so I can feel his fingers and interlace them with my own.

He bends his head, the tiny braids at the front of his hair sliding along his cheekbones. Gently he bumps his profile against mine, nuzzling me. A warm breath slides from his mouth between my parted lips.

For a moment we stay like that, suspended in magical anticipation—the scintillating tension before the kiss, the tingling of lips, hovering close without quite touching.

Then he captures my mouth with desperate urgency, whipping his hand up to grip the back of my head. His lips are hot smooth spice, salty-sweet, with just enough coarseness to send tiny spears of delight lancing through my core.

My whole being hangs on the magic of his mouth, the heat of his tongue. He angles his head, licking deeper, then withdraws to pepper my lips with short, intense kisses. I shift astride his lap, pressing my body to his chest and stomach, bruising my mouth on his because I want him so much. There are far too many layers between us, and I ache to slough them off until we're both bare and warm, sliding against each other, into each other.

"I'm going to kiss you forever," I whisper.

He rumbles his approval, circling my waist with one arm, while my tongue tangles with his. Our kisses sink into a slow, languid rhythm, then grow fervent again, until I'm desperate for more pressure, even through the layers of my clothing.

"You promised you'd finish it," I pant against his lips. "That you'd make me come. Liar."

The Warlord catches my bottom lip in his teeth and tugs it savagely. I gasp, almost a breathy shriek, and he leans back, clapping one hand over my mouth. "You have to be quiet, mouse. Do you understand? If I do this, you have to be quiet."

Frantically I nod.

He sets me aside, off his lap, then rises to scan the surrounding landscape. Next he surveys the tents—all dark, their flaps painted amber by the fire's glow.

"We must be quick," he whispers.

54

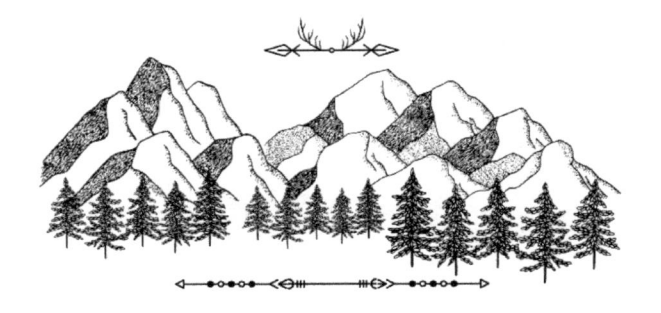

The Warlord leads me into his empty tent. It's smaller than the one he used on our last trip, probably because his company is traveling lighter this time. We leave the flap of the tent slightly open, allowing a bit of the fire's glow to seep in.

In the cramped space, he sits with his legs spread in wide V and makes me stand between them, facing him. Then he tucks up my tunic and pulls down my trousers, revealing the downy cleft between my legs. With a satisfied murmur, he strokes me with his fingers, sighing with pleasure when they slide through easily, no resistance. He pulls them out and looks at the wetness coating them.

"She was right," he whispers hoarsely. "I can't be trusted with you, not when your body begs for me like this."

"Please," I breathe. "Don't stop. Please touch me."

Licking his lips, he grasps my bare hips and tugs my mound nearer to his face. "Spread your legs a little wider then, treasure," he says. "And don't make a sound."

His tongue plunges between my legs, stroking along my folds. Each pass of that silky wet tongue sends a shiver of sparkles through my entire body, so intense I can barely stay upright. My knees weaken under the onslaught, ripple after ripple of glittering pleasure, building toward a single shining point.

With tender lapping and gentle sucking kisses, he works me toward the peak, and when I'm nearly there he swirls a broad fingertip in just the right spot, until I burst, shaking, arching against his hand. The pleasure floods through me in waves of pulsating glory, while I clutch the Warlord's hair and breathe, sharp and shallow.

With a final kiss and a cleansing swirl of his tongue, he withdraws and pulls my clothing back into place. I collapse against his chest, boneless with bliss.

But my hand brushes the front of his trousers, and through the thick material I feel the straining heat of his need for me.

"Your turn," I whisper.

I'm half-afraid he'll jump up and storm out into the cold, to spew himself on the snow as he usually does.

But this time, he tenses briefly. And then he nods.

Heart thundering, I release the laces of his pants and wriggle my fingers into the heated space. He inhales a sharp breath when my fingertips graze his hardness, and he seizes two great fistfuls of the blankets.

Cautiously I ease out his length—thick and solid and smooth. I run two fingers along the soft skin experimentally, delighting in the twitch that results. Another long stroke of my finger to the underside of the shaft, and the Warlord's whole body jerks. "We have to be quick," he gasps. "For the gods' sake, mouse—*faen!*" He crushes a hand over his mouth as I slide my lips over the head of his cock, savoring him with my tongue. I push forward until I can't take any more of him.

I suck him gently, while my tongue caresses the thin sensitive skin, and I clasp my fingers around the part of his length that won't fit in my mouth. His breath cracks from his lips, heavy and ragged—he's writhing, desperate. Then he gives in to his lust and seizes my hair, bucking his hips upward, thrusting himself through the channel of my mouth and hand. With a final hard roll of his body, he explodes, a geyser worthy of the Bloodsalt. And like the Bloodsalt, I manage to take it all down, leaving him clean, without a trace of what we've done.

"Did I do it right?" I whisper, wiping my lips.

He brushes my hair back with a shaking hand. "No woman has ever done that for me. I can't imagine it being any better. Unless—"

"Unless?"

"Unless I could be inside you. Which I never will." He puts himself away and relaces his pants. "And you? You are—pleased?"

"My craven lust is well satisfied, thank you," I whisper back.

In the dim glow through the tent flap, I see him wince. "I'm sorry I said that to you."

I plant a forgiving kiss on his mouth. "I should go back to Zeha's tent before she wakes."

"You should." But he holds my hand in his, stroking the backs of my fingers with his thumb.

Warmed all the way to my soul, I give him a bright smile and pull away.

When I sweep aside the tent flap and step out, I come face to face with a *jäkel*.

55

The *jäkel* looks just as startled as I am, interrupted in the middle of its investigative prowling. But it recovers before I do. With a snarl, it leaps at my face, mouth wide.

The Warlord's huge forearm is there, slamming between the beast's jaws. The *jäkel* chomps, and the Warlord's bone cracks through. His roar of agony wakes the camp.

The Warlord pushes me back and shoves the *jäkel* away, his forearm still lodged between its teeth. He's bellowing with pain and rage. The agony must fuel him, because he catches the scruff of the beast, whips it around, and slams it onto the hard-packed snow with immense force. There's another snap—the *jäkel*'s neck this time—and the creature lies broken, with the Warlord seething and panting above it.

Zeha races up to him, knives clutched in both hands. She lets loose a string of scared, angry words in their language, all the while examining his arm and gesticulating at me and the *jäkel* by turns.

Other warriors approach, woken by the noise.

Olsa is there too, and she casts a baleful look at me, as I sit shaking in the entrance to the Warlord's tent. But she only says, "I will find something to splint your arm, Cronan."

A young warrior steps forward, white-faced. "It should have been me. The Warlord offered to take over my watch so I could sleep."

"And he failed in his duty," Zeha snaps. "You both did. If you had stuck to your task and sat up with him—if there had been two pairs of eyes instead of none at all, this might not have happened. And if certain people had stayed where they were put—" She throws me a savage glare.

The Warlord accepts her chastisement without a word. Sweat glistens on his forehead, and his face is taut with pain. I rise and creep closer despite Zeha's stormy presence, and I touch his good arm. "Thank you for saving me," I murmur. "I'm so sorry. I wish I could fix it."

"You are worth any pain," he answers between gritted teeth.

"We'll have the healer fix him when we reach the Lower Bloodsalt." Zeha's tone is slightly less strident. She shakes her head at both of us like we're irresponsible wayward children.

Someone brings the Warlord a bottle of liquor, and he gulps it eagerly while Zeha and Olsa splint his arm. But mine is the hand he grips while they work over him.

Zeha sets two men on watch and marches me back to her tent, where we catch a few more hours of restless sleep before setting off again. I ride behind the Warlord, holding the reins for him, taking care not to jostle his broken arm. He's been drinking more, and he sways in the saddle, droning an off-key tune.

"This pain is nothing," he slurs once, around noon. "The real pain is yet to come, mouse. You are going to carve out my heart and take it with you."

I press closer to his back. "I would stay with you. But then—"

"I know," he mutters. "No ransom. No land. You would die in the cold wastelands. I'd rather you lived, mouse. I want to know that you're running around in a Southern kingdom, free and well cared for."

Free? I'm not sure being pampered in the Prince's quarters for the rest of my life is freedom. It won't taste like the kind of freedom I feel now, as the Warlord's captive—the keen, icy, bright, savage liberty I've enjoyed in his presence.

We camp again that night, and travel for another day before reaching the edge of the blood-veined forest. Zeha leaves our camp and rides away to fetch the healer herself, rather than sending a hawk. "He may need some persuasion," she says.

Indeed, when the healer arrives, he's scowling. "Again?" he grumbles. "Again I am expected to serve you without pay, with only the promise of coin. You are fortunate you're my favorite of the warlords. I will do this for you, but I am coming with you to wherever you're accepting the ransom, to ensure that I get my rightful due before you give it all away."

"I won't give it away," growls the Warlord.

"You will. Generous to a fault. That's why you never have any coin to pay me." The healer's eyes sparkle with golden lights as he lays his fingers over the Warlord's arm. Within moments, the Warlord can move the limb painlessly. He flexes his fingers and rolls his shoulder, testing it.

Zeha enters the tent with a hawk on her arm. "The girl's parents will meet us at the mountain village," she says. "And the Prince himself is coming, with some of his men. They have laid out the instructions for the exchange." She passes a slip of paper to her brother.

The Warlord inspects the letter. "We leave before dawn, and ride across the Bloodsalt and through the mountains," he says. "We should reach the village around sunset tomorrow." He looks up at his sister, his eyes burning. "The girl stays in my tent tonight."

"No."

"I won't jeopardize the arrangement, I swear. She will remain a virgin."

I flush, twisting my fingers together.

Clearing his throat awkwardly, the healer shuffles out of the tent.

"I can't trust the two of you together," Zeha says. "This connection makes you both foolish."

"You can't tell me what to do," the Warlord replies, and for a moment I hear an echo of childhood arguments in his tone.

"You may be the oldest, but I'm the wisest." Zeha gives him a tight smile, tinged with pity. "She'll be in my tent. Come, Ixiana."

Meekly I rise to follow her out.

"A kiss first." The Warlord leaps up and drags me to him, crushing his mouth to mine, inhaling as if he longs to breathe me in. His hands cup my body tenderly, and I lace my fingers behind his neck.

"Gods," Zeha says, exasperated. "Enough."

With a final firm kiss, the Warlord lets me go.

56

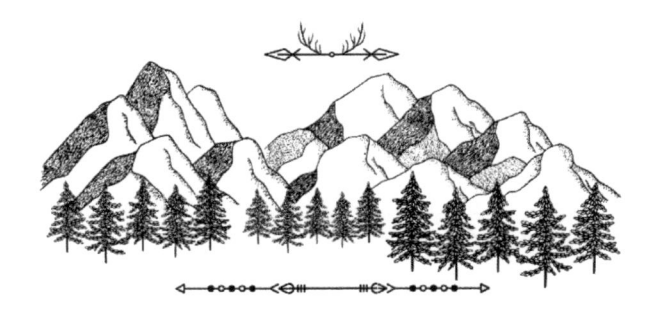

That night, lying in Zeha's tent in my bedroll, I dream that I'm searching for the Warlord. I'm wandering through a forest of white trees whose razor-edged leaves drip blood on the snow. There's a figure ahead, massive and broad-shouldered, glazed with glossy red blood. I run toward that shape, my heart thundering—but Prince Havil steps into my path, cool and composed. Behind him stand my parents, looking dreadfully disappointed in me.

"I will get to him. You can't stop me," I tell them, and I take hold of the dream, banishing them from my path. I forge ahead, and the blood drains away from the distant figure, leaving the Warlord whole and unblemished, gazing up at the sky with his blond hair rippling in the breeze. I'm slogging through waist-high snow now, struggling across an open field toward him.

"Cronan," I call.

He turns, and opens his arms. "Ixiana."

I run to him.

But before I can fling myself into his embrace, he's gone. I'm floating in a great nothing, an expanse of purplish-blue. "Cronan?" This time, my voice has dimension and power—it spans time and space.

He answers, low and rough. I can't see him, but we can hear each other. Instinctively I know that we are communing through the ether again, this time while both of us are asleep. The realization floods me with mischievous delight. No one can interrupt us here.

"Do you think we'll be able to speak to each other like this when I'm far from you?" I ask.

"I don't know," his disembodied voice replies.

"It would be wonderful and terrible if we could."

"It would be torture. You will be married to someone else."

"And you—you'll marry Olsa."

"Maybe."

"You'll have babies with her." My ether voice sounds so much calmer than I feel. "You'll take her body, like I wanted you to take mine."

"And your Prince will take *you*," he says caustically. "He will possess you and put his hands on you. He'll slide his dick between your legs and push his tongue into your mouth."

"Stop." The picture he's painting blazes in my mind, sharp and clear, and I panic. "I—I'm not sure I can let him do that. I don't think I can marry him after all."

"You are part of the deal. You're the reason he is contributing money and soldiers," says the Warlord. "Do you think he'll let you go so easily, or that your parents will allow you to break the engagement?"

"My parents are good people. They'll listen to me."

He laughs, bitter and harsh. "If you want to get out of this, treasure, you can't be so trusting. You have to be the woman who stole my horse and left me in a ditch to bleed out. The people we love disappoint us. They break us, sometimes without meaning to."

"You think I'll break you?"

His voice sinks low, fading into the distance. "You already have."

My consciousness and his drift apart. Try as I might, I can't connect with him again. I wake sometime later, wretched and cold, and I crawl out of Zeha's tent into a gray dawn. I nearly gag on the foul grainy porridge during breakfast. Despite my fur-lined trousers, my inner thighs are chafed from riding, and a persistent ache thrums through my bones and skull.

Our crossing of the southern stretch of the Bloodsalt is uneventful. We climb the great range of mountains a different way this time, skirting close to one of my father's watchtowers. The guards there can surely see us, but they have orders to let us pass unmolested. The Warlord and his people don't leave anything to chance, though. They're all clad in their dark, steely armor, roughly hammered pauldrons and breastplates and bracers. The Warlord and Zeha each wear helmets over their braided hair.

Once we've made it out of the pass, the Warlord calls a halt. "That must be the village. It's called Three Bridges." He points it out to Olsa and Zeha.

Three Bridges is a scattering of tidy cottages along a ridge a little way down the mountainside. The tiled roofs are bathed orange with the glow of the setting sun. A stream snakes between the buildings before spilling down the hill, and its flow is spanned in three places by small stone bridges. A thin line of wagons and people move slowly away from the settlement, down to the foothills.

"It looks as if they're keeping their word, at least for now," Olsa says. "The villagers are emptying the place for us."

"Either that, or they're getting everyone out so we can battle without civilian casualties," Zeha mutters.

The Warlord grunts assent. "We haven't raided this place before, but Erfyn and his people did. They took away plenty of livestock and grain. There may be some patches of ground worth farming here, after all. Olsa, tell everyone to beware, and have weapons ready, but stay back. Zeha and I will ride ahead and make the exchange."

Olsa pulls her horse nearer to his. "I would like to be at your side for this, Cronan."

My teeth clench. I don't like the way she says his name in that intimate tone.

"I need you to make sure the warriors restrain themselves unless I call for them to attack," he says. "I don't want this deal ruined by an impetuous idiot. And ask the healer to be ready in case he's needed. They may try to kill me." He chuckles darkly, and a chill of dread runs over my skin. I wrap my arms tighter around his waist.

Olsa's mouth pinches, and she throws me a vicious glare before wheeling her horse around and riding back to the others.

Zeha's horse and the Warlord's have just enough room to walk abreast as we pick our way down the mountain road toward the village.

"You're really going to do this?" she says quietly to him.

"I am. It's the right thing for our people."

Zeha nods. "It is."

I want to scream at both of them. I want to sob, and kick, and force them to take me back to the settlement—or force my people and the clans to get along. I don't want to do this. I can't do this—nor can I return to the North. Neither path ends well for us—so why can't there be a third option? Some choice I haven't seen yet?

I almost voice my grief and panic to the Warlord, but the rigidity of his huge body tells me he's got enough on his mind. This is hard for him, too, and my protests and pleading will only make it more difficult.

Maybe this can be a temporary separation. Maybe I can talk to my parents, help them see his side of things. Maybe someday I can see him again.

I can't bear the thought of never seeing him again.

We're entering the village from above, clopping along the cobbled street. I suppose they invested in cobbles to prevent erosion, given the placement of their town on the slope. The houses here are well-made, with coops and pens holding chickens, goats, and pigs. It's chilly, but compared to the aching cold on the other side of the mountains, it feels almost balmy.

"A pretty place," Zeha comments. "Our people will like it here."

"Too bad all these families had to be shoved out of their homes," I murmur.

The Warlord doesn't respond, but I know he heard me.

"There they are," he says.

Up ahead, the street levels out into the village square, with a well in the center. There's a dark line of mounted soldiers stretched across the square, spanning its width on either side of the well, from one row of homes and shops to the other.

Glancing back, I see several of the Warlord's people taking up positions along the street, bows in hand. A line of his warriors hold their swords ready, but they keep their distance behind us. Olsa is on horseback in front of them, her chestnut hair shining in the fading light.

My whole body is burning, blazing with nerves, and my inner voice keeps screaming, *I don't want this. I don't want to do this.*

57

When we're close enough to see my parents' faces, the Warlord dismounts and lifts me down. Zeha stays put, holding his horse's reins as well as her own. Slowly the Warlord walks me toward my parents, his hand heavy on my shoulder.

My father's face is pale with mingled anger and anxiety. My mother's eyes blaze, and I think if she could incinerate the Warlord with her glare, she would. Beside them, Prince Havil stands amid his own guards, resplendent in gold brocade. Has he always been so short and slight? He wears an expression of haughty offense, not the caring kindness I remember. There's no leap of excitement in his gaze when he sees me, no flicker of loving joy. Maybe he is pretending not to care too much, lest the Warlord's people notice his eagerness and ask for a higher price.

"Here she is." The Warlord's deep voice rolls across the square.

Prince Havil lifts a white-gloved hand and speaks, thin and sharp. "Bring forward the money and take it to the brute."

Two servants carry several bags of coin to the Warlord. He turns, gesturing to Olsa and one of his men, and they ride forward to accept the ransom.

"Now, give me my daughter." My father's voice—so dear to me, so precious. There's a slight crack in it, the sign of his love. I smile reassuringly at him.

"Come to us, child." My mother reaches out both arms.

The Warlord inhales, low and steady, as if he's bracing himself. His hand falls from my shoulder. Leaving me free to move away from him.

I look up, but he's not looking at me. His features are tense, and his fierce green gaze is fixed ahead. A muscle in his cheek flexes with hardening of his jaw, and his lips are pinned tight.

I place one hand on his chest, over the breastplate. Then I gather his hand and press my lips to his calloused knuckles.

My mother gasps.

My father speaks again, with a trace of horror in his voice. "Come here, Ixiana."

"I love you," I whisper to the Warlord.

Then I turn away from him and walk toward my parents and Prince Havil. I can't see their faces—my vision is blurred and burning with tears.

My mother grips my shoulders, pulls me in. She's wearing armor, crafted beautifully of reinforced leather. She smells like roses and steel. She begins to hustle me toward the horses, but Prince Havil snaps, "Wait. The deal is not yet done."

"What more is there?" my father asks.

"I need satisfaction on a key point," says the Prince. "That my intended bride remains intact. A virgin. I have my own physik here to perform the inspection."

"Surely that isn't necessary," my father says. "Ixiana's word alone—"

"Forgive me," says the Prince, with a genteel smile. "But Ixiana's judgment seems to have been—compromised. I cannot trust her word on the matter." He beckons to the robed physik. "Take her into one of the houses and perform the test."

My mother's hands tighten on my arms. "This is an outrage. We included that wording in the message only to ensure that no one would touch her. There will be no such examination."

"There will," says the Prince. "Or we will give her back to the brute." He turns to my mother. "Haven't I been through enough during this ordeal? Am I not entitled to the assurance that my bride has not been soiled and ruined?"

My mother hisses through her teeth, tensing as if she's about to spring at him, but I step forward, with a scowl of my own to rival any the Warlord has ever delivered. Prince Havil lifts an eyebrow. In the past, I have always been meek and shy in his presence, accepting his tokens of affection with eager modesty.

But I am not the same Ixiana who was taken from her tower.

"What if someone had 'ruined' me, as you say?" I face him with my head high. "In that case, an invasive examination of my person like the one you propose would cause me extreme emotional pain and embarrassment. Do you care about that at all? Do you care about me, or only yourself?"

He sucks in a shocked breath, his pale blue eyes widening. "I have invested money and men in this undertaking, to ensure your safe return, and you question my love simply because I want a pure wife?"

The Warlord speaks up, his voice throaty with suppressed rage. "None of my people touched her. And I did not take her virginity. That remains hers to give to the man she deems worthy of it."

Prince Havil scoffs. "As if I'd believe you, brute." He nods to his guards. "Take her inside. Perform the examination, whether she agrees or not."

My mother shoves me behind her and draws her sword halfway, and my father raises his hand. His guards respond, clustering around us. "Have a care, Prince," my father says.

"No, *you* have a care," Havil replies. "You are nothing without my father's good graces and his support. Without him, you'd be overrun by these stinking barbarians. Stand down, I say!"

My father keeps his hand upraised, and he glances at me. He's ready to fight Prince Havil for me. He's ready to start a war.

And that gives me hope. Because love will always be stronger than hate, and if my parents love me that much, they just might listen when I tell them about the plight of the Warlord's people, and about the man I've come to love.

But to tell them all of that, I need time. I need to defuse this situation, right now, so we can leave this place and I can speak to my parents alone. I cannot allow this standoff to devolve into a bloody three-way battle.

"It's all right." I nod to my father and move past my mother, toward Havil and his physik. "I'll submit to the test."

Prince Havil's face smooths into its usual pleasant, affable lines. "Good girl. We'll wait here until it's done."

58

Spreading my legs for the physik is embarrassing. It feels more like a violation than anything the Warlord ever did to me. Even when he told me he could do what he pleased with my body, I could sense that he would never take me without consent. And I believe he knew that I welcomed his rough attentions—the possessive hand cupping between my legs, the caressing touch at my breast. I loved it all.

But this examination is cold and cruel. If I had truly been violated during my captivity, I would find it unbearably hurtful. As it is, I endure it until the physik is satisfied. He leads me out of the abandoned house and pronounces me still a virgin.

The Warlord looks as if he might explode any second. It's time to hurry away. I avoid Prince Havil's open arms and step to my father's side instead. "Let's go," I say quietly. "Let the warriors take possession of the village. I have things I need to tell you."

My father nods, and we hurry to mount the horses. As our mounts file away, down the village street, I twist around for a last look at the hulking shape of the Warlord.

I'm leaving my heart behind with him. But I carry his with me. If he can only be patient, I'll bring it back to him.

With my parents flanking me on either side, and the guards around us, I ride out of the mountain village. It feels strange to be on my own horse without the comforting bulk of the Warlord.

"You look better than I expected," my mother says, inspecting me. "Thinner, and your clothes are strange, and you have a few scratches, but you're not bruised or bedraggled. You almost look—stronger."

"They were kind to me," I tell her quietly.

She frowns, but doesn't protest. "Your brothers wanted to be here, but we thought it safer if they stayed at home. We couldn't risk one of them being taken. Joss refused to remain at the stronghold, but we persuaded her to wait in Hoenfel. It's a town in the foothills...we'll be spending the night at the inn there. We'll be under heavy guard, never fear. No one will be able to capture you again."

Too bad.

Aloud I say, "That's reassuring."

"I nearly forgot!" My mother rummages in a saddlebag and hands me a tiny pouch. "The potion for your lungs. I brought it along. Thank the gods you did not suffer any attacks while they had you."

"I did," I tell her. "But the Warlord helped me through it."

My mother's forehead creases again. "The Warlord…"

But before she can say anything else, Prince Havil waves to me from up ahead. "My bride! Come and ride beside me."

"I should go and pacify him," I mutter.

My mother tilts her head, eyeing me. "You seem different, my love. Before all this, you worshiped the ground he walked on, or so it seemed."

I can't explain now, so I say, "When we reach the inn, I need to speak with you and Father privately, about something very important."

"Anything, my love."

For the next two hours, I'm serenaded by the limpid tones of Prince Havil as he explains how very traumatic this entire experience has been for him. He exclaims over how brutish the Warlord looked. "No elegance or grace at all, and he probably smelled terrible. You poor darling. Here, have a sniff of my new cologne." He stretches out his wrist, pulling the glove aside to show his skin. "It's delightful."

I lean over and sniff politely. "Mmm. Prince Havil, could I trouble one of your people for some water? It's been a long ride."

"Wine!" he barks at a servant, who produces two goblets and a wine-skin.

"Just water," I protest, but he says, "I insist. You need something to brace yourself after that dreadful ordeal. I know I do."

I smile through clenched teeth and sip the drink. Perhaps it will help me to endure him. How did I ever think he was charming? I suppose he can be, when he's in his court among his comforts. When the engagement was first proposed I thought him wonderful—a man with power who could care for me and coddle me, treat me like a princess. But out here in the mountains, he just seems silly and selfish. A vapid fool.

"We should hasten our marriage," he says. "So you can come live with me, not in this rough backwoods district of your father's."

"This is my home."

"Oh my dear, no. My palace is your home now. You'll be quite safe there. You'll never have to go outside again if you don't want to, except for a quick nip into and out of carriages. In our summer palace we have an entire gallery painted like a forest—such a delight, with much more appealing colors than the real thing. I don't think you've seen it yet, have you, darling?"

"No," I murmur.

I don't speak again until we dismount in front of the Hoenfel inn, when Joss barrels out the front door and nearly knocks me over with the force of her hug.

"Damn you, Ixie," she hisses into my hair. "I thought you were going to die. Gods, what is in your hair? Are those *bones*?" She pulls back, inspecting me. "You look—different."

"Mother said the same thing." I give her a half-smile, and she returns it with a confused, wondering grin of her own.

"Come inside," she says. "They have decent grub here. And I've explained your diet to them."

During the meal, Prince Havil complains constantly about the poor quality of the food, while I devour my portion greedily. I've never tasted anything so good in my life.

My mother is too jittery to eat—she hovers behind me, unbraiding my hair and picking the bones out of it. For a second I think about asking if I can keep them—but then she tosses them into the fire. "We'll burn the rest of these clothes, too, and put you in something decent," she says. "I brought your softest gowns and robes—"

"No," I say sharply, and she stops.

"I'd like to keep the clothes," I say, more quietly.

Prince Havil bursts into disdainful laughter. "Why, darling, whatever for?"

Instead of answering, I rise from the table. "I'm tired. And I'd like to speak with my parents alone before I retire, so if you'll pardon me, Your Highness."

"Of course, of course." He looks a bit disgruntled, but he gives me a permissive wave. "Have a bath as well, darling. I didn't want to speak of it, but you reek of vagabonds and beasts."

"So sorry, my dear." I give him an exaggerated curtsy. "I shall try to be more pleasing to you in the future."

"I'm sure you will." He smiles, his gaze traveling along my body. "I look forward to it."

59

Once my parents and Joss and I are finally alone, seated around a small table in the inn's best and largest room, I tell them everything—all the details of my time with the Warlord, including our connection through the ether and what it means. I omit our sensual interludes, but I try to communicate how our feelings for each other deepened during those days of travel. I explain the history of his people as they see it, and the hardships under which they suffer.

"You see, they raid our villages because they don't have much choice," I say. "They need supplies that they can't make or obtain in their own lands. They lose people all the time to disease, exposure, and monsters. They live among so many dangers—it's terrifying."

My mother presses her hand over mine. "You're a compassionate girl, Ixiana. I understand why you feel for them."

"But it's not that simple," my father adds. "The raiders don't just take what they need and leave. They are cruel and destructive. They poison wells, burn buildings, and rape villagers—men and women alike. They kill children."

"Some of the clans do those things, yes, but not all. The Warlord's people don't commit rape or murder children. At least, not with his permission."

Joss is playing with one of her knives, as she often does when she's unsettled. "When I was attending classes in Oloth District, I heard a version of our history like the one the Northern raiders tell," she says. "I thought the teacher who told it was merely trying to be subversive, or keep us from falling asleep at our writing tables. But maybe he was trying to wake us up to an uncomfortable truth. Still, if you'd seen some of the border villages after the raids, Ixiana—if you heard the weeping of the people left violated and broken in the streets—"

"Cronan would say that these wrongs were done to his people first—that this is vengeance," I murmur. "Though as I said, he doesn't condone rape. *Faen,* there's so much pain on both sides—how can we ever—" My lip trembles, and I bury my face in my hands. Exhaustion and emotion crash together inside me, but I fight the oncoming tears. If I give in and cry, I'm not sure when I'll be able to *stop* crying. A wound in my heart bleeds for the Warlord, gushing more pain as I realize just how great the divide is between our peoples.

I'd had some vague notion of convincing my parents, of single-handedly crafting a permanent treaty.

A stupid idea. Impossible.

My mother strokes my hair. "Darling, sometimes when we are with powerful people, when we are frightened and endangered—our hearts have to adapt. They develop emotions and connections to help us survive the situation."

I drop my hands from my face and pull away from her. "That's not what this is. You don't understand—you don't know him."

"Ixie, be honest. You haven't known him long, either." Joss stares me down. "Are you saying you're in love with him?" Her lip curls.

In her eyes I see that familiar disdain, the contempt for my weakness. Pitiful little helpless Ixiana, falling for her mighty captor.

My parents' eyes reflect it too—pity and prejudice blending to create a reality in their minds, one they can accept. It's easier for them to believe that my soft heart was temporarily overcome by Warlord's looks and brawn—much harder for them to accept that I've awakened to a broader worldview and a deeper truth than any of them understand.

"Did he touch you?" asks my mother through tight lips.

She'll read the truth in my eyes whether I speak it or not, so I say, "I wanted him to."

"Gods." My father's voice shakes, and he rises abruptly. "I can't bear any more of this tonight. Ixiana, you need rest. We're safe here, well-guarded by our soldiers and the Prince's men. Tomorrow we will continue on, and we'll head straight for the border and the Prince's palace. He wants you with him, Ixiana, so he can protect you. And he will likely want to move up the wedding. Once you two are married, you'll be far out of this Warlord's reach, safe under the protection of His Highness's family."

Fury and panic blazes along my nerves. I rise as well, ready to protest—but my sister interrupts. "Whatever you want to say, Ixie, it can wait until we've all had some sleep. Come along—you'll share my room. There's a bath heated for you. You'd best get into it before the water cools."

She ushers me out, and I don't resist. My mind is beginning to blur and my head is swimming—sure signs that my body has reached its limits. I've had a good meal, and once I've bathed and rested, I can attack my parents with the truth again—more effectively, maybe. I need a strategy, some way to convince them to at least meet with the Warlord and talk to him.

The bath is a sheer delight, as is the comfortable bed that I sink into afterwards. In an uncharacteristic display of affection, Joss sits on the edge of the bed and strokes my hair, while my eyes close and my thoughts drift into darkness.

Deep in the night the darkness shifts, turning blue, beautiful, infinite.

And somewhere in that vast blue, I can hear the Warlord screaming.

60

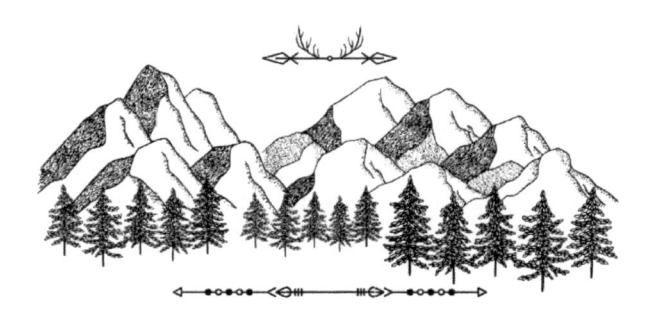

My Warlord is roaring in pain. He's close to blacking out from the intensity of it—I can feel him shifting in and out of the ether.

"Where are you?" I shriek. "Tell me where you are so I can help you!"

He appears, whole and vivid for an instant, his body lacerated and leaking blood, his beard fouled with dirt and more blood. "The Prince," he whispers. "Don't come for me."

Then he's gone, and I'm waking, fighting my way out of the dream. My body is slick with sweat and my heart shudders with terror.

I fling myself out of bed. There are traveling clothes laid out for me—a pair of elegant pants and a long dress with a split up the front so I can ride astride, as well as delicate underthings and a fur cape. I snatch all of it, not daring to dress in the bedroom lest I wake Joss. She's a warrior, and she'll rouse at the mere scent of danger.

In the chilly upstairs hallway of the inn, I strip my nightdress off and sponge the sweat from my bare body with it. I'm not even concerned with anyone seeing me naked. Not anymore. Not when my Warlord is in distress.

I pull on the clothing as quickly as I can. There's a lump in the pocket of the overdress—it's the magical spray that stops my breathing attacks.

Speaking of attacks—on impulse, I slip back into the room and take one of my sister's swords. I slide it out quietly, not bothering with the belt and sheath—they'll clink and jangle too much. It's the shorter of her two favorite weapons—short and thin enough for me to wield. There's no way I could carry her big broadsword.

Prince Havil has Cronan. He's hurting him. And they have to be nearby, because I don't think the Prince would wander far from the comfort of the inn. They must have found a place where no one would hear the screams.

I creep down the inn stairs, wincing at every creak, and glide along the back hall, through the kitchen. The door is barred, and the man on guard there is lolling on a bench asleep, with an empty bottle lying near his hand. I ease the wooden bar up and let myself out, into the frigid black night.

Beyond the kitchen doorstep lie the snow-flecked cobbles of the innyard. The leather boots I'm wearing are finely made, but not overly sturdy, and I can feel every lump and pebble of the ground through their soles. They keep the cold at bay well enough, but I doubt they'd do me much good up North.

I walk between the stables and outbuildings, toward a fringe of dark trees. The inn stands at the southern edge of Hoenfel. If the Prince is doing anything underhanded, he'd probably do it outside of town where the village folk won't notice. Not that they'd fault him for torturing one of our district's mortal enemies.

There's a gate in the low wall around the innyard, the only obstacle between me and the black forest. As I reach for the gate latch, three figures on horseback trot out of the dark and range up in a row, barring my way. Two of them wear the bear's head shield of my father's guard, while the third sports the emblem of Prince Havil's house—a dove with four wings.

I was already holding the sword low, against my skirts, but I quickly shift my right hand behind me to conceal the weapon from the men.

"Hold there," says Prince Havil's guard. "What's your business, woman?"

"It's the child," says one of my father's soldiers. "It's Ixiana, the one who was taken. What are you doing out here in the dark, lass?"

"I need some air," I tell them. "The inn feels too close and confining. I thought I'd breathe the pine scent of those delightful trees."

"Afraid we can't let you take a midnight walk, my lady," replies the soldier. "Too dangerous. Could be ruffians about."

"We caught one earlier," says Prince Havil's man. "Big monstrous brute, lurking in the forest."

"Oh indeed?" I raise my eyebrows, trying to keep my voice steady. "How wonderful that you caught him. And what did you do with the villain?"

"Dragged him in there." The soldier points to an outbuilding, an old barn at the far corner of the innyard. "The inn-keeper's got a cold cellar, thick-walled and all, so His Highness took the brute down there for interrogation. Didn't want to disturb everyone, you see."

"The Prince is going to interrogate the man himself?"

"Oh yes. His Highness is a fair hand at torture. Enjoys it, you might say."

"Lovely," I say through smiling, gritted teeth. "Well, thank you for guarding us so well. I'll just have a short walk through the yard then, before I return to bed. Good night!"

"Good night, my lady."

As I turn, I shift the sword, keeping it hidden in my skirts. I pace casually back toward the inn before glancing back. The men have turned toward the trees, with their backs to me, so I quickly cross the yard and slip into the shadow of an outbuilding—a privy, by the smell of it. I wish I could cut straight to the old barn, but the guards will likely keep an eye on the innyard as well as the woods. To avoid catching their eyes, I'm forced to circle the stables and a chicken coop to stay out of sight, jumping from shadow to shadow like a child skipping across a creek on stones.

At last I reach the door of the old barn. There's no one on guard, so I open the great door a crack and slide through.

All is silent inside.

If Prince Havil has killed my soulmate, I'm going to slice him apart. I don't care if his father and brothers demand my head for the crime.

I slink through the dusty expanse of the barn, my way lit only by a few shafts of moonlight glancing between broken rafters overhead. The place reeks of musty, mildewed hay and rancid rot. At one end, between thick posts, stone steps descend to a door shrouded in black shadows.

That must be the entrance to the cold cellar.

Quietly I descend the steps and fumble in the dark for the handle. My other palm sweats against the leather-wrapped hilt of my sister's sword.

At last my fingertips graze cold metal instead of rough wood. The handle.

I wrench it downward and push, and the ponderous door swings slowly open.

61

As I shove the door wide, gold lamplight floods over me, revealing three figures.

One is a guard, standing just inside the door. He's been watching Prince Havil work, I suppose, but his head swivels toward me as I enter.

The second figure is Prince Havil, clad in a black vest and purple silk trousers. His lean milk-white arms are bare, and the brown waves of his hair are as neat as ever. Only his hands are soiled—smeared and spattered with the blood of my Warlord.

The Warlord's wrists are tied, and the bit of rope between them hangs over a huge iron hook in the ceiling of the cold cellar. His great arms are bulging, sinew and muscle stretched to the limit. He's naked, barefoot, and his toes barely brush the floor enough to take a little of the strain off his arms and shoulders. His ankles are manacled and tethered to the wall so he can't kick his attackers.

His body has been sliced deeply in several places, just as I saw through the ether. His right eye is swollen shut, sealed by dark blood trailing from a cut on his brow. His lips are puffy and bleeding too. I can't tell if he's conscious.

Prince Havil whirls at my interruption. Eager blood flushes his cheeks, and his eyes sparkle. He has been enjoying himself.

A throb of nausea passes through my gut as I realize just how little I knew this man, this prince I've been acquainted with for years. I was going to marry him, when I had no idea who he truly was, or the cruel depths he was concealing.

There's a scratchy raw feeling in my throat—my airway warning me that it might revolt soon. I try to control my breathing, to keep the sword behind the stiff fold of my overdress.

"My dear!" exclaims Prince Havil. "You shouldn't be in here."

"Your men told me you'd caught someone sneaking around." I take a step toward him.

"Yes, the leader of the ruffians himself. Probably planning to steal you again. Or maybe he intended to slaughter your whole family in your sleep. I'm trying to get information out of him, you see, to keep you safe."

"What information?"

"If he's alone, that sort of thing."

"I think it's fairly obvious he's alone. You must have been working on him awhile, and no one has come for him."

"Well, I suppose at this point it's more of a punishment than an interrogation." Havil chuckles and gives me a wild smile. "You didn't think I'd let him steal my future wife and then walk away, did you? A man must have satisfaction, you see. Especially when a fiend like this has dared to touch his property. Now, go back to the inn, there's a good girl."

He nods to the guard, who leans forward as if to take my arm and escort me out.

But I sidestep and swivel, setting my back to the wall and pointing Joss's sword at the guard. "I'm not your property, Highness. And I'm not going back to the inn."

The guard hesitates, casting a shocked glance toward Havil. "Sire?"

"I'm not fond of this change in you, my dear," says the Prince gravely. "You were such a sweet, submissive little thing before they took you, and now—" He shakes his head. "I only hope what they did to you can be undone. It may take some vigorous polishing before my little gem is smooth again. Take the sword from her."

I slash at the guard, and thanks to my brief training with the Warlord I manage to hold him off for a few minutes before he disarms me with his own sword. The guard picks up Joss's weapon and looks to his prince for orders.

Havil waves him away. "Step outside and leave her to me. See that no one else enters this room."

The guard nods and ducks out of the cold cellar with both swords, pulling the door shut behind him.

"I don't want to consider what this defiance means," says the Prince, approaching me. He's much shorter than the Warlord—about my height. To string up the Warlord like this, he must have had help from much stronger men, probably some of the soldiers outside.

Despite his lack of height, Prince Havil exudes a bitter threat I can't help but fear. With the Warlord, my fear was always laced with a sort of jittery expectation, a fevered anticipation of his touch or his words. Havil has been nothing but soft and kind to me for as long as I've known him—but when he placed such value on my virginity as a matter of his own pride, my view of him shifted. I can see him clearly now, the genteel serpent slithering around his tender prey, no less deadly for the pretense of gentleness.

"Why did you come out here, my dear?" Havil asks, stroking my chin with a blood-wet finger. "What do you want? Do you want to watch me flay the man who dared steal from me?"

I jerk my face away from his touch. "I want you to let him go. Fulfill your part of the bargain and honor the truce we've established."

"Truce?" He laughs. "We will take back the village we gave him within the month, and my men will hang all his vagabond followers from the walls of your father's stronghold. Then no one will dare attempt such a thing again."

"So your word is worthless, and you have no honor. Good to know." I bite my lip to steady its shaking.

"My word is good with people who deserve my esteem." Prince Havil pokes the knife toward me in a gesture of emphasis. "Consider this a demonstration, my dear. This is what happens to those who challenge me." He turns back to the Warlord with a flourish of the blade. "Now, where shall we cut next?"

"Stop it, or I'll make you stop."

The Prince doesn't even look at me. "And how will you do that, my dear?"

"I'll tell my father about this."

"Your parents are my lap-dogs. They do as I say, because they need what I give them—more troops to fortify the borders, and a voice in my father's court." He cuts a long slit through the Warlord's pectoral, toward his nipple.

The Warlord hasn't seemed to notice my presence, but as the knife carves through his flesh, his good eye flashes open and he bellows in pain.

"Stop!" I charge at the Prince, tugging his arm back so the knife leaves Cronan's chest.

"Get off me," snaps the Prince, and with a savage whip of his arm he flings me backward. My head bounces against the stone wall. The impact rings through my ears, and for a second I can't right myself, or react.

62

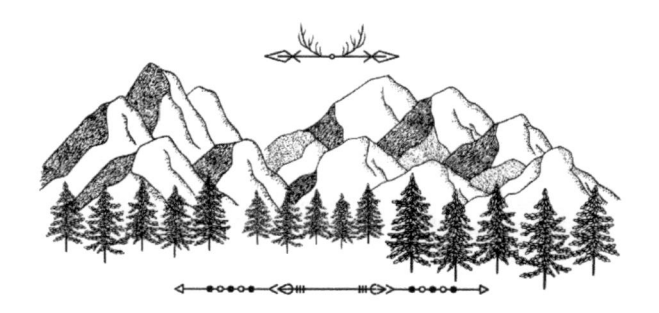

As I collapse to the floor, the Warlord cries out, enraged, and his whole body jerks against his bonds.

His concern for me seems to infuriate Havil. "She's not yours!" he spits at the Warlord. "She belongs to me!" The Prince lunges in my direction, knife in hand, eyes wild. For a horrible moment I'm certain he means to murder me.

"Then why was she begging for my cock, pleading for me to let her come?" The Warlord's bruised mouth hitches up at the corner.

Havil whirls around, his face white. Then he lurches forward and sinks his knife into Cronan's shoulder, twisting it until I can hear blade grating against bone.

The Warlord screams, his head arching back.

"Know what I'm going to cut next?" Havil reaches between the Warlord's legs. "This. I think I'll keep it as a trophy. When I kill a man I like to keep a part of him around, to remember my triumph. I have a lot of fingers and ears, but no dicks yet. This one will do nicely."

I can't stop Havil. He's too strong, and I have no weapons. Nothing, except the bottle in my pocket, the magical spray that opens my airways when they're shriveling up—

The spray that sends healthy lungs into spasms and makes their owners panic and retch.

"Havil." I stagger to my feet and force myself to speak softly, meekly. "I understand now. I think that blow cleared my head, and I can see what a fool I've been. Before you cut off his dick, give me a kiss. I know I don't deserve it, but—please." I let my lips tremble.

Havil eyes me. "I'm still cutting it off."

"Of course. You have every right to your vengeance."

He takes a step toward me. "What about the things he said? He's been talking like that all night. Did you let him put his mouth on you? Did you beg him for release?"

"He's lying to make you angry," I say, with a hoarse laugh. "You know me, Havil. I'm a proper lady, raised to be pure. I'd never debase myself before a man and beg for such a thing—unless that man was my husband." I tug my lower lip with my teeth. "I remember the delight of your lips. Show me how a real man can kiss."

Smirking, Havil sidles nearer, leaning in.

My fingers are in my pocket, flipping back the leather flap that covers the tiny spray bottle, tugging it free, drawing it out—

My forefinger presses down as Havil's parted lips approach mine. I squirt the bottle once, twice, and a third time as he recoils, shock and confusion flooding his eyes.

He inhales, surprised, sealing his own fate. The reaction is instantaneous—he chokes, eyes going wide, hands clutching his chest as his knife clatters to the floor. He bows over, wheezing and retching, and staggers against the wall.

I seize the knife and dash to the Warlord's side. As I reach up to saw through the ropes, my body is flush with his bleeding chest, and my face is upturned to his. He hangs his head, weariness and anguish suffusing his features.

"I told you not to come," he wheezes between swollen lips.

"You must have a death wish," I grit out, sawing against the thick rope.

"Yes."

Startled, I glance at him.

He gives me a slow, pained smile. "Without you, yes."

My heart jerks at his admission, but I keep sawing at his bonds, while Havil gags behind me. "You were a fool to follow us, to hang around this place," I whisper.

"I had to see you again. I was careless—or maybe I let myself be caught, knowing they'd kill me."

"But that's not like you," I murmur. The knife blade snaps through the remaining sliver of rope, and the Warlord's arms fall to his sides. A shattered groan breaks from him, and his breath hitches as he rolls his strained shoulders.

Maybe it *is* like him, after all. He's the kind of person who would sacrifice everything for what he loves and believes in—and if I'm one of those loved things—

"Come on." I tuck myself against him so he can lean on me. "We have to go. The Prince will be sick for a while, but it won't last forever."

Havil is spewing vomit onto the floor, eyes cinched tight. With any luck, he'll vomit until he passes out. Maybe he'll choke on it.

When the Warlord and I stumble out through the door, the guard starts to speak—but Cronan's massive hand shoots out and grips him by the neck. There's a flex, a pained grunt from Cronan, and a *snap*. The guard goes limp, and when the Warlord releases him, he crumples.

But the effort seems to have drained what little strength the Warlord had left. He sways, and his weight hangs heavy on me. I can't support him for long.

"Can you get onto a horse?" I ask him.

His answering mumble isn't reassuring. We hitch along through the cold night, until we reach the shadow of the stables. I'm sweating, and my lungs are tightening, spasming—I'm having trouble sucking in enough air. I know this feeling, and it's only going to get worse.

"Hold on," I manage to gasp. "I can't—you have to sit."

He slides off my shoulder at once and collapses onto the cold mud by the stables, while I take out the spray bottle and inhale one squirt of the potion. Immediately my breathing eases.

I haul the heavy door open, wincing as it creaks. But the three guards must have ridden off to patrol the area, because none of them show up to confront me.

The horse I'm most familiar with is my mother's mare, though I've never had to saddle her myself. But I've watched the Warlord's people saddle and unsaddle their mounts more times than I can count, and although my mother's saddle is a different style, the principles are the same. Softly I croon to the horse while I find the tack and fumble about the straps and buckles with cold, trembling fingers.

Finally the saddle and bridle are on the mare, mostly. I hope to the gods I've done everything right. Otherwise it might all might slide off when the Warlord and I try to mount.

With my heart throbbing in my throat, I lead the horse outside, cringing at every muffled *clop* of her hooves. Thank the gods for the thin coating of snow, and for the mud outside the stable door. It softens the sounds a little. Still, I need to hurry.

Gripping the mare's reins, I bend over the Warlord's slumped figure. "Cronan? Can you mount?"

He doesn't answer, or move. In the dark, I see the faint glimmer of blood shining on far too much of his skin.

Is he…

He isn't dead. Can't be dead.

"Cronan, please." A sob cracks through my whisper.

63

When the Warlord doesn't stir, I run through my options. I could ask my family for help, but I can't guarantee my parents and Joss won't kill him on sight. I have nowhere to hide Cronan, and I don't know where any healer is in this town. The only healer I know of is a couple hours away, in Three Bridges, properly sleeping with his share of the ransom money under his pillow.

I have no idea how long the sickening effects of the spray potion will last on Prince Havil. And when he regains control over himself, he's going to be furious. The wedding is certainly canceled, and it's possible I've started a war between his father and mine. So instead of stopping one conflict, I may have incited a new one.

Brilliant work, Ixiana.

I can't think about that anymore. Cronan is my priority, now and always.

Hitching my hands into his armpits, I tug vainly at his bulk. He doesn't budge, not an iota.

"*Faen, faen*," I hiss under my breath, hot tears sliding down my cold cheeks. "Get *up*, you big bastard. Do you have a spine? Any will to fight? Or are you weak after all?" A sob hitches in my throat. "Pull yourself out of this, or I swear I will dive into the ether and kill you myself." In my helpless rage, I kick him, right in the breastbone.

His body jolts and he hauls in a long breath.

"Oh gods." I bite back more tears and pull vainly at his arm. "Come on, Cronan. You have to do this. I need to get you onto the horse."

I don't like the sound of his thick, wheezing breaths, or the way he groans piteously as he heaves himself mostly upright. Blood oozes from the gashes across his chest, stomach, and thighs, smearing the horse and her saddle as he gives one great pained lunge and throws himself up onto her back. I toss the reins over the mare's head and leap up behind him quickly, wrapping both arms around him and taking up the reins again. I can only pray that I'll be able to keep him from toppling off during the ride to the mountain village.

Peering around the Warlord's bulk, I lift the reins and urge the mare forward in a low voice. She obeys me without hesitation, sweet thing that she is. As we round the corner of the stable, I notice the three guards passing the back gate again, and I tug the reins sharply to halt the horse in the shadows.

The guards assemble briefly before splitting up, two going in opposite directions around the inn wall and the third heading for the woods.

I wait a few moments, then hurry the mare toward the back gate. It won't take the guards long to do their rounds and return here.

I have to dismount to open the back gate, and when I do, Cronan nearly slides off. But I manage to push his shoulder hard enough to get him back up, lying on the horse's neck. She chuffs, apparently disturbed by the size and the slack weight of him, but I keep crooning to her, and when I urge her through the gate into the field beyond, she complies.

I close the back gate before mounting again. Inside I'm chanting a terrified prayer of *quickly, quickly,* mingled with the names of all the gods I've ever heard of and some I probably made up on the spot. I don't head straight for the forest; I angle the mare to the left, toward a long ridge of rocky dirt with no snow on it. Her hoofprints by the gate will mingle with those of the guards, and if we ride along the bare stretch of hard earth, hopefully they won't notice our trail leading away from the inn until we've covered some distance.

We trot along the packed dirt for a few minutes, and then I hear, up ahead, the low voices of another patrol through the fringe of trees. Panicking, I pull the mare up short and hold her there, peering through the gloom. I can barely see anything, but I wait until the voices and the dull tramp of hooves has receded.

We have to stop a few more times to avoid patrols. Once, two pairs of guards intersect nearly on top of us, and we only get clear of them because my mother's mare is quick, even with the Warlord and me on her back. If I'd been on foot, I wouldn't have been able to cross the open ground fast enough, and I would have been caught.

No wonder Cronan was captured. My father and the Prince have laced these woods with a few dozen soldiers, it seems.

After that narrow escape, I consider angling toward the village and hoping for fewer patrols—but then we would have to deal with walls and fences that the mare can't jump with two on her back, and gates I can't risk stopping to open. Plus there would be village dogs who might signal our passing.

We stick to the forest, picking our way through the thickest shadows until it's been a long time since I've seen a patrol. Meanwhile I talk to Cronan in my mind, constantly, in my sharpest tones. I criticize and cajole, pester and praise him. Anything to keep his consciousness rooted to his body, tethered to me. If he's answering in the ether, I can't hear it—but I have to believe that he's there, responding to all my nonsense with annoyed grunts.

He's still naked, except for the horse blanket I threw around his shoulders. I hate to think what the saddle is doing to his privates, or how cold his feet must be, but it can't be helped. When I think it's safe,

I steer us onto the mountain road leading up to Three Bridges.

What follows is a blur of dark trees, the miasma of coppery blood, freezing night air, and rough road. The mare stumbles several times, and with each jerk, the Warlord's body shifts and starts to slide. I have to strain and pull, tugging him back into balance. I'm shaking with nerves, and my nose is numb with cold, yet my armpits and chest are damp with hectic sweat.

Just when I think I can't keep him on the horse any longer, when I think my teeth are going to crack from chattering, I see the glittering stream and the first of the three bridges.

The next moment, someone barks, "Stop."

64

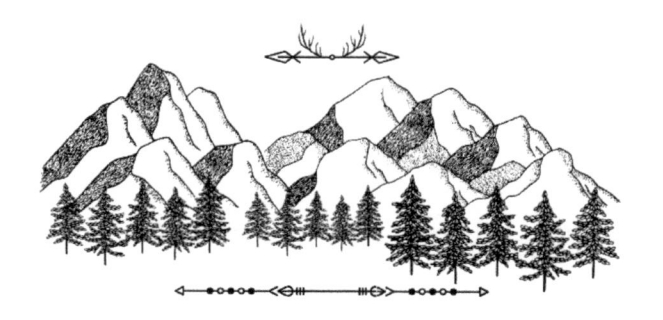

At the harsh command, I halt the mare. I know better than to test the good graces of the Warlord's people. They probably have arrows trained on me already.

"I have the Warlord," I call out. My voice sounds pitifully feeble. "He's injured. He needs the healer."

"The Warlord? Injured?" A lantern flares and bobs toward the mare. "Dismount, and throw down your weapons!"

"I don't have any weapons, and if I dismount he'll fall off," I reply.

Urgent voices speak the Warlord's language, and another lantern springs to life. Large figures approach the horse, and arms reach up to take Cronan down. The men exclaim at the state of him—naked, torn to pieces, nearly frozen.

I sway on the mare's back, sick to my stomach and terrified that I didn't make the right choice, that I didn't get him here in time.

"He's breathing," one of the warriors calls out, and I vent a sob of relief. The healer can fix him. It will take a while to seal those gashes, restore the lost blood, repair any frostbitten parts—but my Warlord will live.

"You." A hand grips my arm and jerks me off the mare. My ankle wrenches painfully, caught in the stirrup, and when I finally get it free and land on it, agony lances up my leg. A shrill cry escapes me, and I collapse onto the cold cobbles of the road.

"Foolish brat." Chestnut braids swing past my face, and I catch a glimpse of Olsa's features, painted harshly in the light of the lamp she carries. "You arranged for him to come to you tonight, knowing it would mean his death!"

"I didn't arrange it," I gasp. "I had no idea he would try to see me. It was stupid of him."

"*You* make him stupid," she snaps. "You've turned his head and wrecked the goals he's worked for his entire life. You are bad for him. For all of us."

She's half-dragging me along, not toward the village where the other men took Cronan—no, she's pulling me off the road, into the trees. The ground slopes sharply downward here, and I can barely keep my feet under me.

"I'm going to do what he should have done," she says. "We have the money and the town. I'll tell him your own people wounded you as you were helping him escape, and you died from the injuries before the healer could tend to you. That will enrage him enough to call on the other warlords and begin the war that needs to be fought."

"But—your people aren't strong enough for a war," I manage, through the pain of my ankle and her iron grip. "You'll lose. He'll die."

"Maybe. Maybe he and I will die gloriously in battle, side by side, fighting for our ancestral land. Or maybe we'll win, and he'll forget you quickly when I remind him what we have together." Olsa throws me against the trunk of a huge tree and pins me there with one hand to my chest. After the exertion of this night, I am too weak to resist her—too weak to do anything but hang there, helpless.

Olsa sets down her lantern and drags a wide knife from a sheath at her belt. She sets its tip beneath my chin, right against the soft tissue there.

Death is before me again, so crisp and clear I can taste its bitter tang, smell the sweet rot of its breath. The night forest is so still, just a whisper of chill wind riffling through the thickets of black lacy branches. The lantern spills orange light onto the rocky ground. Olsa is partly uplit with the glow, and her face looks strange, mad and distorted. In her eyes I recognize the ice of inevitability—the certainty of the end.

My fingers graze the rough bark of the tree behind me, but there are no branches to seize, no makeshift weapons with which to defend myself—not that I could survive against a warrior like Olsa.

Since I'm going to die anyway, I can't resist one last tiny triumph. "Cronan hears my thought-voice through the ether," I say softly. "And I hear his. He can hear me right now, I know it. He can hear me say that I love him. You can kill me, but you'll never have a true soul-bond with him."

"You're lying," Olsa says through her teeth. The knife pricks my skin, driving upward just enough to release a trickle of pain and blood.

"I'm not lying. We told Zeha about it, too. You can ask her."

Olsa cries out, a half-scream of frustration. The knife-tip jerks away from me, and the pressure of her hand on my chest disappears. I slide down against the tree, cupping my injured ankle.

"If you truly have a bond with him, our law prevents me from killing you. Murder of a life-mate is the greatest of wrongs." Olsa strikes the heel of her fist against a tree. "I could still do it, and blame your own people. No one has to know."

She hasn't quite decided either way—to kill me or not. I can sense her tension, her rage, her affection for Cronan, and the law of her clan, all dragging at her, tearing her apart.

I've been in this very spot with Cronan himself, as he teetered on the murderous edge of his passions. But with Olsa, no part of me appeals to her. I can't use my body, my voice, my personality, my helplessness—none of that will sway her in my favor.

All I can do is wait—and maybe play for time.

"You've cared about him for years, haven't you?" I ask quietly. "Have you known each other since you were children?"

"Yes," she hisses. "I've been close with Cronan and Zeha since we were born. I was there when he lost his brother and his mother. I was there when his father sank into darkness. I've been there for both of them, for all our people, my whole life. And for a nasty little worm like you to squeeze into his heart and push me out—it's unbearable."

"I didn't mean to," I say. "It just happened."

"You're probably lying about the soul-bond to save your wretched Southern hide," she snarls. "Admit it. You're lying."

"I'm not—I told you I love—"

"Don't!" She whirls, pointing the knife at me. "I have to do this, do you understand? It's not only for Cronan and me—I'm not such a fool as to kill with the sole aim of bedding a man. No, this is for all of us. Peace simply cannot exist between our people and yours. You must know that. War is the only way to purge all the hate and the hurt, to change the future. With your death, that change can begin. Cronan will incite it himself, as he was meant to do. You will be the spark that ignites the cleansing fire."

"Why do people keep saying that I'm the key to all this?" My words tremble, nearly dissolving into sobs. "I'm no one. I'm nothing. You people should have left me out of it."

Olsa steps toward me again, her fingers flexing on the knife hilt. "Too late," she says.

65

The knife flashes in the lantern-light.

I throw myself to the side, and the blade grazes my neck. There's a spurt of pain, a trickle of warm blood. I want to panic, to clamp my hand over the cut, but I can't spare the time. I'm still alive, for now.

Not for long if I don't move.

Olsa slashes again, but I'm already scrambling away on all fours, like a wounded beast, putting the tree trunk between us. She steps around it, her knife whistling through the air. I duck low and lurch in, seizing her ankle, jerking as hard as I can. She's off-balance—I twist my body and kick her ankle with my good foot, and with a cry she crashes into the leaves.

She rolls on top of me the next second, gripping one of my arms. She clamps the knife between her teeth for a second while she fights to get both of my slim wrists into her large hand. I screech and writhe, but she's big, and well-trained, and she gets both my hands pinned above my head.

I've been here before, in this position. The Warlord's voice rises from my consciousness.

See how I've pinned your hands, mouse? Twist your wrists, if you can. Make your hands small, and try to slip them out. Do whatever you can to distract me while you get free— spit at me, bite at me, strike my forehead with yours.

With her free hand, Olsa reaches up to take the knife from between her teeth.

I lurch upward, head and neck snaking out, and my jaws clamp shut on her wrist. I bite as hard as I can, grinding into the flesh and tendons. A short, harsh scream breaks from her, and the knife falls out of her mouth onto my chest.

All the while I've been working my left hand loose, and with a final squirm it pops free of Olsa's grip.

My teeth unlatch from her wrist.

I seize the knife.

I drive it up, toward her neck.

Your trick gets you nowhere unless you're willing to follow through.

But my hand freezes, the knife's tip barely denting Olsa's skin.

"No," I whisper. "There's been enough blood."

If I have to die to redeem the wrongs of my ancestors, so be it.

And my fingers open, letting the knife tumble out.

Olsa grabs it as it falls. I relax beneath her, closing my eyes and tilting my chin up, baring my throat for the slice.

When it doesn't come, I open my eyes.

Olsa's weight still rests on me, but her hands have fallen slack at her sides. The knife lies nearby in the brittle brown grass.

Hers is a lovely face, flushed with strength and righteous anger. But the anger is fading, leaving behind a weariness that I've felt myself—the soul-deep ache of a warrior who's tired of fighting.

For a long moment, there's only silence, and the rustle of the breeze through the litter of the forest floor. Something passes between us, eye to eye—a wordless acknowledgment, a tenuous link of something that isn't friendship or sisterhood, but might one day turn into both.

Neither of us speak as she climbs off me and offers her hand. I grip it silently and pull myself up, putting my weight on my good leg while I brush leaves from my backside and my hair.

Olsa picks up the knife and uses it to trim the twigs from a long, sturdy branch. She hands it to me, and I use it as a walking stick to relieve the pain of my ankle.

Slowly, haltingly, we make our way back to the road.

We don't talk about how we nearly killed each other. We don't try to make sense of all the complex wrongs of our two peoples. For now, it is enough to exist companionably. To let each other live.

66

When Olsa stops outside a house and gestures to the door, I give her a nod of thanks. She follows me inside. Her silent presence at my back is my only defense against the gauntlet of burly, grim-faced warriors who eye me as I walk through the front room of the house.

In one of the bedrooms, I glimpse a flare of golden light, so I peek in. The healer stands next to Cronan, shining beams of energy into the wounds. It's slow, difficult work, as evidenced by the healer's rough breathing. His dark fingers are tense and rigid, spread in the air over the Warlord's chest.

At the foot of the bed stands Zeha. She glances up at me and releases an aggravated sigh. "What happened to him?"

Quietly I tell her everything, while she shakes her head and mutters in her language. "And what happened to *you*?" she asks when I'm done, surveying my bloody, dirt-covered clothes.

I don't mention the incident with Olsa. "Most of this is Cronan's blood. Also a sharp branch cut my neck a bit, and I sprained my ankle getting off the horse."

"Of course you did." Zeha rolls her eyes. "Fine horse, by the way. One of the men is caring for it."

"It's my mother's." I edge closer to the bed, my eyes locked on the Warlord's ravaged body. Even bloodied and grimed, he's so beautiful.

"We can't be apart," I whisper, gazing at him.

Zeha says something in her language—I'm fairly sure it's a swear. Olsa responds quietly, and picks up a bandage from a nearby table. I retreat when she approaches me, but then I realize what she's doing, and I lift my hair so she can secure the bandage around my neck.

Then Zeha speaks to the healer. "Please keep working on Cronan as long as you can. I'll have someone bring you food and drink, and we'll have a bed ready so you can recover afterward. And you'll be well paid. Again."

The healer snorts. "I might as well travel with your clan from now on. Seems I'm to be the personal healer for this fool. He's going to have scars from this one—I can't make his skin seamless *and* replace the blood he lost *and* save his frostbitten feet."

"Save his feet and his life," Zeha says. "The scars will remind him of his foolishness." She hesitates in the doorway, looking back at me. "Thank you for saving him."

"You're welcome," the healer replies. I smile and nod to Zeha.

She gives me the tiniest of answering smiles, shaking her head. "What are we going to do with you, Ixiana?"

She doesn't answer her own question, and I have no response. She and Olsa leave together, talking in low tones. Probably trying to figure a way out of this mess.

I perch on the end of the bed, watching the healer work until my vision blurs and I sink down onto the blankets. It's still the dead of night. If I leave now I could make it back to Hoenfel before sunrise and smooth things over with my parents and Havil—if that's even possible—not that I want to marry him, but I should try to mollify him somehow, keep another war from beginning…

The bedroom is firelit and warm, and my thoughts drift into a sleepy golden swirl, like molten sunlight. My sleep is punctuated by splinters of pain through my ankle, interrupted by nightmare flashes of vomit spewing from Prince Havil's mouth.

I wake with a jolt—an actual jolt as my whole body is flung over something bulky and warm. I'm hanging head-down, my long yellow hair swaying. The ground is moving, and all I can see is a pair of boots, two muscular thighs, and a well-shaped male butt clad in tight leather trousers. I've been flung over someone's enormous shoulder, someone whose spicy, smoky male scent I recognize.

"Cronan," I gasp. "Put me down."

"No."

"You're healed! You're walking! That's so wonderful… but what is going on?"

"I'm taking you back to your father."

67

"What?" I hammer the Warlord's back with my fist. "I don't want to go back to my family yet! We haven't even had a chance to talk… Cronan, I want to stay with you. Just for a little while."

He doesn't respond. We're out of the building now, in the cold pink air of dawn. Olsa is holding the bridle of my mother's horse, and Cronan tosses me onto the saddle before mounting.

"I'll return," is all he says to his sister before spurring the horse southward along the road.

I keep fussing at him as we ride, but he refuses to answer me for a full hour. Finally, in a seething rage, I elbow him in the ribs as hard as I can. He doesn't seem to notice, and pain shoots through my arm. "Ow! You big horrible ruffian. Why won't you talk to me? I saved your life, you know, after you were dumb enough to get yourself caught—and this is just as dumb, riding back to Hoenfel after everything that happened last night! Havil's guards are going to shoot you dead."

"I'm honoring the deal," he says roughly.

"Finally, he speaks," I retort. "So you came all the way down the mountain and sneaked around through the forest in the middle of the night on the off chance you might get to see me again—got yourself caught and tortured and nearly killed—and now you're just—bringing me back? What was the point of all that?"

"There was no point," he says. "I was an idiot. My craving for you makes me a fool. So while I have the strength, I'm taking you back where you belong. Then I will leave Three Bridges in Zeha's hands and go north, beyond the mountains, where I cannot be tempted. You will never see me again."

"But you—you can't do that." My voice is strained, full of barely repressed tears. "How will you lead your revolution and spearhead your conquest of the South from so far away?"

"Olsa and Zeha are more than capable of handling it. I will return to our settlement and focus on building, hunting, and crafting. I'm useless as a warrior. You've ruined me. If I lead a raiding party, every villager I terrorize and every guard I slay will have your face. When I steal goods and food, I will hear your disappointed voice in my ears." His mouth descends, hot breath sifting into my ear. "If I stay on this side of the mountains, I won't be able to resist coming to you again."

I want to tell him, *Yes, come to me again and again*, but it would be too dangerous for him. "What if I send my parents a message, that I want to stay with you? I told them how I feel about you last night—maybe they would understand. And I don't care about the dangers of the North, Cronan—I survived them before, and I can do it again. I'm stronger than everyone thought, including me. I can be yours, truly yours. Havil is furious, and he won't want to marry me after this, so the bargain is already wrecked. You don't have to honor it. You can take me back with you—you can *take* me—" I grip his thighs and shift my hips, pressing my rear against him.

But the Warlord clamps an enormous hand across my mouth. "You're talking foolishness," he says. "You're being as stupid as I was last night. It won't work, Ixiana. You know it."

I drag my nails across his hand until he releases my mouth. "Then be with me," I gasp. "Right now, right here. Just once, before you leave. We can rut in the trees like a pair of beasts."

He rumbles low in his chest. "If I do that, I won't be able to leave you."

"Perfect." I grind against him again, and he vents a rough moan.

"Ixiana." My name is a rebuke and a caution.

Reckless, I writhe again, and I reach behind me, where the hard column of him presses against my rear and my lower back. When my fingers wriggle into the tight space, stroking upward, he sucks in a breath. "Ixiana, stop."

I stroke upward once more, but he catches my wrist. "Did I ever keep touching you after you'd asked me to stop?"

"I—I never asked you to stop."

"But I would have, if you'd protested."

I scoff. "I was your prize. You didn't need my permission, as you reminded me so often."

"I staked the claim of a Warlord, yes," he says. "But I honored you despite those words. Allow me the same dignity."

Flushing, I extricate my hands and clasp them together.

"As for what I said to you," he continues, "Those rough words of possession—I suspect you liked them."

My stomach flutters, and I pinch my lips tight.

"You secretly wish to be claimed. To play at being forced and overcome by someone like me."

I can barely breathe. How does he know? It's my most shameful proclivity, one I never realize I had until he took me. And he has laid it bare, spoken it aloud in the bright morning.

"Only by you," I murmur, my face flaming. "I only want to pretend that with you."

His chest swells against my back, a massive sigh. "No more talking. When we talk, I lose my reason."

"Or perhaps you gain it," I mutter.

"Do I need to gag you, mouse?"

I smirk, though he can't see it. "Gag me with what?"

I feel the answering twitch of him against my rear, but he growls, "Hush."

As I'm about to respond, we round a bend in the road—and there, on the slope below, riding up to meet us, is a contingent of district guards, with my father at their head.

My people noticed my absence, and they have come to fetch me.

68

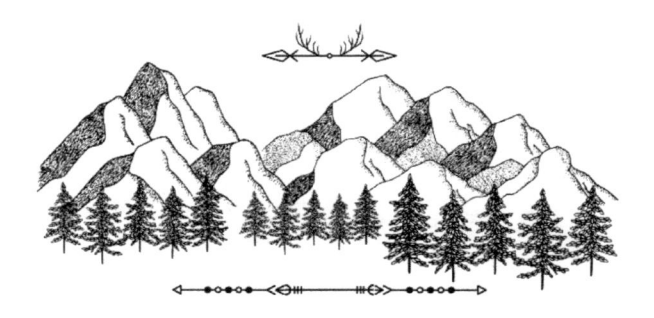

Cronan stops the mare at once and swings off. He unbuckles his giant sword from the back of the saddle and throws it onto the ground, a clear sign that he does not plan to fight them. His gaze locks with mine, and he jerks his head toward my father's group. His eyes demand that I ride on obediently, and go back to my family like a good little mouse.

I set my jaw and shake my head.

My father and his people have stopped, too. They're a couple dozen paces away, able to witness my exchange with Cronan in the clear morning light. I'm glad of it—I want them to see that I'm not being coerced, that I want to stay with Cronan.

To make the point, I lift the reins and whirl the mare around, pointing her back up the mountain road toward Three Bridges.

My father gives a surprised cry, and Cronan growls his frustration.

The mare and I only manage a few strides before the Warlord sprints up beside us, seizes the bridle, and hauls the horse's head back around. "Stop this, Ixiana," he says.

"At least let's talk to him," I beg. "Let's tell him I want to stay with you."

He lifts his hand to smack the mare's rump and propel her toward the soldiers. But I slide off the saddle, cringing as I land on my damaged ankle. The mare trots away, toward my father and the guards.

"Stubborn little ass," the Warlord grits out, and he picks me up, slinging me over his shoulder like he did earlier. He strides toward my father with determined purpose.

Swinging upside-down behind Cronan, I can't see my father's face or the actions of his guards, and that terrifies me. What if they decide to attack the Warlord, even while he's carrying me? Lucky for him, none of Prince Havil's guards are present, or he'd likely have an arrow through his eye by now.

But he walks unmolested down the road, heedless of my feet kicking and my hands clawing at his back.

When he sets me down, I'm flushed and flustered, tangled in my own hair, and very angry at not being heeded.

"What in the gods' names is going on?" barks my father, his hand on his sword. "I wake this morning and Prince Havil is gone, with all his men, and there's a letter telling me the wedding is off and our alliance with his kingdom is over—and then I discover that my daughter is missing once more. My wife is riding after Havil as we speak, to try to mend the situation. What happened? Did you steal Ixiana again?"

"Does it look like she was stolen against her will?" the Warlord snaps.

"No," says my father slowly. "It does not." He surveys me, confusion and anger mingling in his eyes. "You went to him, then."

"I want to stay with him," I blurt out.

"She cannot stay with me," Cronan interjects. "The North is a dangerous, barbaric place. She won't survive, and I cannot allow her to die. She belongs with you." He pushes me forward.

I turn, sharp words ready to fly from my tongue. But they dissipate when I see the Warlord's face, taut with restraint, his eyes brimming with bright pain.

My father sees it too. He clears his throat. "You care for her," he says gruffly. "As she does for you."

I stay quiet, watching the two warriors. Neither of them is comfortable speaking of this—that much is clear—but they're trying. The battle-ready tension in the air has eased, leaving only a warm, tenuous awkwardness.

Cronan's face reddens, and he forces out a few words—beautiful, vulnerable words, spoken to his greatest enemy. "I love your daughter."

My father grimaces. It must be so hard for him to accept those words—and yet he does. I can see it happening—the softening of his mouth, the relaxing of his brow. He's tender-hearted, and when Cronan stands before him, weaponless, having delivered me back safely, speaking a vow of love—my father can't resist.

"Well," he says. "Perhaps we should have a talk, you and I."

Cronan opens his mouth to protest, but I clamp a hand on his arm. "Please," I say urgently.

He looks down at me. Nods.

"Stay where you are," my father tells his men. "And keep an eye on *her*." He points to me before striding a little way into the woods with the Warlord.

They stay within sight, barely, but they speak low. I want to know everything they're saying to each other, but this conversation isn't mine to hear.

It's a long talk, nearly an hour. By the end, Cronan and my father are sitting a few paces apart, one on a rock and the other on a nearby log. Their gestures are slow and casual, not tense or threatening. The Warlord's shoulders aren't as rigid as they were at the beginning; they're relaxed now, bowed slightly forward. My father's hand is nowhere near his sword-hilt.

At last they return to the road, side by side, and the hope I've been nurturing tightens in my chest. I rise from the stone I've been resting on and limp a few steps toward them.

My father walks up to me and folds me into an embrace. He holds me close, rubbing my back without speaking, just letting his love flood over me. My lower lip wobbles.

When he releases me, I have to whisk away a few tears. "Well?" I ask.

"I can't decide anything without your mother, you know that," he says. "But I am open to talks with Cronan's clan. If this connection to Havil's kingdom is really over, there may be a way to ally with Cronan and his people—safe haven for them on this side of the mountains, while they act as liaisons with the other clans of the North. There is much to be discussed, of past wrongs and future changes, but—I am open."

Careless of my ankle, I leap for him and squeeze him around the neck, so tightly he wheezes, "You've gotten stronger, my dear."

"A little." I move back. "What does this mean for me and Cronan?"

69

My father puckers his lips and glances at the Warlord. "It seems the two of you are connected. He explained this ether-speak to me, this soul-bond. It's strange, yes, but I've heard a little about it before, from Northern prisoners. We'll talk with your mother before this is all settled, of course, but I believe it would be cruel to keep you two apart for very long. So if all goes well with our negotiations, you and he can—" he winces, "you can be together, and live on this side of the mountains." He keeps talking, but I barely hear anything else… something about reparation from each side to the other… I will listen more carefully later but in this moment I can't. I simply can't.

My vision, my mind, my entire being consists of the Warlord, as he stands with the morning breeze ruffling his yellow hair. He's still a little blood-stained in places—he hasn't washed thoroughly since the events of last night—but to me he's the most glorious man who ever walked the earth.

He draws me to him just by his existence—without moving, without speaking, with a single magnetic look he summons me, and I'm in front of him before I realize it. I can tell by the heat in his eyes that he wants to kiss me, but he won't, not with my father there, not with this truce still so new. Instead he clasps both my hands in his.

We separate then, for a while. I go with my father to Hoenfel, and the Warlord returns to Three Bridges.

Joss is waiting for us at the inn, tense and tight-lipped. She stayed in Hoenfel to question the guards on duty last night, and by the time we arrive she seems to have pieced together some of what happened. She's holding the Warlord's clothing and weapons from the ice-house. Apparently he came skulking around with only a couple of knives for defense, the big idiot.

When she hears the full tale of what happened, she rolls her eyes. "Love? Really? And you believe him, Father?"

"You didn't see the way the man looked, Joss," my father says. "The way he toted her back to us, gave her up for her own good—"

"Now *that* I would have liked to see—Ixiana flailing on his shoulder while he brought her to you." Joss allows herself a tiny smirk. Then she whirls on me. "You should have woken me last night. I could have helped you."

"You would have let him die," I snap.

Her lips compress, a wordless confession.

"We'll sort it out this afternoon," my father says. "Your mother will be back by then, and Cronan is coming down to Hoenfel with his sister and some warriors, for food and negotiations. Joss, tell the kitchens to prepare a feast, the finest they can muster on such short notice."

"Since when did I become your rutting messenger?" Joss mumbles as she stomps away.

When my mother returns with her handful of accompanying guards, her eyes have that rageful flaming look, the one we've all learned to respect.

"That pompous little cockatrice!" she spits, swinging off the horse. "If I never have to see that self-indulgent ass-wipe again it will be too soon."

"Hello, my love," my father says. "I take it your meeting with Prince Havil went well?"

My mother stalks right past him, toward me. "You!" She jabs her gloved finger at me. "You took my favorite horse, Ixiana."

"Because she's nice, and strong, and fast, like you." Giving her my most charming smile, I retreat a few steps. "What did Havil tell you?"

"I'm more interested in your side of things." She plants both fists on her hips. "Explain. Now."

70

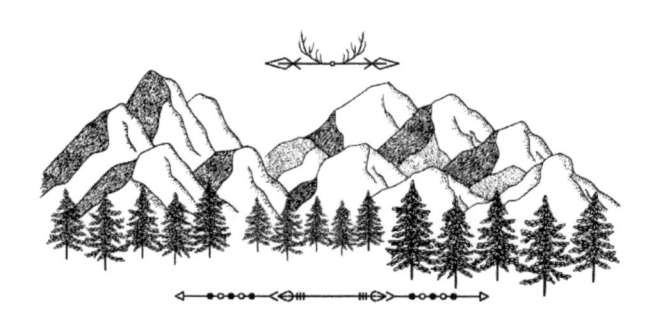

I explain as quickly as I can, and my father takes over once I reach the part about him and Cronan talking by the road. He explains the idea he and the Warlord are working on—a partnership between our peoples.

"So you want *one* clan of thieves and murderers to help us defend against the *other* clans, and possibly bargain with them?" my mother snaps.

"Essentially, yes." My father smiles, wide and apologetic. "Come, Marisa, you know the alliance with Havil's kingdom wasn't working. It hasn't been, for months now. Haven't you told me yourself a dozen times that you weren't sure about Ixiana's marriage to him? And that was before we saw his true colors."

"That doesn't mean I feel any better about her marrying a brigand of the North!" shouts my mother.

"For the gods' sake, Paltrin, have you lost your mind?"

"Yesterday evening I felt as you did, Marisa," my father says, his voice taking on a more serious tone. "But if you'd seen the man—the way he looked—"

"Cronan respects me in a way Havil never did," I interrupt. "He protects me, but he also pushes me to be better, stronger. I can't say it any other way than this—he's mine, and he was meant to be mine, always."

My mother's nostrils are still flared, her eyes still blazing, but her fists relax. My father nods to me, easing backward and moving away, allowing me and my mother to speak alone.

Leaving the guards to tend the horses, she and I walk along the main street of Hoenfel. It's nearly noon, and the sunshine has warmed the air so much that we remove our cloaks and carry them. I tell my mother some of what I omitted before—how the Warlord made me feel, and how we touched each other, body and soul. I tell her more of his past and his pain, his nobility and his penchant for self-sacrifice.

We reach the end of the village and walk farther, between cottages and farms, to the foot of the mountain road. And my mother tells me of her first meeting with my father, how she despised him before uncovering his true worth. She blushes as she speaks of it, and I know she is starting to remember, and to understand.

We're sitting side by side on the low wall of a pasture when figures appear in the distance, coming down the mountain road. My heart shivers with delight, and I press a hand to my stomach. "I'm still covered in his blood," I murmur. "I should wash, and change."

My mother chuckles softly. "Very well."

We rise and walk back toward the inn, at a quicker pace this time.

"There is something I've been meaning to ask you," I say. "Why did you reject Cronan's first offer of ransom?"

"He asked for far more than we could give, my love," she answers. "It killed us to say no, but we thought perhaps we could find you on our own and rescue you without having to pay him. We sent out a dozen search parties into the Bloodsalt and the forest beyond, but they came back empty-handed, and a few soldiers died. So when we received the second demand, which was far more reasonable, of course we accepted it." She reaches over and takes my hand. "We didn't handle it well. I know that. We had Prince Havil speaking in our ears, and neither your father nor I had ever dealt with such a situation before. Our timing and our decisions could have put you in more danger, and for that, I am bitterly sorry, my sweet girl."

"Lucky for you I was in good hands after all."

She squeezes my fingers. "I'm beginning to believe that."

71

When Cronan, Zeha, and the warriors arrive, the peace talks begin, and they continue for three weeks. Word of the negotiation spreads south through my district and north into the Warlord's lands. Thankfully, Cronan and my parents are able to establish a foundation of trust and a practical plan within the first two days, because tension mounts when the other warlords and village councils clamor to be involved. Everyone has a stake in the outcome; everyone has grievances and demands.

The Warlord and I are at the center of the negotiations for the entire three weeks, which is strange for me, as someone who was always left out of politics and never wanted to participate. But every time talks begin to break down, my parents urge Cronan and me to speak about our relationship and how it developed. It's awkward, but it seems to work. We're a strangely matched pair—my slight frame and his hulking one—and the leaders at the peace tables are fascinated enough to listen as we talk about ancestral wrongs and a better future.

It will be a painful change. Our district is more lightly populated than some others, so there is room for additional families to live; but most of the land is owned by the district government or by private citizens. My parents have many long meetings ahead of them, bargaining and compromising with landowners and town councils. But if everyone sacrifices something, we can create space for Cronan's clan to join us here, and perhaps other clans in the future. And we won't be dependent on Prince Havil's kingdom anymore.

For those three weeks, I'm scarcely ever alone with Cronan. We're always with people—my family, his sister, his clan members, the two other warlords who have come down for negotiations, their warriors, members of town councils from this region, the villagers of Hoenfel, the inn staff—people, endlessly, people all the time. He's used to people—he's a leader of his clan, after all—but I've always led a much quieter existence, and the constant presence of *people* grates on me. I long for a quiet evening with a book, in a room I don't share with Joss—or maybe a ride with the Warlord across the Bloodsalt. Strange how both of those wildly different scenarios carry a sense of comfort for me.

On the night that the three warlords, my parents, and several council members finally sign the historic Treaty of Hoenfel, there is feasting in the village like no one there has ever seen. Giant tables line the main street of the town, each one burdened with delights—

whole roasted deer and hogs, shining with grease; dishes of syrupy fruit preserves; piles of fragrant bread; vegetables swimming in creamy sauce; heavy stews and soups in giant tureens; cakes crusted with sugar. There are round tables loaded with jugs and bottles, the best drink the region has to offer, and there's a massive cask from which Hoenfel's lead councilwoman fills foaming tankards and hands them off to citizens and warriors alike.

I'm recovering from a few days of stomach troubles, so I can't partake of most of the food, which makes me grouchy. I wander along the tables, through the haze of lamplight and smoke. Bonfires have been built at intervals, offering warmth against the chill of the deep blue night. Everything smells of wood smoke and crackling roasted meat, of ale and hot sugar.

I know most of these people now, by face if not by name. Some of them nod to me, but they're all occupied with their own merriment. One of the other warlords is engaged in a drinking game with my mother, and she appears to be winning. Olsa is chatting with a village councilman. Joss and Zeha are red-cheeked and guffawing, dancing arm in arm to a fiddler's tune. When the music stops, they stand face to face, laughing, eyes shining—and then Zeha grabs Joss by the back of the neck and pulls her in for a hard kiss. Shouts of gleeful approval erupt around them, and the fiddling begins again.

The moment makes me glad—glad for them, and glad for our people. The more love connects us, the better.

But as I wander on, the smile slips from my face. I haven't seen the Warlord all day, mostly because I spent the morning in the privy and then, once I recovered, I took a long bath, which is why I came late to the festivities.

I'm unsettled inside, and not only because of my health. I miss Cronan. I miss the excitement we had together, the push and pull between us, the dangerous, enticing thrill of his formidable presence.

I ask a few people if they've seen him, but they can only tell me that they glimpsed him earlier, when the feast began—so eventually I quit asking.

Farther I wander, past the end of the merry gathering and along the dark, quiet street. There's an unused cottage at the very outskirts of the village, near the road to the mountain. That's where the Warlord and some of his people have been staying, while the other warlords are camped farther out, in the fields.

My feet carry me to the wall surrounding the Warlord's cottage, to the gate that leads to its door. The gateposts are built solidly of stone, higher than my head, and the garden beyond them is thickly overgrown, with leafless branches curling onto the paved path.

I push the gate open slowly. And then I hesitate, because I thought I heard a sound behind me—heavy footfalls on the road.

But when I turn around, nothing lies behind me except the shadows of a few trees, and the distant hum of merry voices and music.

Shrugging, I step through the gate.

A strong arm lashes around my body, pinning my arms to my sides, immobilizing me in a savage grip. As I inhale to scream, a palm seals over my mouth.

72

I twist and thrash, trying to bite the hand over my mouth. A low chuckle rolls from my captor, vibrating my heartstrings. "Little mouse," says the Warlord, in a voice rich with approval. "You haven't forgotten your lessons. But you still have no chance against me."

My body thrums with searing delight, and I relax against him. When he removes his hand from my mouth, I breathe, "It's you. I've missed you."

"You've seen me every day, in the meetings."

"It's not the same."

"No," he rumbles, his hand sliding across my throat. "It isn't."

Another thrill courses through me at the familiar possessive hold. And when his other hand moves down to hook between my legs through my skirts, I give a soft hitching sigh of satisfaction.

"Do you regret not marrying your Prince?" His voice is a predator's purr at my ear.

"Never," I whisper.

"Good. I'm told Havil has already found another prospective bride."

"I'm glad of it," I say. "I was worried we might have to deal with some sort of reprisal from him."

"His father the king sent your parents an apology of sorts," the Warlord says. "You are not the first ally the Third Prince has offended. And apparently their kingdom is currently dealing with another threat. They have no desire to avenge Havil's wounded pride."

"And why didn't my parents tell me of this?"

"You were indisposed for most of the day."

"Oh. Of course." As usual, my poor health made me miss out on something important.

"Are you better now?" There's a heated roughness to the Warlord's tone that sends tingly quivers along the crevice between my legs. His hips roll forward, pressing his hardness to my rear.

"I am much better," I say, breathless.

"Well enough to play a game?"

I can barely inhale enough air to say, "Is it the game I've been wanting to play?"

"It is." His face dips to the curve of my neck, and he inhales deeply. "What better way to celebrate peace between our peoples?" His thick lips press my skin, and I shiver with anticipation.

"I know this has been hard for you, all this talking and compromise," I say. "Giving up your dream of conquest can't have been easy."

"It was easier than I expected." He kisses along my skin, pushing my dress aside, off my shoulder. "Remember, I took you because I wanted a more peaceful route to my goals. Yes, I was ready to shed blood, but only because I saw no other way." He cups my shoulders in both his huge hands, pulling me to his chest. "You showed me another way."

The immensity of his hulking form behind me makes my heart stutter. I'm afraid of what's going to happen, yet I crave it, too.

"The game," the Warlord says, his tone husky with desire. "Are you ready?"

"Are you going to hurt me?" I ask, an echo of the day he took me out to the woods for "punishment."

The Warlord turns me to face him, clutching my chin in his hand. His thumb pulls at my lower lip, sweeping along the inner edge, dragging against my teeth.

"Yes." In the dark his eyes glitter, green and feral. "I am going to hurt you."

"Good," I whisper. "It's about time."

His fingers sweep around my hair, gathering it together. He wraps it around his hand once and gives my head a brief tug so that my face tips back, turned up to his. But he doesn't kiss me—he only bends his huge frame, his lips hovering a scant finger's-breadth from mine.

"*Faen*," I hiss. "Kiss me, you bastard."

His tongue flicks out, teasing my lips; but when they part for him, he withdraws, grinning. With his free hand he bunches up my skirts, reaching beneath them. Thick fingers dive into my underclothes, straight between my folds without warning.

"You're soaked," he murmurs. "Needy little mouse." I lunge for his lips, but he tugs sharply on my hair. "Not yet."

He dips a finger inside me, and I yelp. We're outside, where anyone could see if they walk down the road. My heart rate speeds up, and my body inflames, tortured and trembling.

The Warlord takes his hand out of my clothing and pulls me along the path to the door of the cottage. He kicks it open and hustles me inside. There's a low fire in the front room, but we don't pause there. He drags me straight to a bedroom and flings me face-down onto a bed that smells like him.

I lie there on my stomach, frozen with eager shock. Behind me I can hear the Warlord unlacing his pants.

"I'll pull out," he promises me. "I won't risk your health with a pregnancy."

"I've been taking an herbal tonic for two weeks, just in case," I tell him. "You can come inside me."

He releases a long, shaky breath. Then, "Lift your sweet little rump for me, mouse."

73

Hot blood rushes to my cheeks as I lift my rear high for the Warlord. He pushes the skirts up around my waist and pulls down my underthings, exposing my naked bottom fully to him. A thick finger traces my folds, and he gives a deep, satisfied hum. "I have never seen a woman so wet for me."

"How many have you been with?" I manage.

"Two," he replies.

My thighs tense. "Olsa?"

"No. Both times were quick trysts with women from other clans I was visiting. They wanted me, but not this much. You are a river of lust, treasure. I will slide into you easily." He kisses one of my ass cheeks, and the tingling press of his mouth there makes me whimper with craving.

He grips my hips and tugs me closer. Then he moves one hand to the small of my back. "Breathe with me," he says. "Let your body relax. You're ready."

Closing my eyes, I inhale, slow and steady. The broad, hot tip of him nestles against my folds, pressing deeper each time we breathe together. Deeper, and deeper still, sinking into me, while every sensitized bit of my skin thrills with the invasion. All of a sudden he pushes firmly, seating himself to the hilt, and I squeal because it burns—he's so thick, and I'm stretched around him tight, too tight. At the same time I'm thrilling inside, pulsing through the burn of it.

"The worst is done," he says in a strangled voice.

"You fit," I murmur, smiling, with a little wriggle of my rear.

He gasps broken words in his language and groans, "Hold still, mouse, or I'll come before I want to."

But I need him to move. This tight, slow stretch is too much—I need motion.

"Play the game," I say. "You are the Warlord, and I am your prize. I know you've wanted to claim me. Do it." And I shift my hips backward, pushing him even deeper into me.

The Warlord responds with a guttural snarl. He tangles one hand in my hair and pushes my head down to the mattress. His hips begin to rock, tugging his length halfway out before slamming in again. The sheer brute force of him overwhelms me, enraptures me. It burns, it burns—but it's feeling better already as my body liquefies even more for him. The rush of him thrusting, thrusting—the heavy press of his palm holding me down—the harsh low grunts bursting from his throat—it's primal, forceful, savage. It's everything I need.

My fingers scrunch the sheets of the bed, and I breathe in tandem with its rhythmic creak as Cronan thrusts. I'm being taken by the Warlord. His entire length is ramming into me, over and over. This is what my primitive self has wanted from the moment he called me back from the edge of death.

Tension coils low in my belly, tightening and thrilling, tighter, tighter—

"Oh gods, Cronan." His name is a hoarse cry from my lips, and he pushes deeper, so deep that my body arches involuntarily, and I lift my head from the mattress.

His hand leaves my skull and wraps around my throat, urging my spine to curve even further, but he doesn't squeeze my neck. He knows that playing with my breath could be perilous.

"Touch me," I plead. "I'm close, so close—touch me—"

His hand leaves my throat. "This damn dress," he huffs, shoving the skirts aside again as he struggles for access to my intimate parts.

"You should have taken it off me."

He reaches beneath my belly, and his rough fingers tuck themselves right against the spot between my legs, right where I need friction. As his fingertips press and play, he thrusts slow and heavy, while the most tantalizing raw moans issue from his mouth.

The pad of his forefinger is the sun of my world, and his shaft is the thick, molten core. I am coalescing, clenching—he speeds up, abandoning himself, roaring his lust, and I let myself cry out too, as everything in my body tightens and bursts, a shining geyser of ecstasy so strong I can't stand it, I can't—I can't breathe—the Warlord's length flexes inside me, heat jetting from him.

"Breathe with me," he commands, and I do, while he slides gently back and forth just a little, soothing both of us through the glimmering pleasure as it fades.

Then he slips out, and crashes beside me on the bed.

"Are you well?" he asks.

"Mmm," I respond dizzily, smiling.

He chuckles. "I'll be ready again soon. I can go six times in a night."

I gape at him. "How do you know?"

"I have tested myself. What else is a man to do, faced with hours of watch duty in the wilderness, while everyone else sleeps?"

"You disgusting barbarian."

He laughs and sits up, grasping my shoulder and rolling me over onto my back. With both hands on my thighs, he spreads my legs wide and surveys his work. I can only imagine what he's seeing—how flushed and swollen that part of me is, how wet with my own arousal and dripping with his essence.

The Warlord lifts his eyes to mine. "I love you in many ways," he says softly. "Riding away on my horse and leaving me to die. Running back to save me from the Bloodsalt. Looking at me so earnestly while you tell me what I need to hear. And like this…" He trails a finger along my slit, and I sigh and squirm, craving him again. "I love you like this."

I reach for him, and he crawls over me, settling part of his weight onto my body. But he's careful, even now—careful not to compress my lungs, or crush me with all that packed muscle.

"Bond with me," he whispers. "The healer who travels with us is a Shaman of the Bloodsalt. He has taken the rites, and he can perform the soul-bond. It will be yet another proof to the clans that this peace can work."

A glow rushes through my heart, a joy that I don't think any sickness or ill fate will ever be able to dim. No matter what happens to me or to him from this point on, we will always have this night, and this moment—the moment when my captor and my enemy asked if he might tether his soul to mine.

The enormity of it makes me want to cry, so to stave off the tears I murmur, "How practical of you. Always thinking about your people, and your goals."

"That's not the only reason I want this," he growls.

I trail a finger across his broad, smooth lips. "I may need some convincing."

74

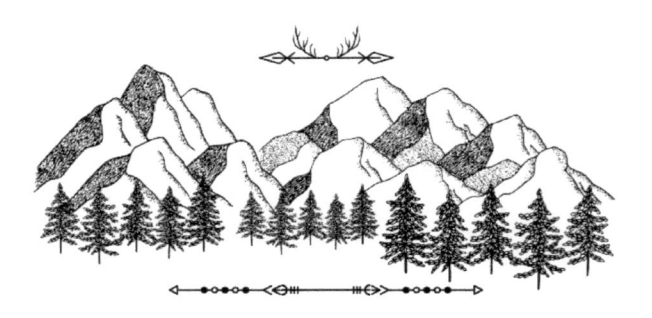

The Warlord rises from the bed, takes off his boots, and removes his unlaced trousers. He shucks aside his tunic—and there he is, bared to me in all his glory. The magnificent expanse of him that I've only been able to admire from a distance, and touch one part at a time.

"Are you going to let me touch all of you?" I whisper.

His throat bobs as he swallows hard. "Get up, mouse."

When I try to obey, my legs wobble, tremulous from the pleasure in which he bathed me. Cronan steps in, whirling me around and unfastening my gown with impatient jerks of his fingers. Finally he grabs the voluminous skirts in his great hands and pulls the whole thing off, over my head. My hairstyle is completely wrecked, loosened and tumbled about my bare shoulders. He dismantles the rest of my clothing—corset, shift, underskirts. And then he steps back, with a quick inhale and a brightening of his green eyes.

I tremble before him, naked as I was all those days ago, when he said my tits were too small and my body was inadequate.

His length hangs limp and thick against his thigh, but when he looks at me, at all of me, it bobs and lifts, stiffening, a mute testament to how much he enjoys what he's seeing. My insecurity softens and slides away, melted by the incandescent heat quivering through my belly.

I rake my gaze slowly up his body, devouring every bulging muscle with avid delight until my eyes reach his face.

His jaw is hard, his broad lips pressed tight; but his eyes are alight with craving. "Come here, mouse," he says.

Slowly I walk to him, and I place all of my skin against his, slipping my arms around his waist. His burning shaft is fully erect now, pinned against my stomach. Experimentally I slide my palms lower, smoothing over his rounded ass.

His hands sweep along my back, gathering handfuls of my hair and fondling it, before releasing it so he can savor my skin again.

We were bare together under the furs on the night of the blizzard, and bare together in the bath as well, but this time there is liberty to explore each other. I draw circles on his firm rear, shift my hands to his front and wander freely across his pectorals. As my hands pass over his nipples, his dick twitches against my stomach.

He pushes me back a little, sinks to one knee, and takes one of my breasts in his mouth, licking its tip. Spots of scintillating pleasure prickle between my legs, and I whine, my hips swaying forward. My body wants him inside again, yearns for that stretched fullness. The Warlord traces a finger along the seam of me, then draws a wet line up my belly before taking his lips from my breast and capturing my mouth instead.

His kiss is brutish, demanding, and he picks me up as he rises to his full height again. I curl my legs over the ridges of his hips. So much of his enormous body is pressed to my flesh—I can barely stand all the sensations screaming along my nerves. Smooth abdominals, broad chest flecked with curling gold hair, iron muscle rolling under hot skin.

He handles me as if I'm nothing, as if I'm a rag doll with limbs to be arranged at his pleasure. His teeth tug at my lips, and I bite him back fiercely, which makes a laugh rumble through his chest.

Hands braced under my thighs, he hitches my whole body up and sinks me down, his shaft poking through, entering me abruptly. I squeal, breathless, clamping both hands on his shoulders. It doesn't hurt, because I'm completely liquid for him, dripping with embarrassing need.

He lifts me, sliding me up until only the tip of him lingers between my folds—then down, pressing me firmly while his length rushes up inside my channel again. The giant muscles of his upper arms bulge as he works me up and down, casually, easily, as if I'm simply a toy for his lust.

The Warlord gives me a feral smile, darkness and delight. "I've wanted to do this with you since they threw you at my feet after your capture. You're the perfect size to be used like this."

"Bastard," I gasp, but my eyes are rolling back in my head. "Maybe I don't want to bond with you after all."

With a snarl he shoves himself up into me, driving a sharp cry of anguished pleasure from my mouth. Then his arms wrap around my back, clasping my body to his chest. Still shoved deep inside me, he walks to the wall and presses my spine against it. Then he keeps pumping, but this time there's more friction of his lower stomach against me, rubbing, rubbing—I release tiny desperate yelps, over and over, while he bucks forward at just the right angle—and a squiggling line of sheer white-hot ecstasy snakes through my belly, branching along my legs.

I scream, and the Warlord slams his mouth over mine, driving his tongue deep as if he wants to taste my pleasure, to swallow it into himself. As my body spasms around him, he starts to pant, heavy and helpless, into my mouth. Dazed, enchanted, I watch his handsome features tighten and shift—and then he comes with a violent quiver of his thigh muscles, his body hardening briefly before it relaxes. He presses his forehead to mine, his eyes shut while his chest heaves with pleasurable agony.

75

Somehow the Warlord manages to get us both on the bed, where we lie, floppy and blissful, him on his back and me on top of him. I can't suppress a wriggle of happiness while I stroke his collarbone and bicep. There's a soothing relief in the rush of my skin against his, as if it's a sensation I've been craving all my life without even knowing it, and I'm finally, fully satisfied.

After a while he rises, wanders from the room naked, and returns with water and fruit. After we eat and drink, he closes and latches the bedroom door, at my insistence. After all, the other warriors staying in this house could come back from their reveling at any time.

"In some clans, a couple's first mating is witnessed by all," the Warlord says.

"Mating?" I raise an eyebrow at him. "Sounds too much like animals, not people."

"We *are* animals," he breathes, climbing over me. My breath stutters in my lungs as his scent envelops my senses—the smoky rich maleness of him. I can practically taste the lust on his tongue as he dips it across mine.

Then he rolls onto his back, flipping me on top of him again. But he doesn't stop there; he spans my waist with both hands and lifts me bodily. Before I can protest he has me seated astride his *face*. My knees press into the pillow on either side of his head, and my hands instinctively grip the frame of the bed. I can feel the brush of his short beard against my inner thighs and more sensitive places—I'm practically dripping into his mouth.

I squeal in protest and try to move, but he holds me still, just a little space between his lips and my core.

And then his tongue sweeps through my quivering center. He keeps me there, held in place, my thighs trembling, while he tugs and nips at my tender folds with his teeth, while he lashes his hot wet tongue over me again and again. After a minute or two I manage to relax a little, to enjoy the delicious attention on that sore, stretched part of me. The flushes of pleasure are growing closer together and more intense—I'm burning again, hot and wanting.

"Can you breathe?" I manage, between the surges of sensation.

"Shut up, mouse."

So the answer is yes. I clutch the frame of the bed harder and yield to his ministrations. One of his hands cups my rear, and now and then those fingers move, stroking my skin. His other hand braces my thigh, supporting me.

His tongue is a thick swirl, and then a delicate, tender lapping. There's a nip of his teeth, a nibble in the right spot—and a dot of exquisite pleasure centers there, quivering. "Please," I sob. "Please." His teeth pinch me again, and his tongue flickers, and his lips press a suckling kiss and—gods—*faen*—*faen*—I'm shattering, shaking, gasping shrill and undone. His bearded mouth presses upward, soothing me, gentling me.

I'm boneless then, completely lax as he arranges my loose limbs on the bed. He kneels between my spread thigh, his muscled torso filling my sight.

"*Faen*, treasure," he says, his cheeks red, his golden hair shining in the lamp-glow. "You are so beautiful." With his knees planted apart, he strokes himself, soaking in the sight of me. Flushed and sleepy, I smile at him, tracing my fingertips along my body. He comes within seconds, sprinkling my skin.

We drift into sleep then, our limbs interlaced. A few hours later we're wakened by the drunken return of some merry-makers, but the noise quiets quickly as they fall into their own beds in the other rooms.

The lamp has burned low. In the near dark, Cronan attacks my mouth with silent urgency, and I crush my body to his, just as violently needy. My fingers find his length, pushing it into me, and even though I'm still faintly sore, I don't care. I need him like I need breath in my lungs, like I need sun on my skin. I love him better than my own comfort. I crave, I hunger, I am absolutely feral for him. The sensation of his thick length filling me up is more addictive than I ever dreamed. My body draws him in, locks him inside, pulses around him until every drop of his pleasure is spent and he's left weak and sated.

When I'm done with him, I crawl onto his chest and touch his face while he lies panting and limp. I stroke the light beard, and the bold cheekbones, and the beautiful straight nose. I smooth the broad lips and trace the arches of his brows. My fingers travel to the nape of his neck, touching the braid that holds the bones of the people he loved and lost. I can never replace them. Nor can I promise to never leave him bereft in that way.

But I can promise to love him and be with him for as long as my body and spirit remain together.

"I love you," I tell him, stroking my fingers over his heart. "And I would like nothing more than to bond with you."

His torso heaves, a rush of relief. "Gods, mouse," he whispers, pulling me up along his chest until my face is near enough for him to kiss. "You are my undoing and my healing. I think I would give up anything for you."

"You won't have to." I kiss him softly again. "Because we don't just share a soul-bond, or the same 'craven lust.'" He rolls his eyes, and I chuckle before sobering again. "We share a common goal. Maybe justice isn't possible, not really, not at this point—but joy is possible. Peace is possible. We're going to show everyone it can be done."

He hums deeply in agreement, stroking my hair.

"Oh, and one more thing," I say. "Enough of this shit about me being too weak to bear children. If I want your little war-babies someday, you'll give them to me. Understand?"

"*Faen,* treasure," he murmurs, with a delighted grin. "You know I will give you anything."

76

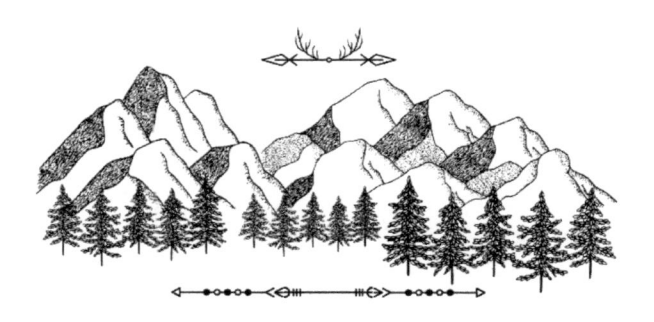

The next day, Cronan and I are soul-bonded by a Shaman of the Bloodsalt, under a hastily-constructed archway of naked tree branches woven with fluttering ribbons. Our union is supervised by the Hoenfel priestess, at my mother's insistence. All the representatives of the clans and the district villages stand witness as we speak the vows, as the healer weaves white threads around our hands and sets them ablaze with golden light. I feel the power of the soul-bond racing along my left middle finger up to my heart, into my blood—and it feels more right and more healing than anything else in my life.

At the feast following the ceremony, feeling invincible, I indulge boldly in a slice of rich cake. Of course my mental state cannot correct the flaws of my body, and I regret it for hours afterward. But when it's over, Cronan is there, and he doesn't complain about any smells or the fact that I'm in no mood for joining with him. He simply brings me a cup of water and holds me as we lie in his bed.

Word of our soul-bond will spread far and wide, and my father has plans for the Warlord and me to travel from village to village through our district for a while, as he and my mother announce the terms of the treaty to everyone. Cronan and I are a symbol; we can help our people visualize the future.

My mother promises we'll travel slowly, so as not to risk my health, but travel doesn't hold the same terrors for me now. I've learned to manage in the worst of scenarios—I can handle a journey through our district. And afterward Cronan and I will live in Hoenfel, in the same cottage where we made love for the first time. Cronan has plans to fix it up and decorate it in the style of his lodge. His father and the others from the northern settlement will join us eventually, moving into Hoenfel and Three Bridges and other border towns.

While Cronan and I travel with my parents to persuade the southern villages, my sister Joss will ride with Zeha from camp to camp beyond the Altagoni mountains, speaking with the warlords. Joss is perfect for the mission; her strength and skills are better suited to the North than mine. She understands the mentality of a warrior better than I can, and with Zeha the diplomatist at her side, I have no doubt she will win the respect of many a clan. The two of them seem very content with the arrangement, and I suspect some of their nights will be spent as blissfully as mine and Cronan's are.

Despite all our efforts, integrating the clans into our district will take decades, or longer. There will be misunderstandings, prejudices, ill will, and disputes. Our two people groups will need every talent we possess. They'll need Zeha's clever diplomacy and the Warlord's pure zeal, my parents' lifelong political experience and Joss's brash confidence. They'll need Olsa's sense of honor, my brothers' eager openness to new ideas, and the healer's grouchy kindness.

And they'll need me—the girl who gets up every morning without knowing what her body might do, or how close she might come to the edge of death. They'll need the girl who survived the North and saved her captor from death. The one who felt his pain and learned to listen.

As for me, I need only one person—the one who greets me with a kiss as I wake each morning. The one who possesses me and sets me free, respects me and commands me. The one who stole my body and my heart. My husband, my life-mate, my enemy and my friend.

My Warlord.

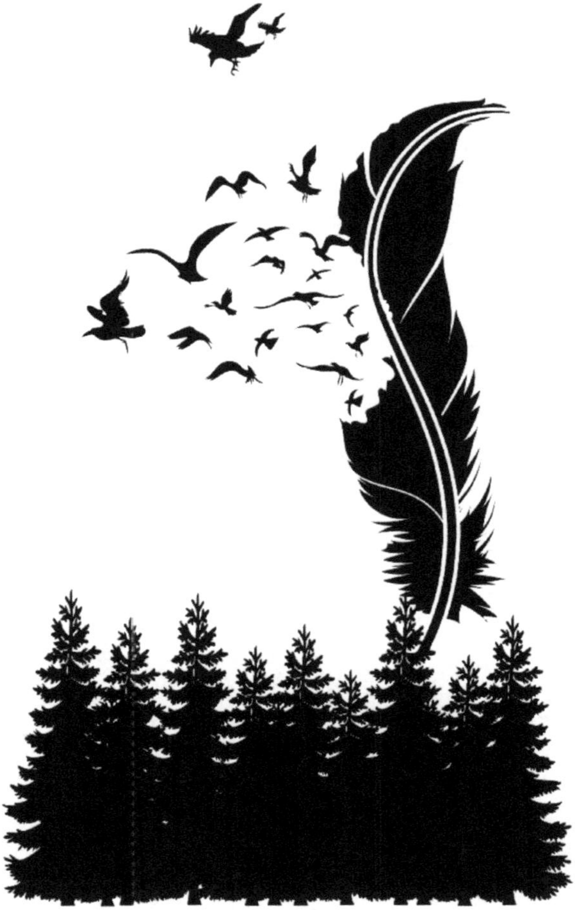

REBECCA F. KENNEY BOOKS

The IMMORTAL WARRIORS adult fantasy romance series

Jack Frost
The Gargoyle Prince

Wendy, Darling (Neverland Fae Book 1)
Captain Pan (Neverland Fae Book 2)

Hades: God of the Dead
Apollo: God of the Sun

Related Content: *The Horseman of Sleepy Hollow*

The PANDEMIC MONSTERS trilogy

The Vampires Will Save You
The Chimera Will Claim You
The Monster Will Rescue You

The SAVAGE SEAS books

The Teeth in the Tide (Savage Seas Book 1)
The Demons in the Deep (Savage Seas Book 2)

These Wretched Wings (A Savage Seas Universe novel)

The DARK RULERS adult fantasy romance series

Bride to the Fiend Prince
Captive of the Pirate King
Prize of the Warlord
Healer to the Ash King

The KORRIGAN trilogy

Korrigan (Book 1), *Druid* (Book 2), and *Samhain* (Book 3)

The INFERNAL CONTESTS adult fantasy romance series

Interior Design for Demons (Book 1)
Infernal Trials for Humans (Book 2)

The ASHTON SHIFTERS adult fantasy romance series

Lion Aflame
Panther Ensnared

MORE BOOKS

Lair of Thieves and Foxes (medieval French romantic fantasy/folklore retelling)

Her Dreadful Will (adult contemporary fantasy with romance coming April 2022)

The Monsters of Music (a YA gender-swapped Phantom of the Opera retelling)